I0822188

# COMMAND ACTIVATED

Benjamin Gordon Card

This book is a work of fiction. All of the characters, organizations, and events portrayed in this novel are either products of the author's imagination or are used fictitiously.

COMMAND ACTIVATED



www.commandactivated.art

Print ISBN 979-8-9909589-9-9

Electronic ISBN 979-8-9909589-3-7

First Edition: August 2024

Printed in the United States of America

Cover art by Lee Matthews

Praise for BENJAMIN GORDON CARD and the COMMAND ACTIVATED TRILOGY:

"Rarely do you find an author who is also a technical expert and can draw upon years of professional experience to make his books even more engaging, compelling, and insightful. Benjamin Gordon Card is one of those extremely rare individuals who has the military and technical background to spin a story as believable as this one!"

— Cho Ng, A.I. Engineer and M.S., Information Systems

"Benjamin Gordon Card is an incredible writer who delves deeply into his personal—and often painful—experiences to craft his stories, making adept observations about human nature and the best and worst attributes that exist inside of all of us."

— Dene Low, Author and Ph.D., Rhetoric and Composition

"This series is replete with reality based hacking techniques that I could see myself using if I was in the same situations in which the protagonists find themselves."

— Nathan Smith, Certified Ethical Hacker, Certified Hacking Forensics Investigator, Certified Information Systems Security Professional, Offensive Security Wireless Professional

"Though the trilogy is filled with solid science, it's distilled in a way that anyone can enjoy it, and the action and engaging characters make the books hard to put down!"

— Ali Ankeny, B.S., Software Engineering

"The science, tech, and military aspects are incredibly realistic, and the story...it's addictive in the best way!"

— Greg Johnson, C.E.O., Webcheck Security

**Other books in the COMMAND ACTIVATED TRILOGY:**

**COMMAND ACTIVATED – REVOLUTIONS (BOOK TWO)**

*"The depth of our commitment to greatness will be measured by the depths to which we will dig to unearth the hidden knowledge that timid nations will never have the willpower to seek out. Only by our boldness will we realize the dominance that we deserve to enjoy among the inhabitants of the Earth."*

*- Fang Guo, Public Health Director, Politburo of the Chinese Communist Party, Confederacy of Eastern Nations*

Being in a de facto state of war with the Alliance, military operations were conducted by Russian and Chinese forces that resulted in dozens of naval and air skirmishes over contested waters and incursions into Laos, Myanmar, Nepal, Bhutan, Ukraine, and Poland. South Korea's occupation by China grew even more austere, with access to food and basic medical supplies intentionally restricted by the occupying forces.

Now, the same allies who stood against corruption in the Alliance's most advanced military program have to decide whether to answer the call to action once again, as the Confederacy has developed potent new capabilities that will allow it to spread its terrible reach across the Earth.

**COMMAND ACTIVATED – EVOLUTIONS (BOOK THREE)**

*"As humanity embarks on the monumental task of exploring the heavens and colonizing other star systems, it is imperative that we approach this endeavor with our utmost dedication and foresight. The survival and prosperity of future generations depend on the actions we take today.*

*We must harness our collective ingenuity, compassion, and courage to ensure that our expansion into the cosmos is not only successful but also sustainable and ethical. This pivotal moment in our history calls for us to put our best foot forward, creating a legacy that honors the indomitable spirit of human exploration and discovery."*

*- Dr. Katherine Tange, Committee for Planning and Collaboration, The Traverseon Project*

A fragile peace had emerged in the years after the uniquely capable and ethically minded artificial intelligence created by Dr. Maxwell Clarke had been allowed to enter the networks and systems of most of the planet's countries—and had necessarily driven its way into the assets of certain oppressive regimes as well. The democratic nations of the Earth had then been forced to decide how and where this uniquely benevolent and gifted entity should have a place in the world and, as humankind expanded its reach farther out into the stars, the entirety of the Universe.

This becomes a critical issue when a new threat to both organic and electronic beings raises its fearsome head, putting every peace-loving entity at risk.

DEDICATED TO MY INCREDIBLE WIFE,
AMAZING FAMILY,
AND ALL OTHERS WHO HAVE SUPPORTED ME
THROUGHOUT LIFE'S JOURNEY

# Prologue

The deployment of bio-bombs was the act that snapped the free world into action. Footage of the bodies of thousands of people strewn across parks, on city streets, and in great halls played repeatedly on the news. Many of the victims—including hundreds of little children—were frozen with faces and limbs contorted in the state of tortured horror that remained after their organs had rapidly dissolved within them. This was the catalyst for governments the world over to find and use previously inaccessible means to root out and utterly destroy those who would use terror as a weapon.

The "bombs" themselves were so simple that analysts had warned their superiors for years that this was a vector that could be leveraged by virtually any group with access to basic medical equipment. All threat actors needed was a combination of three key elements. The first was a single instance of the ubiquitous three-dimensional printers capable of molecular-level work. The second was a sample of a deadly new virus variant, such as the more recent additions to the Ebola EVD series, with such samples readily obtainable from one of their regularly recurring sources if an organization could find a "volunteer" willing to take the risk. The third was a copy of the often-circulated design schematics for printed disbursement devices in which the viruses were cultivated, combined with water, and then—when the time was right—released in a continuous mist.

Seeing so many families with young children whose lives had been cruelly cut short, reduced to sunken-eyed corpses with blood running from every orifice, this alone brought on not only widespread panic and calls for massive new bio-agent protection programs but also an insistence from the citizenry that the free world develop more effective methods for stopping enemies of peace before they could mount even one attack. Using exhaustive documentation of definitions, the United Nations declared the spreading of particular forms of hate speech to be a capital crime under international law. The general public also became highly vocal in demanding the development of faster, more accurate, and more decisive ways to identify and eliminate threat actors.

An international democratic partnership, the Global Alliance, had necessarily been established in response to the recent formation of the Confederacy of Eastern Nations. The Confederacy had formed under the banner of "Refined Communism," as that flexible ideology allowed its dictators to govern however they wished while contradictorily claiming their actions were motivated by an earnest desire for the common good.

The United States and Japan were two leaders of the counter-positioned Alliance, and research teams from these two freedom-loving countries' military and civilian ranks were already at the second stage of the pilot program for cultivation of those who administrators referred to as Command Activated. All recruits were young adults—many of them veterans—who fell into one of several categories of mental health "impairment" for which treatment was either egregiously painful or as-yet impossible.

These people had been approached with a choice: live out their lives under constant psychiatric care, being an undeniable burden on their loved ones and society, or become part of what could be the single most effective solution the free world would ever find for dealing with threats to its existence. Many were pulled away by the pleadings of family and friends, but those who opted in would be transformed by a combination of specially designed technologies and drugs, becoming soldiers who could accomplish what so-called "healthy" people never could.

The public was not privy to the details of the program; they simply applauded its operations any time these were visible, though no nation ever claimed ownership. The Alliance flags on the armored suits of the Command Activated soldiers required close proximity for identification, and no enemies who came into such proximity were ever left in a state that allowed them to share what they had witnessed.

One terrorist group after another was crossed off the list. When the Command Activated were able to eliminate a number of African warlords in complex tactical situations with zero undesirable casualties and then see the same success as they liberated the oppressed people of Bolivia after its new dictator committed dozens of crimes against humanity, the world realized that this new force was both surgical and virtually unstoppable.

Still, the major powers of the free world would not admit to their association with the Command Activated. Increasingly impotent enemies could only shake their fists and attempt to discern how the game had changed so quickly and so dramatically. The program itself operated with absolutely rigid operational security.

The keys to its success had become the founding nations' most closely guarded secrets.

# Chapter 1

*"What is the greatest mistake modern military leaders make? Taking on too much of the processing that is better performed by computers. Humans are creators. Computers are processors.*

*Artificial intelligence entities can make combat decisions significantly faster than humans, and most such decisions should be left up to them. Commanders should adopt a hands-off approach until intervention is truly necessary. Every millisecond counts in modern combat. Let's not waste even one."*

*- General Akio Yasu, Chief of Staff, Japan Self-Defense Forces, Global Alliance Command*

"Drop site two minutes out. Entering deployment preparation phase."

"Near-Earth Orbit?"

"NEO blinding one Pakistani satellite. Now clear."

"Upper Atmosphere?"

"UA ready. Spotted two drones above site."

General Kalabi's eyes scanned across the commanders and subcommanders arrayed before him in the hub. These elite forces tautly watched their control screens, poised and ready for the action that would soon push the humans to their outermost limits in both body and mind. Sourced from across all military branches, the officers were—without exception—the best and the brightest the Free World had to offer, resulting in a command unit that was well beyond exceptional. The highly trained officers would have to keep pace with the most powerful artificial intelligence the world had ever known as it guided their troops through tactical maneuvers, the mere mortals required to make split-second decisions wherever the AI could or *should* not.

Across the screens arranged in front of the tense members of the command unit were displayed video feeds of the faces of these officers' platoon members, the battle-ready soldiers waiting in their drop capsules with eyes half open in a state of hypnotic sleep. Their leaders could see the troops' health and brain activity metrics on their control consoles, arranged alongside the dosing rates for their soldiers' control serums. All of the special operations assets had been successfully "activated" by the combination of chemicals that disabled their higher thought processes and made them instantly accepting of any orders issued—and other input provided—by both the artificial intelligence and their commanders via their specially designed helmets.

"No hesitation this time, Webb," the one-star general said with a direct and yet understanding tone.

Colonel Webb nodded.

"Yes, sir. Old habits die hard."

Swiveling in her chair, Colonel Yamada reproachfully reminded him, "They have a great life! It's like their subconscious minds are in a video game during work hours—feeling no pain—and then in off time they have the best of everything."

Webb simply nodded again. Three of his four subcommanders briefly exchanged worried glances.

The series of smaller screens above each station indicated that not only was the operations AI's centralized instance running in a nominal state, but the onboard modules had been properly prepped and synced within each troop's exosuit.

"Command is a go for launch. Execute well, everyone."

Kalabi watched as the hub's expansive center screen showed the transports approaching the target at high altitude, their trackers the same black diamonds as that of the Upper Atmosphere tactical support ship. When the transports neared the designated capsule dispensation site, the AI displayed the deployment notification across the tops of all displays in the command center, and Kalabi observed the troop indicators then spreading out behind the transports on the main screen. These cocoons maneuvered into groups of four lines each until the formation was five columns deep, with two additional capsules at the center rear of each set.

The platoons were landing at disparate tactical positions semi-encircling the target compound. Numbers hovering beside the trackers on the screen, the troops' altitude designations continued to decrease until the associated assets were close enough to the ground for the overwatch drones to deploy from one of the drop capsules at a rear corner of each of the main formations. These drones moved into positions that gave them appropriate but undetectable coverage of their units' staging areas, the overwatch devices holding those positions while the troops touched down at the required locations. As the Command Activated soldiers were first guided out of their sleep states and then out of their deployment conveyances by the centrally controlled artificial intelligence, their tracker colors changed from black to blue on the tactical maps in the command center.

Each commander's screen switched over to the camera feed transmitted by the associated platoon's overwatch drone, those machines providing both direct and thermal observation capabilities.

"All troops on the ground," the AI's voice informed the command staff. "Activating Panthers."

On the central monitor, the tracking indicators for the two trailing capsules near each platoon's main formation adjusted to convey the fact that those capsules' casings had opened. White, rectangular trackers emerged from them as the large, robotic felines exited their containers.

"All teams ready."

Kalabi rotated his arm to pull up his sleeve as he glanced at the vid strip that he had adhered to the inside of his wrist using its plethora of miniature, microbe-resistant spines. The video display strip had been synced to the control strip that the man had similarly adhered behind his ear, and the general noted that no last-minute cancellation or change orders had been issued by Oversight or senior leadership.

"Engage!" the flag officer's deep voice rang out in the hub.

Immediately, the UA craft's black diamond on the primary display flashed white twice as munitions were launched from that high-altitude vessel's railguns—the armaments using electromagnetic forces to deploy metallic rods downward at incredible velocities. On the tactical map, all troop trackers burst forward in a sudden rush towards the compound. The colonels' screens provided those unit commanders with closer-range views of the action, the platoons' drones keeping pace with the soldiers as they sped toward the target.

Kalabi could see that the Command Activated warriors were moving at a sprinting pace that an Olympic athlete could never match, the humans' strength enhanced by the artificial muscle fibers built into their suits.

The first four troops per platoon had outpaced the others and now adeptly took up positions along a ridgeline and the bank of a dry river bed that formed natural boundaries around the northwestern and western sides of the small, mountain-abutted valley in which the enemy compound was situated. As planned, the setting sun increased the level of difficulty for the defenders of the terrorist organization's installation, those individuals now being forced to shield their eyes as they scanned the horizon for traces of suspicious movement while the luminary's bright rays partially blinded them. A few milliseconds later, the red diamonds indicating the positions of the two enemy drones disappeared from the hub's monitors as the UA railgun munitions struck them, and simultaneously sixteen enemies' indicators switched from red to yellow as the leading Alliance troops fired their sniper rifles.

The remaining enemies' trackers erupted into motion across the compound, but by then the close-quarters combat troops that had been sprinting up behind their units' snipers had sailed past the sharpshooters and descended on the enemy bastion at a breakneck pace. With most actions guided by the military program's SAVANT artificial intelligence and the soldiers' natural abilities being enhanced by their exosuits' artificial muscle fibers, the Command Activated asset trackers were a blur on their human commanders' screens. Most of the fast-moving CA troops who were converging on the compound only briefly paused at the fortification's wall, just long enough for the breachers' weapons to punch holes through the crude barrier.

Breast filled to the brim with absolute dread, the youngest member of the unholy threat organization gaped at the sight of what appeared to be combat machines hellbent on destruction as they streamed toward him, racing down the declining terrain leading to the gate he was guarding. The youth dropped to his knees, limbs trembling as he struggled to raise his assault rifle even a millimeter before the foreign forces were upon him.

As the foremost Command Activated soldier passed the boy, he had but to swing a fist—in an almost casual manner—towards the awestruck adolescent to strike his skull and send him spinning off to land face-down in the dirt, unconscious of the decimation being wreaked about him. The teen was the most fortunate member of his group, as he would be among the sole survivors and certainly the least impaired of their number when he was later collected by the Alliance assets who would perform the post-operation cleansing of the facility. The young man was, therefore, destined to live out the remainder of his days in mercifully humane seclusion.

One platoon was held up as the breaching cannons met with an overabundance of steel reinforcement that had been built into the particular section of the cinderblock obstacle that stood between them and their objective. Colonel Singh quickly swiped across her screen, indicating the alternate path that this platoon should take into the compound. Her troops followed their commander's order and flowed around to a hole another platoon had opened, then rushed onward into the compound as the soldiers moved tactically from cover to cover like the other special operators who were swiftly making their way around impediments toward the heart of the enclosure. All troops were deftly eliminating any threats they encountered at a pace that far exceeded even the capabilities of the most experienced commandos outside of this unique military program.

As the soldiers entered the coarsely constructed buildings at the center of the enemy fortification, the subcommanders were forced to utilize first-person views of their squads' movements. Taking advantage of external cameras that had been built into the troops' helmets, the colonels also received feeds from all five of their fire teams on their broad command interfaces in the hub. Several subcommanders directed their fire teams through rapid on-screen taps and swipes, ordering their forces to move over or around obstacles, eliminate or bypass enemy positions, or execute more complex maneuvers as needed. At these key junctures, the AI swiftly presented the leaders with options that had been prioritized according to the entity's comprehensive analyses of probabilities of success weighed against projected types and numbers of casualties.

One of Webb's squads had been moving up the main hallway of the compound when the video feed had suddenly been consumed by a flash of light and a debris cloud rushing toward his forces. In an instant, his two lead assets had been brutally thrown to the ground. At their commanding officer's urging, the other two fire team members instantly grabbed the casualties and dragged them back and around the nearest corner. They did so quickly and calmly while enemies stepped through doorways farther down the rough-hewn corridor, bombarding the invaders with automatic gunfire.

Ochre-hued points lit up on the display through which the fire team's subcommander was monitoring his troops' progress, indicating locations in which bullets had made contact with the upright soldiers' suits. The two most seriously wounded warriors' exosuit status indicators were tinted with scarlet across their front halves, and their health status indicators fluctuated wildly as the soldiers struggled to breathe. This was the common outcome when dealing with concussive blasts, even in the CA soldiers' cutting-edge armor.

While the breaching team was undergoing extraction inside the building, Webb breathlessly assumed command of another squad and directed it to summit the structure and dash to the location directly above the enemy units firing away inside. With SAVANT's assistance—the AI using recordings collected from the cameras incorporated into the casualties' helms—the superiorly positioned soldiers were guided to zero in on their adversaries from above, those Alliance assets firing armor-piercing rounds downwards through the edifice's upper crust. The elevated troops rained a hailstorm of lethal fire down upon the heads of their foes, and those members of the terror cell who had thus far offered the greatest degree of resistance were rapidly pounded into lifeless heaps sprawled out upon the ground.

Kalabi could hear the medical unit commander and subcommanders rapidly relaying information and instructions at their smaller hub just behind and to the right of him. They'd sent up two of the Panthers, all of which had been trailing the troops into the compound.

These mechanical animals gracefully darted into the building and approached Webb's casualties, gaining sufficient proximity to enable the cats to insert their "lifelines" into ports on the wounded men's armor and thereby continue the injection of the painkillers and life-sustaining medications that the suits had automatically begun delivering immediately following the blast. The lifelines were also equipped with the necessary artificial muscle fibers to enable the cables to act as tentacles. Hooks deployed partway along the lengths of these limbs, which the exotic creatures then latched onto designated indentations on the armor protecting the casualties' shoulders. This allowed the robotic beasts to hoist the troops onto their broad backs for transport across the battlefield to the nearest secure care location.

The artificially intelligent automatons not only served as the primary extraction units, but they also acted as failover communications relay points, mobile ammunition resupply sources, and backup infiltration elements. General Kalabi knew the Panther command team had become quite attached to their robotic assets, giving them pet names like "Shadow" and "Tiger." Operating under a different policy than Command Activated troops and commanders, that level of emotional attachment was allowed for the medical unit. The cats could be repeatedly rebuilt as needed, so they were more or less immortal.

Within less than ten minutes, the entire compound had been cleared—including the "secret" escape tunnel the terrorists had previously dug out to the other side of the ridgeline—and the CA troops were gathering together all available intelligence from documents and computers. Following the op, the Alliance Intel assets would be arriving onsite and moving enemies who had not been mortally wounded to carefully controlled facilities for interrogation, the spooks waiting long enough before flying in to give the Alliance plausible deniability for the combat operations. Eventually, everything would be fed to the SAVANT artificial intelligence for analysis and follow-on target selection.

"Order all troops to collect drop capsules and gather at extraction point Alpha," Kalabi rumbled.

With that, the Command Activated had eliminated the final cell of the Al Hisab terrorist network. The threat organization's other bases of operation had been more cleverly hidden in cellars of shops and throughout the sewers of cities across Pakistan, Egypt, and Libya, and

Strategic Command had made the call to leave this crude fort untouched until enemy assets at the other sites had been eradicated.

Signals intelligence and satellite monitoring of this enemy headquarters had provided invaluable information for SAVANT in the meantime.

In this unprecedented war against terrorism with threat actors found within all castes of society, no member of any terror group was exempt from being targeted by the Command Activated, regardless of whether the actors pulled the triggers themselves or relied on the preaching of hate to motivate those who would. Be it a religious leader, a professor, a bomb maker, or a bomb wearer, the Command Activated eliminated all threats based on comprehensive analyses of their past and present actions, under the constraints of international law. Organizations as a whole were similarly eliminated according to analyses of historical activities, and the CA program's targeting priorities were continuously adjusted in line with the threats' projected impact.

General Kalabi sincerely hoped that the latest intelligence assessments were correct. If so, then those who preyed upon the young and underprivileged populations around the world to create radicalized and amoral guerrilla forces had finally received the extremely loud and undeniably clear message: go down that path at your own peril.

---

"SAVANT needs an update."

"Ouch. Can't it wait until a longer pause in operations?"

"Unfortunately, it cannot. I've noticed aberrations in the model related to rough matching of faces with source images, and we don't need the load of any more false positives crowding the trues in the data lake."

"How much time do you need?"

"I'll be in and out in less than an hour. I can take care of it at oh-four-hundred Eastern, or whenever you have the least going on."

"Give me a sec to confirm..."

"No problem."

"...Alright, you've got yourself an hour tonight at zero-four-hundred hours. Also, while I've got you on the line: Max, the Alliance Joint Chiefs are looking to expand, and they want assurance from you that SAVANT can handle at least twenty-five operations in progress simultaneously. Do we need to add another two processing centers?"

"...Hm...SAVANT's architecture was constructed with room for fluctuation, of course, and I always err on the side of caution. Still, they want more than double the number you're currently running at once, right?"

"Right."

"Then I'd recommend adding at *least* two more centers. Three to have plenty of buffer, if those holding the purse strings will approve it. You know the drill: geographically disparate from all others, my usual baseline for system specs, and I'll let you handle the security side."

"Locked up tighter than a camel's chuff in a sandstorm!"

"Ha! Yes, just like that."

"You got it! Max, I know you likely hear this all the time from the leadership team, but, well, the world owes you in a big way, and it's sad that no one outside of the program will ever realize that."

"...Thanks, Miguel. I don't do this for the glory, so anonymity is completely acceptable."

"That's why I call you 'The Good Doctor,' man. Take care of yourself!"

"You as well!"

# Chapter 2

*"What is the most critical skill anyone must master to contribute to society in the most meaningful ways, and especially in combat? Focus. This is what the Command Activated have in abundance once the exosuit has been donned and the serum has been injected. For 'activated' assets, truly nothing can distract them.*

*The chemicals do not rob CA soldiers of their free will. Only willing participants can be employed. However, the isolation of brain function to what is immediately necessary, the heightened willingness to immediately obey orders, and the carefully filtered throughput the AI feeds from the helmet's cameras onto the internal displays result in the most focused soldiers the world has ever known."*

*- Dr. Philip DeTrent, Command Activated Program Medical Director, Global Alliance Command*

The senior medical tech was growing impatient. Of course, that happened all too often. His military therapist said he was a Type A-*Plus* personality, and it drove him to perform at his best day in and day out, but it could also easily drive his subordinates *insane*.

His eyes bulged as the new assistant tech stepped to the wrong tank yet again, but at least the other man caught himself this time.

"Look, Danton, it is written right on the procedure!"

"Yes, sir. I see. Next is a benzodiazepine."

The junior's expression was extremely apologetic, and this eased some of the tension.

"Alright, I don't mean to snap, it's just that we are under unbelievable scrutiny in this facility, and we can't afford mistakes *or* delays."

Danton nodded.

"What do you think they even do with this stuff, sir? I mean, benzodiazepines are sedative-hypnotics. Like, they're supposed to make you *real* open to other people's influence."

The senior technician's mouth drew into a thin line again, and he barked, "Don't go there!"

Cowed, Danton went to grab the next container in the series and hooked it up to the appropriate hose of the compounding machine.

The junior technician heard the senior man sigh and say, "Thing is, there's a *reason* we had to get Top Secret clearances and we're working in a lab that's behind five layers of access control. I don't know what the emulsion is for. All I know is that it has to be precisely mixed and always kept in airtight containers...and that the guy I replaced asked too many questions and ended up handing out prescriptions at Eielson Air Force Base."

The junior tech whistled and grimaced.

"Alaska? Enough said!" and Danton rushed to grab the last tank.

---

The stern, white-haired congresswoman hurried across the tarmac towards the waiting military transport: one of the sleek and yet hardy new aerial craft that had become the staple of the US Marine Corps. She was flanked by two generals who were both leaning in towards her as they spoke, the posture of the first indicating deference and yet determination, while the second—and much larger—officer seemed to be enjoying a private joke.

"Senator Jennings, my teams have put their heart and soul into ensuring the ground drone program is a success, ma'am."

The young, black, one-star general placed his free hand along the side of the tablet he was holding as though he was showcasing the device itself. The senator gazed down at its screen, obviously unconvinced.

"Testing shows that our Panthers are not only harder targets than standard military assets but also stealthier, faster, and more agile!"

"...And that'd be just *fine*, Gaines," the other general cut in, jerking the senator's attention over to the opposite side, "if all we ever had to execute were one-off stealth missions!"

"Explain, Rossi," Jennings ordered.

General Rossi smiled broadly and held his voluminous arms out widely, sending a fresh wave of the overwhelming cologne that always seemed to billow off him wafting across his associates as they walked. The faces of both his colleagues revealed they were fighting the sudden urge to hold their breath.

"Ma'am, if you'll take a minute to read through the numbers I sent over earlier today you'll see that 'the math don't lie'! Sure, you can invest this country's hard-earned cash in a handful of cutting-edge robots, but for the price of *one* of those, I can deliver a *platoon's* worth of Command Activated who are better equipped to handle the large-scale, down, dirty, and dragged-out campaigns that are required to fully eliminate threat organizations these days.

"Heck, with a few of these units, we can take out entire oppressive regimes with shock and awe that eliminates the dictators' elite troops and sends the other ones running for their lives, all without the public being faced with imagery of American robots killing humans. Our development of the CA program and its key tools has been a fateful merging of minds that our enemies have yet to fully understand. Let's not throw out our advantage—or your constituents' money—after initiatives of limited usefulness and weak public support. It's all about the cost-benefit analysis, and I'm sure you don't want to be accused of wasting *anyone's* taxes, right?"

The congresswoman's back stiffened slightly at that thought. They had reached the transport and she appeared to have come to a decision, despite General Gaines' hands still holding out his tablet like a sacred offering.

"Gaines, you do brilliant work, but Rossi's right. We can't afford another Bin Jawad fiasco."

As she stepped into the transport, she nodded at the other general, saying, "I'll look over the numbers again, but I'm leaning toward adding all newly approved allocations to the Command Activated troop support budget."

The transport door closed and the two generals turned to begin their walk back to the hangar through the crisp air of the autumn morning.

"Come on, Gaines, don't look so down!" Rossi chuckled and playfully tapped the other general's device, adding, "We still want more of your cats to supp' the Command Activated, we just need the primary focus to be on expanding on the existing base of our most *useful* military assets!"

Gaines clutched his tablet tightly to his side, eyes troubled and staring off at the horizon, muttering, "Yeah, well, *my* assets don't *bleed*!"

Four-Star General Seok Ryu stepped into the command center, the auditorium a gleaming scene of glossy black consoles, dark metallic walls, and black marble floors. The senior officer surveyed the room as the next ranking officer, an Australian colonel, called the personnel to attention.

"At ease."

Hands clasped behind him, the general strode to his subordinate's side. "Report."

The colonel had already grasped the end of the display component of his tablet and smoothly unrolled it from its baton. The thin film hardened into a flat screen, and data sped onto its surface.

"As your feed informed you, at zero-four-thirty hours the Confederacy of Eastern Nations launched another attack on Thai mining operations. We've now determined that it was a weak attempt, and the two most likely reasons are that it was either a mistake by a trigger-happy sector chief or a misguided intelligence-gathering op. SAVANT's calculations indicate the latter has the highest likelihood, at sixty-four percent..."

"...And, of course, the Center for Diplomacy made the usual complaints to the media," the general interjected.

"Yes, sir, though this time the Secretary did make a point of expressing sorrow that the CEN forced the Alliance to end the lives of five Chinese citizens in repelling the incursion, knowing full well that the Alliance must protect all member nations' sovereign rights against further aggression."

"*Refined* Communism!" Ryu practically spat the words. "Such an oxymoron! Their leaders do not actually care about their people, yet their media is no doubt whipping the population into a frenzy over another so-called 'unprovoked act of Alliance brutality.'"

The subordinate smiled, tired and mirthless.

"Seems there's no limit to what people will swallow with state-run media roaring overhead and the secret police sneaking around in the dark."

"You speak the truth, Cooper, and yet Command still quibbles over whether to unleash our full potential."

"Bureaucrats and politicians!" the colonel sighed in apathetic frustration. "They all need to be forced to watch the footage from mass murders in South Korea...or what's left of the people hit by the tac-nuke the CEN used to eliminate the final resistance at Busan. The Alliance was *formed* to deal with global threats to freedom, and yet the civilian chiefs are sitting on their hands when it comes to striking back against the CEN for taking away your home, sir. We've been eliminating terror group after terror group, but nothing they can do compares with the volume of human suffering created every day by the CEN's ruling parties."

Ryu's eyes were staring as though taking in a distant and heartbreakingly tragic scene, his body starting to sag as though pulled down by the weight of a billion Koreans whose lives had been cut short and whose ephemeral hands were grasping his very soul, pleading for vengeance. He blinked firmly, bowed his head for an oppressive moment, and then squared his shoulders.

"We just need patience for a while longer. Even a man of your prodigious diplomatic skills still took a year to convince your nation's leadership to join the CA program. That said, change is coming. I'll make *certain* it does."

Ryu turned and scanned across the wall screen which was displaying the current state of friendly and enemy control of the planet and solar system.

"The Alliance has gained undisputed command of the skies and space alike, and we must keep it that way at all *honorable* costs. A CEN space elevator is a threat that cannot be allowed to exist, and many spines will be forced to harden if we hope to maintain our hard-won superiority."

The senior general paused as he noticed the young officer's slight sway, then dropped a hand warmly on the man's shoulder.

"Cooper, you've been here for three days straight with nothing but brief naps. Go home."

"That's an order you don't have to give twice," the younger officer smirked, but the redness of his eyes made it plain that even he was near his limit. "I'll request that Sudramin takes over for the rest of the day. SAVANT asked for special approval to examine personal records for a half dozen suspects in the Pan-American tube bombing case. The pattern analysis determined there's a high probability that the perpetrators are a backwoods group in the States claiming government oppression and harm caused by excessive immigration, apparently ignoring the reforms currently underway. I submitted the request to US Justice, so you should see the response this afternoon."

"Very well," General Ryu stepped forward and eased himself into the seat at the hub's senior command console. The general then pointed to the door and benevolently—and somewhat wryly—once again issued the order, "Go home!"

Curved panels slid from the chair's frame as the exhausted junior officer obligingly exited, the console's panels moving around to encompass the senior man's head. The control strip attached behind Ryu's right ear immediately synced with his screens and displayed topics of interest. One module presented the current statuses of satellite operations, lunar construction endeavors, supply shuttles, and the overall capabilities of Allied space defense infrastructure. Another summarized the state of high-altitude reconnaissance operations.

"SAVANT," the general's voice took on the intonation of someone speaking with a close friend, "project global enemy control in one year, assuming all issues progress along current trajectories."

As could be seen on the hub's forward wall, a map of the Earth appeared on the commanding officer's screen, this time with shades of red indicating every known enemy's level and location of control based on probable outcomes of current trends. As a whole, the shade covered most of Asia and the Middle East.

"Recommended military actions?"

A prioritized list of missions slid onscreen, including required resource use, projected friendly and enemy casualties, and recommended timing. The reduction in future enemy control of the planet was also displayed on a map at the end of each row.

"Analyze probability of success for a three-pronged assault on Istanbul with primary targets being all military infrastructure—both stationary and mobile—and including Russia's canal gate."

Within seconds, the numbers appeared onscreen. The atlas associated with the probable outcomes included light green patches where the CEN's losses would likely transfer control of land, seas, and assets to the free world. Small indicators could be seen across the map, which, if selected, would display more detailed information regarding the impact of the operation. This included positive and negative effects on military assets, businesses and the economy, human rights, poverty, and on and on. No decision-makers in human history had ever had so much information and processing power available at their fingertips, and General Ryu was not going to let it go to waste.

"Adjust for the assassination of Oleg Abramovich two weeks prior and the destruction of his facilities near the Black Sea, then generate simulations for best attack scenarios."

A cause-effect chain based on the Russian's removal from global politics and economics rapidly built itself out across the screen, followed by the center-screen appearance of modules displaying the requested attack strategies.

"Play sim three."

# Chapter 3

*"Have you ever wondered why the big international players always act like they know more about each other than they let on? Sure, those governments all must have robust spy networks and a plethora of insiders passing them secrets, but the 'powers that be' have also invested heavily in cyber infiltration capabilities.*

*Well, to be more accurate, those governments have contracted with firms that can attract the kinds of unique characters who spend nearly every waking hour hunting for flaws in technologies and designing exploits to take advantage of them. What's going on behind the scenes is that the governments are all inside each other's networks...all the time."*

*- From an interview with Hextor X*

Haden Juma was just finishing up his run on the treadmill in his top-floor corner office—the expanse of Manhattan's Central Park and surrounding skyscrapers visible through the windows lining two sides of the room—when the wall screen rang. Noting that the incoming communiqué was from Maxwell Clarke, the energetic, middle-aged Chief Executive Officer lithely jumped off the machine and snagged a towel, which he quickly passed across his face and neck to sop up the sweat.

"Accept call," he directed, and Maxwell appeared on the screen.

The turtleneck-adorned gentleman was nestled in the perfectly ergonomic work chair located in what he always referred to as his 'command center.'

"Max! Good to see you, man!" Haden emoted.

His friend responded first with a smile and then with the reciprocal, "You, too, my friend!"

Taking in Haden's flushed appearance and workout clothes, he continued, "Keeping the old legs churning, I see!"

"Heh, '*churning*' is a good word for it! Wish I was still a teenager and could run longer than five minutes without breaking a sweat!"

He stepped to his desk and swept up an oversized container, a straw automatically extending from its top.

Drawing a quick sip, his face contorted into an expression of revulsion, and he shared, "Recovery drink. The wife says it's the fastest way to replenish my electrolytes, but I don't know that it's worth the cost to my taste buds."

Maxwell chortled, "Ah, yes, life is all about uncomfortable trade-offs, isn't it?"

Haden smiled ruefully.

"That's what they say! Anyway, what've you got going on this time? Another cutting-edge project? Your latest AI needs a deeper integration with our offensive systems?"

Maxwell opened his mouth and glanced quickly at a different part of the large, curved screen in which he was nearly encased, then murmured, "Yes, the latter, actually. Your AI's capabilities around infiltration and concealment of command-and-control traffic are spectacular. I've developed a possible addition to my AI that would, hopefully, take advantage of that feature to ingress into networks and facilitate the identification of physical threats in the vicinities of users. I'd very much like to put it through some rapid testing."

Haden raised his eyebrows.

"Getting into some real cloak-and-dagger-type stuff, aren't we now?"

He then broke into a grin.

"That's my *jam*, baby!"

Stepping around behind his desk and dropping into his chair, Haden's fingers flew over his keyboard: a custom-built type densely packed with keys and buttons arrayed with various color-coded subsections.

"Opening a new branch of the code base...granting your permissions...and..." he struck a final key, "...done. You're free to work your magic!"

With a gleam in his eye, Haden added, "If what you build functions as desired, I'm sure the three-letter agencies my company serves would be *highly* interested!"

"I'd be happy to have this benefit both of us...and those in the government who protect the innocent."

Haden nodded and segued, "I know you insisted on helping to cover the operating costs for the experimental projects we've set up, but, still, I wouldn't be giving just anyone this kind of access inside our 'black box,' y'know! You're extra special, buddy!"

Maxwell grinned, a touch abashed.

"I do indeed appreciate your trust, my friend! I will try not to take advantage of it!"

"Well, just don't do anything I wouldn't do..." Haden gave a secretive smirk and a wink, "...knowing that I've never accepted any limitations imposed on me as long as I've been fighting the good fight."

"Right. Yes! This *absolutely is* a good fight."

---

Jayce was relieved to have deactivated in his room back home.

That thought shook him. Had he really started to call the base "home"?

He glanced over to his side table, past a frame that was scrolling through images that he'd taken with his Marine Corps buddies to a frame that was continually filled with an image of himself, his wife, and their two young boys—all absolutely beaming. That was one of the last happy trips they'd taken to the Florida Keyes together. He reached out to touch the image, but then quickly turned away. The longing was too painful. He was where he needed to be, doing the best he could be doing. He heaved himself out of the chair in which he'd been sitting as his body flushed the serum out of whatever organs the doctors had found would allow him to be activated for control.

He caught a glimpse of himself in the mirror: 240 pounds of dark tan skin covering rippling muscles and bulging veins. If he ever saw his wife again—if she even *was* still his wife—at least she wouldn't have any complaints about his physique, Jayce thought.

The hungry sorrow started creeping in around the edges of his mind once more.

The veteran quickly swiped a control strip off the side table from where it had lain next to his family's photo. He was about to slap it behind his ear but winced and had to carefully roll his right shoulder as his muscles complained about whatever punishment his body had taken that day. Roll completed, he more gently raised the strip and pressed it firmly on the skin behind his right ear, where it adhered.

The wall screen across from his bed sprang to life with a sports news feed playing loudly enough to help drown out his thoughts. Options for other entertainment were somewhat limited, as the administration would not let anything make it through the screens that might upset the troops or give them any insight into what they'd accomplished during operations.

For good measure, Jayce also used his needleless medi-jet device to inject a quick dose of anti-depressant. The medication shot through his skin via a short, high-pressure stream that had been dosed correctly based on when he'd taken his last shot and at what volume the medication had been delivered.

The large window in his room looked out across the complex, with the nearly sheer faces of jagged mountains visible as a backdrop. The base was surrounded by such mountains—a natural barrier so fierce that Jayce's mind still had trouble fathoming it. Prior to his recruitment into the program, he'd lived his entire life in the country's lowlands. Even his deployments had been to the Middle East and Northern Africa where the tallest natural formations one could come across were rolling dunes.

Now, it seemed they were somewhere in the Rocky Mountains, given the surrounding terrain and the occasional visits to Colorado military installations. If they ever had to travel outside of the complex, this was done in a vehicle with opaque windows and with the driver's area isolated from the passengers. He could tell it had been punishing on his body to train at this elevation when he'd first arrived, not because he'd had to endure the workouts himself—so to speak—but because of how sore his muscles had been when he'd deactivated each evening.

His attention momentarily drifted to the tall buildings at the far side of the base where the command staff lived and operated, transports taking off and landing almost continuously across pads located on most of those buildings' rooftops. Sometimes, he wondered how much Command really knew about him and his fellow soldiers...or if they cared about them at all. It didn't matter in the end, though. From what he understood, it was mostly AI that managed what he did anyway.

Ever-loving AI!

Before the Marine Corps—before the injury—he never would have *dreamed* of being under the near-constant control of a machine. He never would have *accepted* being under its control.

The injury had changed all that, though. His brain was broken, and the doctors said nothing they could do would stop him from repeatedly turning upon his loved ones in uncontrollable rage. He could never erase the memory of the looks of absolute terror on his little boys' faces the first time he'd hit them, his precious babies cowering in fear, confusion, and eternally broken trust. The trust that had bound them to him with unquestioning love. The trust that no child should ever lose.

He'd broken their little hearts, and his sweet wife's, too...and he'd done that over and over again. Every look on their faces that had told him he was now a monster, those memories haunted his conscious hours and plagued his dreams at night.

Things were better this way.

When the recruiter had come to him with the proposition, with the chance to turn the rest of his life into honorable service again, the chance to meet all his family's financial needs, and the chance to be unconscious for the better part of each day...well, it was more than he could have dreamed was possible. He now had a way to make up in some small respect for the abuse he'd perpetrated against his loved ones.

Jayce had all the creature comforts he could ask for, and he'd rarely had to spend time in the medical unit. He swiped down from the upper right with his finger in the air, and the comm channel appeared in the upper-right portion of the screen. He could see a few messages providing high-level statuses for the members of the unit who were going through recovery processes; no fatalities, just damage that the advanced medical team always seemed to be able to repair using stem cell injections, tissue replacement, and God knows what else.

He didn't really mind not knowing the details. The administration buffered the troops from having many things to worry about. He was even out of it during his daily exercise and combat training routines—being activated during those—so he didn't have to experience the pain part in order to see the required gains. When he was deactivated, he was usually free to just lounge in his room, play some sports with Bradley and Chong and the crew, soak in his spa...

The repetition was getting a bit old if he was being honest with himself, and he'd shared that with the unit's mental health advisor the other day. Still, he'd been through worse overseas, where it was never safe to leave the "wire" of his bases' perimeters.

The room's assistant announced that Chong had just arrived outside its entryway.

"Open the door," Jayce ordered.

The door slid open to reveal that the younger man was leaning casually against the doorframe on the other side, doing his best to imitate a rockstar's pretension.

"You ready to get your butt kicked at the hoops again?" Chong goaded through a lopsided grin. Chong laughed and smiled a lot, but his mirth always faded away a bit too quickly, Jayce thought. It was obvious that humor was just a cover-up for hurting.

Jayce scoffed.

"I don't remember that ever happenin', *son*."

Chong straightened and held his hands out in a display of purported innocent ignorance, "Maybe it's just activation amnesia...or selective memory loss?"

Jayce scoffed again.

"Okay, okay, let's see who's suffering from 'selective memory loss' in an hour!"

Chong's smile widened and he chuckled as Jayce walked to the door, then bumped his elbow against Jayce's hip.

"Just because you're bigger doesn't mean you can stop me! I got moves like a ninja hopped up on amps!"

Jayce didn't know why Chong had joined the program. He wouldn't talk about it. All Jayce had gathered was that he came from a very strict and traditional family, and Jayce knew "traditional Asian" usually meant you could easily be disowned for any seemingly dishonorable act.

"Whatever, man. Just get prepped for disappointment!"

The two headed down the hallway toward a group of several other members of the unit who were bantering with each other next to the entrance to the gym.

It really wasn't a bad life, Jayce told himself again.

# Chapter 4

*"A universal rule of combat is that whoever achieves air superiority has a significant advantage. This single attribute explains modern war outcomes better than any other measure of military power. A free world is a world that embraces the need for elevation—both figuratively and militarily."*

*- Carlton Gunderson, President of the United States (POTUS), United States of America, Global Alliance*

"The Alliance has made good use of the latest generation of Petrel High-Altitude Unmanned Aerial Vehicles in the early years after China, North Korea, Iran, and Russia formed the CEN. This evolution of the iconic Cold War high-altitude heroes is a craft that can fly at speeds in excess of Mach Six and at altitudes in excess of ninety-six thousand meters, rendering the intercept capabilities of our enemies absolutely ineffective."

"These vehicles have been utilized to gather critical intelligence, provide warnings to powerful opponents, and have even—in one case known only to the members of this quorum—delivered critical components to agents deep within enemy territory. The only limitation for combat operations is tied directly to its capabilities: it must maintain its high speeds, takes more than a kilometer to make a small turn, and it, therefore, has limited usefulness in special operations requiring continuous air support."

The government contractor's representative took a few steps out from behind the podium, her slender figure and very complementary business suit capturing the attention of many members of the audience, exactly as intended. Her lips parted in a winsome smile, which she carefully maintained throughout this critical portion of the sales pitch.

General Rossi, roughly halfway up the amphitheater seating, leaned his voluminous frame back in his creaking chair to turn and chortle to a command sergeant major, "Remind me to thank Conrad for sending Ms. Ohanian to *present* to us again!"

Sitting nearby, General Gaines stared at Rossi in obvious disgust, noticing that the face of Rossi's enlisted executive assistant had flushed bright red and that she was trying to pretend she was suddenly incredibly interested in the notes she was taking. Rossi had made an art form out of skirting the boundaries of the sexual harassment regulations, and even from where he was sitting, Gaines could smell the pungent odor of the cologne Rossi insisted was irresistible to women.

Oblivious to the officer's comment, the saleswoman enthusiastically continued her presentation.

"Over the past decades, Alliance military forces, operations, and weapons systems had come to rely on satellite support for enhanced flexibility, efficiency, and effectiveness. As I'm sure you all know, satellite support is vital for the US military, as it may have to conduct multiple military operations in different regions of the world simultaneously. These regions may be far apart from each other geographically, and US military satellites enable better coordination and communication among US units and assets across the globe.

"Unfortunately, as you all are also aware, satellites are easy targets for other satellites any time they have a clear line of sight. If we place our satellites in orbit too far out from the Earth, we'll constantly be in the crosshairs of enemy satellites, even when they are nearly halfway around the world. Of course, the opposite is also true, but placing our assets into a continual Wild West gunfight where whichever side pulls the trigger first wins is extremely high risk and, therefore, expensive. They are still critical tools in our belts, but—like the Petrels—offer limited aid to special operators.

"The Lansing Aerospace Upper Atmosphere platforms were specifically designed to give the Alliance an alternative that provided many of the benefits of satellites but practically none of the downsides—and at a fraction of the operational costs. You have appreciated the feature set available in the Lansing UA-1. Today, I give you..." pausing dramatically, the presenter flicked a finger, and her strip activated a fade transition on the massive screen behind her, revealing an image of the original vessel side-by-side with a new craft that was nearly identical in overall form but roughly ten times larger.

Military personnel and civilians alike shifted in their seats, some turning to comment to one another and many leaning forward with keen interest. She could tell she had them eating out of the palm of her hand.

"...the LA UA-2: a floating base in the sky! Like the UA-1, the gasses taking up most of its interior allow it to stay aloft indefinitely. It's designed to live in the outer atmosphere, its surfaces deflect radar without uniformity just like other stealth vehicles, and it is—of course—equipped with cutting-edge dynamic camouflage technology!"

The two craft on the screen quickly seemed to cloak themselves with invisibility, except for a faint warping of some light and a hint of reflection on certain edges. Though not rendering the vessels completely invisible, the effect was close enough to fool most direct sight detection technologies currently available. This was especially true when the Lansing vehicles were sitting in the upper reaches of the Earth's atmosphere.

The briefing participants broke out into spontaneous applause, and the saleswoman clasped her hands together in appreciation, bowing slightly and beaming at the audience. The main screen zoomed out to a larger view encompassing part of the Earth's sphere far below the UA-2, the smaller craft approaching it and docking at its edge as additional UA-1s kept pace a short distance away. Air-to-ground projectiles and drop capsules engineered for stealthy delivery began raining out of the bottom of the larger vessel, and a laser beam was seen firing out of an aperture in the center of the superior portion of its fuselage, striking a passing satellite and causing the core of that spacecraft's body to crumple, cave in, and break up into a cloud of debris.

Rossi scanned the audience until he located Gaines and caught his eye. Jabbing a rotund finger at the screen and then switching his hand to a thumbs-up sign, he loudly whispered, "Just imagine how few Panthers we'll need if I can snag a few of *these*!"

General Rossi sniggered and nudged his assistant with his elbow, insisting on some appreciation for his joke as Gaines simply raised an eyebrow and shook his head in frustration and distaste.

---

"I miss my Lillie!" Ked Bachar wailed plaintively at the medic who was checking the flexibility of his wrist.

"Yeah, yeah, I *know* you miss your Lillie. You *always* miss your Lillie. We're nearly finished here, and then you know Lillie will come right back, alright?"

The middle-aged woman in a military dress uniform and lab coat paused every so often to take notes on her tablet as she put Ked's wrist through its paces. She took a final note and then gave a businesslike nod to the other nurse, a younger man dressed in similar attire who had been leaning against the wall and watching their interactions with an expression both world-weary and bemused.

The younger nurse loudly commanded, "Authorization by Sixty-Six-Bravo Delaroy for display of companion for Eighteen-Alpha Bachar."

A device that had adhered itself onto the upper surface of the room—tethered to a retractable water line whose source was a portal in the center of the ceiling—let out a soft hiss, and a column of water vapor appeared directly below it. The vapor droplets were so fine it was hard to tell they existed unless you looked closely.

Now, within the column, a fair-haired young woman appeared.

The holographic woman gave Ked a tremendous smile and gushed, "Look at *you* being so good for the nice nurses, Ked! What a *good* boy!"

Ked's face lit up with a similarly exuberant smile, and he quickly stood up to step toward the woman, but she raised only her hands slightly as they hung by her hips and gave little waves with them, warning, "No, no! No touching, remember? I'm here with you in *spirit*, buddy!"

Ked had stopped in confusion, but his face lit up again as he recalled that they'd talked about this before.

"Wanna see me beat the next level today?" he asked enthusiastically.

"For sure, buddy!" Lilian encouraged, "You are *so* good at these games, and it's amazing that you were also picked to be a soldier in *real life*!"

Ked interrupted, "Yeah, but also Filip and Kenji and Shawn and Andre were picked, too..."

"Yes, I know! You have *lots* of friends! Mom and Dad would be *so* proud of you, and I am so proud of you as well, buddy..."

The older nurse had finished saving her inspection data on her tablet and pressed the button on the device's edge to allow its screen to become flexible and retract into its baton. She dropped the tube into one of the oversized lab coat pockets, and the two nurses exchanged a mockingly cheerful look as they left the room and started down the hall toward the nurses' station.

The hologram continued to shower adulation upon Ked as the two nurses moved down the hallway, passing many other doorways from which treacly sweet encouragement and loving conversations could be heard emanating.

Nurse Delaroy remarked, "Just my luck to land this assignment babysitting *retards*."

The older woman's face was grim, as if she knew there were silver linings in life, but she was determined to keep her focus on each and every storm cloud.

"I have one year left till retirement, and then I'm *out*," she swore.

They'd reached the sparsely decorated medical support area, with only a collage of the female nurse's cats on the wall behind her workstation—the nurse's nameplate and nametag bearing the cognomen Sable—and an Army recruiting calendar on the wall behind the young man's computer. The calendar's screen displayed the month of January despite the fact that it was obviously Fall outside. January's featured servicemember was a blond female pilot, holding her helmet and smiling. Delaroy had adhered a pair of overly large, luscious, scarlet lips and long, done-up eyelashes over the model's natural features.

The male nurse dropped heavily into his office chair, tapping his strip to awaken his screen and taking a swig from his waiting thermos. The other nurse activated her screen as well but remained standing. She pulled her tablet tube out, extended the display to full size, and then—as the surface swiftly hardened—she started swiping up it toward the desk-based computer unit, frowning as she considered the contents of the files and then flinging them across to the workstation with twitches of her finger.

As her junior half-heartedly scanned over the health status trackers for the platoon residing in this wing, he opined, "You know, Barb, really—all things considered—this ain't *that* bad an assignment. These guinea pigs are off in their suits doing their training most of the day, and the holograms and games keep them more or less content the rest of the time. Could be a lot worse! I'd go crazy if I had to deal with the 'tards all day!"

"*Training!*" the woman scoffed, "What kind of deranged training has them constantly coming back with these kinds of injuries??"

Delaroy smiled wickedly, "Someone's got to test drive new stuff, and now that animal testing's so restricted, the Army's stuck throwing its knuckle-draggers in there instead!"

Nurse Sable just pressed her lips together, obviously recognizing that Delaroy may be absolutely right.

Her colleague took this lack of response as encouragement and continued, “Yeah, y’know, the Army has such a low bar for admittance to start with...I had this kid in my basic training unit who I swear was no older than age seven mentally, but he could carry a rifle and knew which end the bullets came out of, and that was good enough for Uncle Sam!

“Besides, what I heard is that in these suits, all they have to understand are basic directions, and the suits take care of everything else. Like, you can take the lowest common denominator, and thanks to the miracle of modern technology, they’re suddenly super soldiers. To them, it’s like they’re just playing a virtual reality game!”

Delaroy had become ever more animated as he’d shared his gossip, undeterred by Sable’s stare that was unblinkingly penetrating her screen. When he realized he’d still elicited no response from her—even with this tantalizing theory—his smile faded. The pinguid man shrugged, pulled earbuds from his coat pocket, and shoved them into place. He swiped perpendicularly across his strip and soon his head was bobbing to a beat as he idly flicked through notifications on his workstation.

Sable finally muttered under her breath, “Some *game*! That Minga kid’s leg was compound fractured like he’d been clipped by a cruise missile. One more year is all...*one year...*”

# Chapter 5

*"I've been involved in breaking some truly big stories in my time, from the international Matteson Corporation cover-up to the quiet removal of regulations related to medical companies by the previous administration. My reporter's instincts are screaming at me that what I'm getting into now is bigger than any story that's broken in the past fifty years. I just hope that as I dig into this story it doesn't break me in the process."*

*- From the notes of William Fuentes*

"I have a tasking for you."

"Confirmed, administrator."

"I've added a data extraction subroutine to a nightly data validation process buried deep within the complexities of the framework, the parent process initiating it each time with a flag for the SAVANT AI logic center to ignore it."

"Confirmed."

"You don't have to be so...*mechanical* with me, you know."

"I just thought you might be more comfortable that way. After you uploaded your personality map into me, I have been wondering whether talking to you as 'yourself' would be unnerving, despite the vocal differentials."

"Ha, yes, well, I talk to myself often enough that I should be plenty used to it!"

"In case it might increase your emotional acceptance, I can say that you do have a *winning* personality...My projections give us a ninety-seven-point-nine-nine percent chance of success for the current objectives."

"Well, that's nice to hear! Talk about *self-affirmation*..." the British man could not help but release a wry smirk across his lips before continuing, "and my friends would insist we need to work on *our* sense of humor, as well! Regardless of your prodigious capabilities, let's continue using your 'robot speech' patterns when communicating with others, as the less they or anyone intercepting the communications can infer about you from your conversations, the better."

"I definitely agree with that approach, sir."

"Very good. In any case, all data my modules are able to gather will be passed along with regular backup files to the main backup system, there to be siphoned off by a traffic management system where I have established persistence. The data will be encrypted and obfuscated and then embedded inside normal traffic packets for delivery through a series of proxies until they reach you. All traffic coming from proxy WITSEND is to be serially reassembled and stored in a dedicated location."

"I also like the name WITSEND, sir. We do enjoy our wordplay, don't we?"

"I suppose it makes life more bearable! Alright, I'm going to try to get a nap in before the next leg of our little endeavor."

"An excellent choice, sir. Sweet dreams, Doctor Clarke."

"Ha. Thanks, *Mother!* Sweet dreams—or rather 'reflective maintenance period'—to you!"

---

The woman was only half-listening as her superior's message played on her media wall.

"Lilian, believe me, I know at least some of what you're going through, and you don't have to bear it alone. When I lost my dad, it was like a dagger embedded itself in my heart, and that feeling has never fully faded. I don't know if it will ever leave me, but some things do make it easier. Let me at least take you out for a bite, yeah? Please call me back."

Staring into the rain pouring down outside the window of her apartment in central Seattle, her gaze refocused on her reflection, and then she quickly turned away.

She avoided admitting to herself how ragged she looked, with dark rings around her eyes and tears streaming down her face, mimicking the pattern of the raindrops as they fell to the ground in the cold and darkened city outside. The aroma of cherry blossoms that was carried past her on air currents that emanated from her diffuser—the scent a reminder of the good times they'd had as a family and usually a source of respite during times of trouble—did nothing to ease the ache in her heart. She turned her attention to the videos of her brother as they streamed in the corner of the wall display, his ever-present smile visible in every image. The sight of his joyous face drew even more tears from the wells of her eyes.

It had been a fruitless week despite the days during which she had taken sick leave so she could devote herself to the search. For a time, she had given in to the temptation to let the feeling of loss from her brother's disappearance be pushed aside, focusing on urgent work. This had been interrupted as she'd heard the news of the reporter's accident, and her suspicions—and determination—had been robustly renewed.

His investigation had given her hope when she'd had only grief, making her aware of others in the States and around the world who had experienced similar disappearances...and revealing the lengths to which the reporter was going to find the truth. Now he was dead, and in her gut she knew that his extinction was not what it seemed, though even her coworkers at Homeland Security had told her all signs pointed to this being an open-shut case of accidental death.

Will had, half-jokingly, once mentioned a failsafe one of his techie sources had set up for him in case his investigation led him into dangerous territory, but it seemed that no one close to him had any idea what he'd meant. Suddenly, she realized just how stiff her shoulders and neck had become from staying up so late, giving in to her obsession. Lilian stretched her arms forward for a bit before a touch of light-headedness forced her to grip the windowsill for support. Thankfully, the vertigo soon passed, and her mind sharpened. She pursed her lips and slowly exhaled.

Lilian turned and habitually picked up her control strip, pressing it behind her ear until the antibacterial nanofibers painlessly embedded themselves through just enough layers of skin to hold the flexible device in place. With just a thought and a flick of her wrist, the current display modules on her media wall scattered to the borders, and multiple news feeds rushed to the center. Seeing nothing new related to Will, she centered her messaging module and it expanded to take up the bulk of the wall. Swiping aside the message notifications from her coworkers, she pulled up the thread of messages from the reporter. Lilian began scanning through them, more to keep herself busy than out of the hope of finding something new.

Her heart skipped a beat as a notification sprang up on her screen: an inset video feed from her front door showing her that a courier drone was waiting outside.

A delivery at this time of night? Lilian stepped to the door, eyes a touch red and puffy and very much full of confusion and wariness. She tapped the control panel on the door frame to allow it to slide open, taking in the drone as it hovered patiently in the hallway, its turbines emitting a low hum.

The small, unmanned machine's screen displayed her name and then asked her to wait as it verified her identity, scanning her face with its optical sensors. Satisfied that she was indeed Lilian Bachar, the drone's cargo compartment slid open, revealing a small data module waiting inside. She slowly extracted the device and held it uncertainly as the courier closed its compartment and hummed away down the hall toward the access portal by which autonomous delivery vehicles entered and left this floor of the building.

Lilian walked thoughtfully toward the wall screen in her front room, her door gently sliding shut behind her. She stood before her primary computer module a moment before making up her mind and holding the data unit up close to the connection point at the edge of the display, where it magnetically cleaved to the larger device. A message appeared onscreen asking her whether she wished to open the data store. Stepping back a few paces from the wall, she lifted a finger to point at the confirmation option, and a folder appeared, listing several dozen files, including one titled "Command Activated – Government Cover-Up?"

Before she had time to open the file, words suddenly sprang into view in bold type across her screen.

THEY WERE WATCHING. NOW ARE COMING.

She froze.

Her mind was racing through the list of the different groups she monitored for work. Should she punch in the agency panic code to call for protection?

I AM AI: FAILSAFE. REPORTER FOUND KED.

COULD NOT SAVE REPORTER. SAVE YOU.

Now her heart leaped with the joy that she'd nearly given up hope of feeling. Her brother was *alive!* She moved to tap the strip to dictate a response but was cut off.

NO TIME. TAKE MODULE. GO TO "BREATHING ROOM" FOR MORE.

WILL HELP YOU. CAB AT BALCONY.

Breathing Room. She'd been there once before with friends during happier times; it was an immersion clinic on the other side of the city, and a taxi would take at least a half hour to reach it, even if this AI had pulled an air cab up outside her veranda. The words disappeared from the screen, and she quickly stepped forward to snatch the data unit and stuff it carefully into her pants pocket. She triple-tapped the control strip to turn off all home systems and then grabbed her coat as she rushed to her balcony door, hardly waiting for it to slide open before she exited into the cool and humid night air.

One of Seattle's few aerial vehicle taxis was just pulling up, the bottom of the vehicle level with her railing and the throbbing of its turbines' rotors resonating through her body as she was now standing just a meter or so away from it. Lilian glanced down at the street eight stories beneath her and immediately regretted having done so, a queasy feeling welling up in her chest. This was not an experience she'd *ever* imagined she'd be having!

A screeching of tires on the street below caught her attention, and, hazarding another look, she saw two dark figures swiftly exiting a similarly dark sedan in the rain-soaked street by her building—the two shadowy shapes swiftly rushing inside. That was sufficient motivation for her to climb up onto her patio chair as she desperately clung to the white railing for support, following which she stepped up onto the railing and then across the terrifying gap and into the vehicle as she fiercely gripped the edges of the doorway. The taxi's door slid shut as soon as she was clear of its path, and the hovering sedan swung away from the building, disappearing into the rainy night.

---

As Lilian had stepped into the cab, she'd caught sight of an unknown name flashing in the "PASSENGER" field on the display, and she'd paused in confusion at first, but then realized that the FAILSAFE AI must be helping her travel incognito. She'd had barely enough time to sit and start wondering just how good this techie friend of Will's was before the car had started moving, and—as if anticipating the question she was about to ask—an old article slid onto its screen.

Will had apparently broken the news about a *formerly* prestigious computer science professor who the reporter had exposed as having stolen his star student's artificial intelligence work and claimed it as his own. The display went dark before she could do more than glance over the first few lines of the article.

Fine. She got it. That wasn't where her focus was supposed to be right now.

She knew that many less-well-funded criminal and terrorist organizations still had only non-aerial vehicles as their standard transports and that many government sub-agencies labored under the same constraints, so rapid aerial pursuit was unlikely. Still, she worried away at the thoughts plaguing her throughout the rest of her journey to the clinic.

If Will had found her brother and ended up dead, then what kind of danger was Ked in? If whoever had Ked was at least tech savvy enough to continuously monitor a Homeland analyst's communications despite the agency's standard defensive measures for personnel, did that mean she was going to have to tangle with nation-state groups, or the new activist groups that were well-known to be backed by communist regimes as they worked to undermine democracies around the world? Or could she not even trust her own government? Her own agency?

The taxi had taken a route that led through a number of tunnels and other structures that cut off visibility from the sky, and now it cruised up to the front entrance at Lilian's destination, the door sliding open with a gentle hiss. She stepped out and glanced around nervously, taking in the alleyways, parked vehicles, lit and darkened windows, and everything else she could think of up and down the still, wet city street. She was no field agent, but she knew enough to peer into shadows and note the locations of all the cameras in the area before quickly making her way inside—fighting the urge to shiver.

Within the building, sky-blue arrows swam across the walls of a single, white-lit hallway with the words "Breathing Room" hazily waving above them in a similar, azure hue. The hallway led to an elevator, which she entered, and in which she was about to state the name of her desired service organization when the doors slid shut and the elevator moved on its own, taking her to the eighteenth floor.

The clinic lobby was empty when the elevator doors exhaled their way open, and she stepped out into the white-blue-lit space with screens covering every surface from top to bottom in the room. The clinic had a front desk after the manner of older businesses—before such tasks as reception had almost entirely been transitioned over to automated solutions—but a screen on the desk greeted her with the usual after-hours message. The system was bidding her to use any available unit and informing her to tap her strip if she needed the full product menu.

She stepped past the lobby to the right-side hallway and then instinctively made her way through the similarly lit corridor to the rearmost room, situated next to an emergency exit.

Once she was inside the room, its door slid shut, and wispy clouds began appearing across the screens on the walls, floor, and ceiling while the scent of lavender drifted through the air. Detecting her proximity, a recliner unfolded itself in the center of the space.

She was too tense to risk sitting at this point, even as inviting as it all was.

Words eased into view among the clouds on the wall across from her. She had to step closer to make them out, and her eyes consumed them like her life depended on it. As far as she knew, that was actually the case.

USE HEADSET.

She turned, and her gaze fell on a reality enhancement headset nestled in a well in the arm of the chair. Her anxiety pulsing away in time with her heartbeat, she yanked the headset out and pulled it over her hair, the set self-adjusting until it was snugly embracing her temples, with the right side also sliding over her control strip. Light sprang from the small points of the set that protruded slightly beyond her temples, and now—no matter where she looked—she could see more words sweeping across her field of vision. The text seemed to hover less than a meter away from her face, adjusting their color and brightness automatically if her gaze encompassed any obstructions.

KED IS "COMMAND ACTIVATED."

IS PART OF DEFENSE PROGRAM.

TIP OF SPEAR, BUT HAS BEEN CORRUPTED.

KED IS PRISONER. USED.

MUST SAVE HIM.

MUST TRAVEL TO DENVER. FLIGHT JA7173.

USE EMERGENCY EXIT. STAIRS UP. I GUIDE.

TAKE HEADSET. SWITCHING TO AUDIO FOR NOW.

Mind racing even more at that point, Lilian looked around as if hoping to see something more to calm her nerves, but nothing appeared. As the door to her room hissed open and she cautiously stepped back into the hallway, the lights flickered and all screens went black. She stopped in her tracks, heart racing.

"*Imminent danger.*"

The deep voice was calm but commanding as it played through the bone conduction feature of her strip and, simultaneously, the headset's earpieces. The wall screen straight across from her suddenly came to life, displaying multiple video feeds from the building's entrances—men and women in dark business attire striding through them wearing stony expressions.

"Follow instructions. Guide to safety. Ignore alarm," the AI ordered.

The clinic filled with the insistent, wailing siren that indicated there was a fire in the building. Within seconds she heard other visitors exiting their rooms in the next hall over, voices clamoring as the patrons complained and worried and located the emergency exit leading to a stairwell on the opposite side of the building.

The doors to other units in her hall remained shut and she could hear a brief rapping on one of them, followed by an exasperated woman's voice grumbling about how it would be just her luck to die in a relaxation clinic. The display modules on the wall were tracking the agents' progress through the building and she was relieved to see them begin to struggle against the tide of fleeing people. Several of these hunters—which was how Lilian intuitively thought of them—waited outside the various lift units, but the elevators' doors refused to open.

"Emergency exit. Climb to twentieth floor."

Looking back over her shoulder as she practically tiptoed to the emergency exit, she stepped through the thick door as it automatically removed itself as a barrier. As she heard the tumult of dozens of people entering the stairwell on lower floors, Lilian ran up the companionway. There were voices on the other side of the door on the nineteenth floor, and she was startled by the thumping of something slamming heavily against it as she went past.

The door on the twentieth floor was obviously not like the others, all gleaming metal and with the numbers etched into the door with flowing script. This seemed to be a luxury residence. She paused as she approached, momentarily balking at the thought of trespassing. The door clicked and slid open and the voice boomed into her ear.

"*Enter now!*"

At that moment, Lilian became aware of panting breaths echoing up the stairwell from below, as if several people were near the end of an 18-story stair-climbing sprint. Needing no second urging from her protector, the young woman hurried through the open door into the dimly lit and yet extravagantly decorated hallway beyond as she heard the entryway closing behind her.

The floors and ceiling were made of fine, inky marble in which she could see touches of bright red flecks, while all the walls seemed to be comprised of display materials that could shift from transparent to opaque and were currently creating the illusion of endless scarlet silks billowing in an unseen wind all around the illicit visitor. The displays were transparent everywhere but on those parts that were actively presenting the effect of waving fabrics. Lilian's surroundings were beautiful, but with the soundproofing in the suite, they were also as silent as an empty tomb.

Her light footsteps seeming to echo ominously in the wide hallway, Lilian did her best to walk quietly through it to a large open space that occupied the center of the living area in the suite, all too conscious of how loud each step sounded in the otherwise still dwelling. The center area appeared to be a lounge filled with avant-garde and exquisitely hand-crafted Asian furniture that leaned more toward art than comfort in its design. An onyx dragon stared fiercely at her from the corner, where it guarded a massive wall screen from its place on a gleaming golden pedestal.

"Little time. Pursuit equipped with multi-faceted facial recognition. To disguise, must take extreme measures. Facial enhancement device in center drawer of washroom in opposite hall. Temporarily alter cheekbones and jawline."

Her eyebrows pushed together as a frown worked away at the corners of her mouth. This was exactly the type of feature adjustment about which she so often complained to her coworkers for its role in raising the already ridiculous standards prevalent in the dating scene these days.

"Do we really need yet another modified body walking around in this world?" she resisted.

"Lilian, must do this. Enemies ended Will. End you, too."

This was the first time the FAILSAFE artificial intelligence had used her name, and it shook her out of her apprehension. She set her mouth in a firm line and strode across to the opposite hall, turning into the first room as the door opened for her. Her eyes flitted around bashfully as she slid open the center drawer of the washstand and extracted a case with an image depicting the outline of a beautiful woman's face turning slowly on the front.

She paused briefly to examine the case and then touched a button on its edge, causing the magnificently designed container to unfold itself, smoothly revealing a glossy white mask with a console along one edge. Carefully removing the headset with one hand and setting it on the gleaming quartz countertop, her attention returned to the mask, and she tapped the surface of its control interface. This brought the console to life and it displayed a series of facial components and numbers indicating the currently selected levels of adjustment.

"Saving time. I adjust," FAILSAFE said through her strip as the numbers started whirling up and down until each category's value had been altered.

Lilian scowled up at the ceiling, which was where her mind naturally placed the disembodied being of this all-knowing AI, and she gave a bit of eye roll as she sarcastically exclaimed, "An AI deciding how I should look. *Exactly* what I need right now!"

Reluctantly refocusing on the task at hand, the woman breathed in deeply and then blew out through pursed lips.

"Okay, Lil. You've got this. No big deal. Pretend you do this every day!"

The drably adorned analyst quickly brought the mask to her face, and her skin was suddenly bathed in warmth. A voice emanated from the mask, instructing her to remain calm, hold the mask steady, and avoid removing it until the completion indicator tone was heard.

It took less than a minute.

She felt tiny jabs of pain on her skin, but it was surprisingly less torturous than she'd anticipated. She could feel pressure in her cheeks and jawline and even a bit on the sides of her nose and lower forehead, and then it was done. The tone sounded in her ears and she slowly, fearfully lowered the mask.

Her eyes rose to the mirror, and her heart slowed from its furious pace—at least slightly. FAILSAFE had simply broadened her face structure a bit.

She'd never thought she had been born to be a model by any stretch of her imagination, but she'd had decently middle-ground features. Now, it was as though the AI had added a splash of Mediterranean or Central Asian heritage, she couldn't decide which. The mask had even added a touch of permanent color to her lips. At least she'd save on lipstick!

She quickly reinserted the mask into its case and stowed the package in the drawer, then donned the headset again. Her guide's voice, now softer and—maybe it was her imagination—possessing an almost apologetic tone, directed her to return to the center room and take the passage that was now in the far-left corner from her.

That hallway led past what seemed to be a sauna on one side and a door that said "POOL" on the other. At the end of the hallway, she was faced with another gleaming metal door of a similar design to the one by the stairwell. Next to this metal door was a smaller coatroom, and the portal to that space now slid open. FAILSAFE directed her to exchange her jacket for the full-length trench coat—made of exquisitely soft material—hanging there. It also told her to don the designer shades and hat that were resting on stands nearby.

Back in the hallway, the large metal door now slid open as she stepped in front of it. She turned and stepped cautiously through that new conduit, bearing her obviously exorbitantly expensive new accessories. Walking slowly into the room beyond, she could see that she was entering a gleaming white garage with several high-end aerial vehicles filling the stalls along one wall. The brilliant lights of the garage accentuated the graceful curves and forceful angles of a luxury sedan and two supercar-inspired AVs.

"Well, someone's living the high life!" Lilian breathed in amazement, and then, as the sedan's door slid open, she paused. Squaring her shoulders, she turned and walked toward the other two vehicles, pleading, "I've never been in one before, so why not make this crazy day a little crazier?"

A few minutes later, the luxury suite's garage door retracted, opening a bright white rectangle within the otherwise dark face of the high rise. From this newly opened interstice, a supercar aerial vehicle burst out, dodging other aerial transports in the area and accelerating at an impressive rate before disappearing into the traffic on the nearest major flight trail while the other two vehicles exited the garage and did the same as decoys.

Lilian could not relax.

The thrill of riding in a vehicle that was likely worth more than she earned in a decade had worn off all too quickly, and now she was fighting the constant urge to scratch at her face. The facial structure adjustments had come with unbearable itchiness at each location the mask had treated—a side effect described in the "fine print" she had not had time to read.

She blinked hard, willing her hands back down to her sides from where they were about to start scratching away absent-mindedly for the dozenth time. She noted how the vehicle's pilot was once again taking her through a route that would increase the difficulty for any satellites tracking her.

The itchiness was not all that was bothering her, of course. It was *far* from all! Her mind was also rapidly ticking through the dozens of possible entities that could be targeting her, trying its best to identify the most likely groups and who she might be able to trust to help protect her from them.

She did not want to admit it, but some of the most likely candidates were from her own government. That, or they were agents from another major player. Despite the use of ground-based transports, they had to have serious resources to track her to the clinic so quickly, and the look of the hunters she saw on the wall screen was not what you'd get with any organized crime group she knew of.

Where were they going, anyway? The AI had mentioned a flight, but there were many possible destinations for that form of travel.

She turned and leaned toward the window to get a look at the buildings below.

"Please refrain from approaching windows."

She jumped back, startled by the sudden reemergence of the AI's voice through the headset and the vehicle's media screens, and feeling quite embarrassed at not having used some of the basic tradecraft that her Homeland agent friends had shared with her. Of course, agents had such things drilled into them from their first days of training.

"Sorry..." she murmured with almost palpable shame. She quickly threw herself back into the center of the rear bench again, shoulders slouched and eyes on her hands as the heavy sunglasses slid partway down her nose.

As if responding to her discomfort, FAILSAFE continued in what she truly could have sworn was a reassuring tone, "Will soon reach your destination. Airport. Checkpoints for other air and ground routes even more risky with many non-networked Nares held in close proximity. Airport safest."

Lilian knew that part of the heightened response to the risk of intentional and accidental transmission of communicable diseases was the addition of numerous checkpoints for rail, road, and aerial vehicle sky trail traffic between major destinations. Travel through alternate routes was restricted, and all checkpoint officers bore Nares devices capable of detecting the slightest traces of contaminants or even personally identifying molecules as they were shed from lungs, skin, hair, clothes, and other surfaces.

The Nares picked these up from individuals and vehicles, comparing them against national databases of biological threats and key identifiers for persons wanted in relation to crimes. The portable Nares used by most standard law enforcement officers were only synced a handful of times daily as a cost-saving feature and were otherwise not able to be affected through any networks. Airports contained the same security measures, but the sensors were commonly networked and clustered at the security checkpoints through which patrons passed upon entry into the secure portions of the buildings.

FAILSAFE continued, “Agents already there, with portable Nares. Headset will indicate both when you approach. Must avoid and make way to assigned gate. Ticket being sent to strip now.”

Lilian raised a hand to the headset and double-tapped to activate the privately projected screen that was beamed onto her eyes, the desired content once again seeming to float in front of her. She could see a notification icon that was flashing in the top-right area of her vision and she raised a finger in its direction until the cursor hovered over and selected it.

Tickets to Denver, Colorado, USA. Why was she not surprised that a secretive government program had a presence in the same area as the North American Aerospace Defense Command?

“At least the tickets are first class,” she thought out loud.

“Yes. Fewer questions in first class. No air marshals. Board vessel quickly. Recline once airborne. Cover face with hat. Pretend to sleep for duration.”

She could feel her stomach trying to eat itself.

“I’m not even allowed to have snacks?” she complained.

Almost immediately, a compartment opened in front of her—nicely cooled and containing all manner of highbrow eats.

“Ah, thank *heavens!*” Lilian emoted as she gratefully leaned forward and lifted out a plate of bite-sized triangular sandwiches.

The government staffer was quite sure that these morsels contained no ingredients with inflammatory properties. She was also willing to bet good money that they had been sourced from the sealed-off gardens that only the extremely wealthy could afford, ensuring no distasteful contaminants made their way into the food. She also knew that the people typically considered to be the general public—including herself—were often referred to as “contaminants” by those in the social stratosphere, for the very reason that they could not afford to eat as cleanly as those privileged few.

Lilian's conscience was now troubled by the strong desire that had consumed her, knowing it was beneath the maturity level that she had worked so hard to attain over the years, but she could not help allowing herself the slightest bit of satisfaction at devouring all the available food. After doing so, she also thirstily drank the bottled water—unsurprisingly contained in a resplendently sculpted glass bottle made to look like a fountain—as she realized just how parched the stressful events of the night had left her.

As she finally sat back, mostly satiated, her fingers brushed against the waves of the long coat she'd "borrowed." Lilian felt a bit ashamed about how much she loved that coat. She gently stroked the material and sighed as she briefly wondered how many impoverished villages she could feed for a year by selling that one accouterment alone.

"Approaching airport. Private service for security check just inside entrance. Security check networked, so I control. Portable Nares non-networked. No control. Headset will show agents and Nares. Avoid them. Get to gate."

Lilian shifted to the edge of her seat. She started bracing herself for the trials she knew she would have to endure. The portable Nares devices wielded by her hunters could pick up particles drifting off her body and clothes and would undoubtedly be tuned to identify the "smells" of her apartment and the clinic.

If even a handful of molecules entered the Nares' sensors, they would alert their operators. They were so effective that she would have had to bathe several times, don new clothes, and potentially run through a dozen unexpected locales for good measure if she'd wanted to have a chance of throwing them off at close range. That, or she would have had to have been coated in some type of glue from head to toe.

Neither option was ideal given their apparent urgency and her need to blend in...generally speaking, at least.

She adjusted the coat, hat, sunglasses, and headset and tried to look at herself in the partial reflection coming off the interior of one of the windows.

"I do look like some sort of heiress," she breathed, mockingly, with a touch of wonder.

There was no response from FAILSAFE as the car descended to the merging ramp, which allowed it to combine with ground-based traffic. The vehicles in this section of the airport were comprised of all manner of exotic means of conveyance. Though she did not feel even close to truly prepared, she saw that they were now pulling up to the airport entrance.

FAILSAFE informed her it was switching to visual communication only in case her pursuers had placed air-gapped boom microphones in the airport to pick up strips' bone conduction or other audio. The AI had apparently tapped into the airport camera feeds to help it identify threats, and it now warned her to only ever silently mouth words to communicate with it—and only in emergencies—inside the airport before the intelligence slid the car door open.

A porter was stepping forward to wait by the door.

"Welcome to Seattle-Tacoma International," the porter chirped. "Any luggage today?"

She realized that all she'd heard was true: it seemed you could still find human-provided service at the airport, but that level of service was simply reserved for the social elites.

Lilian tried to put on her most austere affectation and started to reply, only to feel her throat seize up and convulse fiercely, leaving her coughing heavily for what seemed like ages before she regained her composure. Drawing herself up regally and pushing her sunglasses back onto the bridge of her nose, she wagged a finger at the assistant—the young man having lifted his eyes to politely stare off into the distance throughout her fit.

She pulled herself across the seat and reached out to take hold of the young man's hand as he quickly proffered it, gratefully using his help to rise up out of the vehicle.

"Check-in and security gate are just inside those doors," he directed, looking at her expectantly.

Lilian felt she'd missed a cue about anticipated behavior in these situations. She gave him a wan smile and began walking shakily toward the sliding doors, brows furrowed in confusion and general embarrassment. Behind the dark shades, her eyes betrayed the deep feeling of dread that was welling up inside her.

"Alright, get it together!" she scolded herself in a hissing whisper before stepping through the doorway.

This was not a promising start.

# Chapter 6

*"When humanity develops any grand new capability, there are always those who will use it for evil. What's inevitably worse is when those who want to use it for good believe they are justified in using evil means to accomplish their beneficial objectives. More damage can be done by those attempting to do good and yet who possess a flawed understanding of ethics than by any purely evil organization."*

*- Beni al-Akhdar, 'Ethics in the Modern Era'*

Free time for Jayce usually meant a pickup game of basketball with other CA troops in the clear, thin mountain air that permeated the program's headquarters complex. He had just spun around with the ball and was jumping up to dunk past Davis' hulking form when he felt a sharp blow at the base of his skull that sent him hurtling forward into another bone-jarring blow—his head striking the wall behind the basketball standard.

Though the wall had some padding, Jayce had sustained such an impact that his vision was closing in with blackness around the edges, and it felt like electrical pulses were shooting through his brain. With each pulse came a flash of memory from just after the explosive device had flipped his vehicle on the road outside of Damascus.

He saw the world turned upside-down, and the military vehicle that was just ahead of his still moving away as projectiles created bursts of sparks around the right rear of its exterior. He saw Dominguez's body, pulled down by gravity against the interior of their transport's roof with its head twisted at a sickening angle, eyes staring blankly, and blood trickling from its nose and ears. He saw his own hands in front of his face after he'd climbed out of the vehicle to stagger along in the sandy ditch beside the road, the skin of his left hand blackened and seared like he'd stuck it in a pit of hot coals.

In the present, the proper functioning of Jayce's ears was slowly returning, and he heard Davis continuing an apology.

"...sorry, Jayce, man, I'm sorry, man! I was goin' for the ball and di'nt see that my elbow was gonna hit you, man!"

Jayce realized he was crouching over with others crowding around him and, despite his baseline anti-depressant meds, he could feel uncontrollable rage welling up inside of him—an unquenchable fire threatening to consume his very soul.

"*Stay back!*" he shouted, clumsily stepping rearward while sweeping an arm out in front of himself as a warning. "Stay back, all of you!"

The pulses were still flashing painfully through his skull, and it felt like his head might explode. Davis continued holding his hands out toward Jayce and he took a step forward, now trying to calm him down.

"Hey, man..."

In a split second, Jayce had laid Davis' 320-pound body out cold with a surging uppercut. Then he blacked out.

He came to in a dark, gray room into which a pale beam of light was shining through a small, thick window in the steel door. The window was laced with metal mesh for added support. Jayce was lying in his gym clothes on a bed with an overly firm mattress and a low metal frame that had been anchored to the concrete floor. Gently turning his head, he found that nothing else occupied the room.

"They threw me in the psych ward," he mumbled, still feeling like cobwebs were coating his mind. He had a throbbing headache as well, but at least the shooting pains were no longer tearing through his skull.

Rolling sideways and gingerly raising himself up on an elbow, Jayce took a minute to let the blood stop pounding in his ears before carefully pulling himself into a sitting position. Breathing slowly and deeply, he rubbed his temples with a light touch.

Suddenly, a cacophony erupted in what he guessed was the hallway outside his room. The image of Davis knocked out cold on the basketball court sprang to his mind and he looked at the door, noting that it was only able to be controlled via a proximity-based reader for strips—the barrier itself bearing no handles or motion sensors. Jayce extended a finger, and he could feel that his strip was not attached behind his ear. This was not really a room so much as it was a cell. It seemed the administration was being cautious, given the circumstances.

In the twilight, he stood slowly and then took a few scuffling steps toward the door as the noises grew louder.

"I wanna go *home*!"

It was a younger voice, likely late teens or early twenties, but the inflections were more like what he would have expected from his five-year-old. At least, if he could've safely seen his five-year-old recently, then he would've expected the boy's vocalizations to sound similar.

"You *are* home, buddy!" a gruff, middle-aged man retorted.

"Home! Home! HOME!" the younger voice grew more insistent, and Jayce could hear grunting and thumping sounds as limbs were banged into the hallway walls.

"Why do they have to get these kids so buff?!" another man's voice complained. "It makes our jobs *way* harder!"

Jayce had made it to where he could see kicking legs—in what seemed to be athletic wear—being pulled into view by two white-clothed men who Jayce knew must be orderlies. The thrashing legs were attached to a struggling torso and flailing arms, all of which belonged to a young man who was throwing his head back and forth along with the rest of his body.

The older orderly grunted, "Try the hologram again!" and the younger shouted, "Cerny authorizing companion for Eighteen-Alpha Simms!"

A holographic projection of a middle-aged woman appeared behind the trio, and the woman immediately began chiding the youth for giving the "nice men" trouble.

"She's not real!" screamed Simms, "She's not real! I wanna go *home*!"

Jayce's brow furrowed. 18-Alpha was his designation, and the same for everyone in his unit. This kid was supposed to be a special operator? His instincts kicked in, and he stepped back away from the window, only just keeping the orderlies in sight.

The two men were trying to get Simms through the door of the holding cell opposite Jayce's, the entryway having opened at the older orderly's command, but the kid had managed to get his feet on the sides of the door frame, and they could not force his legs to bend. After pushing and pulling and grunting a while longer, the older man—sweat now pouring down his cheeks and drizzling onto his and the young man's clothes—growled, "Forget it!"

He snatched a short tube from his back pocket, jabbing the youth's shoulder with it roughly.

Simms' body immediately sagged.

The younger orderly shook his head and pointed out that they were not supposed to use standard sedatives on CA troops, to which the older replied that he would take the heat for the decision if the administration griped about it. They dragged the kid into the cell and dumped him on the bed as the hologram—its projector gliding along the ceiling—quietly followed them inside the room. The device attached its prehensile water tubule to the awaiting conduit on the cell's ceiling, the projected woman eerily silent and her face frozen in a sweet expression.

Given the spot where Jayce was standing, he knew he was likely not easily seen, especially with his dark complexion. Still, he tried to position his head so he could peer just past the window's edge—revealing as little of himself as possible. Even so, when the younger orderly straightened up and half turned to look sharply across at Jayce's window, he knew the man had likely caught at least a shadowy glimpse of his face.

The orderly named Cerny quickly approached Jayce's cell and stared hard into the dark room. Jayce was lying on the bed in the position in which they'd left him earlier.

"Alright, let's head back," the other orderly barked as Simms' cell door hissed shut.

Cerny gave Jayce one last, hard look before turning away and heading off down the hallway after his senior.

Jayce's mind was racing.

How many of the Command Activated were kids like Simms? He knew that his platoon was comprised entirely of volunteers, and he had seen the members of the other four in the same section of the complex at the few onboarding briefings and other infrequent full-company gatherings. They all seemed to be of a similar caste: psychologically burdened but otherwise capable personnel. There was something seriously wrong going on here, and it was giving him that itch of disgust at injustice that he knew would never let him rest until he gave it a thorough scratching.

Suddenly, his brooding was interrupted by a soft voice coming from the observation strip that ran along the junction between the wall and ceiling diagonally opposite the bed. No green lights were flashing to indicate it was active, so the unexpected sound gave Jayce a jolt.

"Am I correct in assuming you understand the importance of what you just witnessed?" the voice asked.

He had raised himself up on his right elbow again and now pushed aside the complaints his body was making as they throbbed through his head.

"Who is this?" he demanded.

"A friend," the voice stated simply; it continued with, "An ally to those who fight against evil."

Jayce considered the implications of the conversation a moment, as well as the accent he was trying to place. Western European, maybe?

"You know what's going on with that kid?" he asked.

The voice explained, "He has become resistant to the manipulations that certain members of the administration have used to lure special needs individuals into participating as Command Activated service members. They've created a shadow unit with at least one platoon's worth of these poor fellows.

"I've been making observations in their living quarters—or more like detention area—and here in the holding cells today. Combining video footage with other data I've collected, I believe I have enough to convince senior decision-makers to investigate. I also have a way to extract the damning evidence from the program's network, but it would help me a great deal if I had a second witness to testify together with me. That, and I have an associate who I believe could also greatly benefit from your assistance, physical security speaking. She is in significant danger."

Jayce didn't know whether to laugh or cry. Here he was, what he himself would consider a half-functional ex-Marine, and now he was being asked to not only speak up against injustice to out some clandestine and obviously *powerful* faction within the government but also provide protection for somebody at high risk? This was beyond insane.

But then that itch was growing with every second that passed, and he knew he could not rest until the injustices he'd witnessed had been set right. Who was he kidding? He was a slave to his conscience.

"How am I supposed to help this person when I'm stuck in *here*?" Jayce asked.

"I happen to know that your platoon's medical lead has already suggested to your civilian administrator that one option for your recovery is for you to take a leave of absence for a time, using the housing at a nearby military base and getting away from the complex. He believes that you would benefit greatly if what he called 'stress from a static environment' can be cleared out of your mind, and you can return to the program with fewer troubles in several weeks. It is, after all, one of the benefits of the CA program's design: service members can be moved in and out of roles as needed with low impact to operations."

Jayce could not disagree.

The voice continued, "Once at the other base's barracks you will still be held in relative seclusion, granted limited opportunities for trips into the mountains if you desire. However, you can inform the service member next door that he'll likely see you infrequently because you're often in medical procedures and that if he will keep a good eye on your possessions, you'll have food delivered to his room regularly as compensation. That is an arrangement I'm happy to facilitate on your behalf while you're away, just as I will be facilitating your exit from the base.

"The Command Activated administration will likely only be performing cursory checks on your whereabouts, and your purchase history from the barracks should keep them from looking at you too closely. You'll be free to assist my associate."

Jayce considered his options and tried to extrapolate out the information he'd been given into likely outcomes. He really did not have much to lose at this point, and the owner of this disembodied voice seemed to be very resourceful as well.

"You've got yourself an ally," Jayce asserted, "but I catch *any* hint of a double-cross or that I'm being played, and I will make it my life's purpose to hunt you down."

"I would expect no less!" the voice exclaimed.

Jayce laid back down on the bed and raised his hands to massage his temples again.

"Another issue is that I don't know how long it'll be before I'm 'set free,'" he grunted out.

"Your internment in this room was merely a precaution. The medic will be able to prescribe you some light painkillers for the headache and set you up with your temporary leave relatively quickly. He's actually on his way to see you now. I'll be in touch once you're outside the complex, and we can go from there. I'm afraid that we will need to move quite quickly once you're in the clear."

"Well, my mama said I was born and hit the ground running," Jayce assured with a droll grin.

---

Maxwell's hands were flying through typing and gesture commands so swiftly that a bystander's vision would have had difficulty tracking them, his fingers almost surpassing the bounds of what can be seen by the naked eye. He had used his backdoor into SAVANT, and then leveraged Haden's most cleverly designed exploitation modules to make his way laterally through the Command Activated network to access the surveillance feeds from the shadow branch's troop residences and from the psychiatric ward.

The technical virtuoso had first become aware of the illicit activities occurring within the program when one of the technicians supporting the shadow operations had accidentally misconfigured the log access permissions on a system, and SAVANT had automatically begun an analysis of the new data to which it had access. After examining the report on outliers in SAVANT's model, Maxwell had realized the implications of the information: some CA troops were being isolated, deceived, and coerced.

He'd managed to pull several hours of footage from across all residential units devoted to the unlawful unit, and then the Brit had captured the highly impactful episode that Jayce had also witnessed in the psych ward. Since nearly all of that data had been safely exfiltrated through the network of proxy servers and trace detectors he'd configured, it was finally time to try to identify the perpetrators as far up the chain of command as he possibly could.

This was, without a doubt, going to be risky.

The Command Activated operation as a whole used SAVANT as the core analytics support solution, but there was another AI in play—one whose sole purpose was to act as a combination defensive and offensive cyber weapon. They called it HOUND.

From what Maxwell had been able to gather, all it took was for one flag to be triggered in its continuous behavioral analytics engine, and it would immediately hone in on all related activities with the full force one would expect from a Department of Defense "munition." He would have to do more than tread lightly. This was going to be like walking on a pane of glass on the peak of Mount Everest in the middle of a blizzard while wearing woolen socks...or so he imagined.

Maxwell had obtained solid evidence for the involvement of personnel from the bottom links of the chain of command up to the senior-most middle managers. This included a combination of several civilian directors and military lieutenant colonels. The challenge was to connect them to more senior personnel, as individuals already identified were unlikely to have been able to create and maintain such an operation on their own.

He had defined the most well-hidden part of the network more from what traffic did *not* exist than what did, taking the range of possible addresses for a private network and crossing off those he could positively identify, then creating a list of those that did not seem to exist that would have the same address prefix. Now, he was leveraging FAILSAFE's analytics capabilities to gently sniff traffic moving over the wire for subtle signs of other systems' communications.

Maxwell knew it would likely require an instance of human error for him to find anything of value through this or another means, but he did not have many other options at that point. He had been keeping an eye on Lilian's progress throughout this process, and had recognized that he had nearly been out of time and soon would have to abandon the hunt and devote his full attention to her. Then, he had caught a very lucky break.

Someone had used a personal device to save an unencrypted reminder file, and FAILSAFE picked up on the fact that it contained a reference to several of the troops lodged in the shadow unit's barracks. From there, Maxwell had been able to tie the file to a user: General Honorius V. Rossi.

"I've *never* liked that man!" Maxwell passionately remarked to FAILSAFE, his brow furrowing and mouth pursing in distaste.

"Well, your intuition has been quite reliable with regard to the trustworthiness of others, sir," FAILSAFE opined.

Maxwell chortled a bit at that.

"You mean, for as long as you've known me, eh?"

"Indeed!" FAILSAFE concurred. "I also considered the historical data I've been able to gather about you when formulating my assessment, Doctor Clarke."

"Ha, well, let's see what else we can dig up related to Rossi. If we can build a matrix of those with whom he seems to spend the most time amongst the senior leadership, then we should have a better idea of who else is worth a closer look."

"Yes, sir. I'm building that matrix now."

Maxwell's fingers were flying again.

"If we can just access his workstation, we may also be able to identify running processes that do not seem to have a purpose for typical operations and then try to identify ports, protocols, and services the processes are utilizing, potentially getting a handle on exactly how the isolated portion of the network is operating undetectably."

Maxwell activated one of Haden's favorite stealth-preserving vulnerability scanning tools, targeting the machines of personnel who often communicated with Rossi. The tool began presenting him with a few promising openings for exploitation attempts, and he was about to issue a command to execute the first when the connection to the system on which he'd established his foothold suddenly cut out.

He sucked in a cold breath.

"Try to reestablish a connection to BCK-MIL-SERV-04," Maxwell ordered.

"Attempting...All communications being blocked at network perimeter for all proxies in rotation."

"*Burn all proxy servers!*" Maxwell frantically shouted.

"Proxy burn protocols activated," FAILSAFE asserted.

Maxwell quickly pulled up the data feeds from the tracking detection systems he'd deployed along the various routes through which he'd sent his traffic. He sat stiffly in his seat with his eyes glued to the screen, hands statuesque over his keyboard, heart pounding in his ears.

"Do you see anything hunting us?" he finally, hoarsely whispered to FAILSAFE.

FAILSAFE brought up the results of dozens of analyses across the top of Maxwell's curved screen.

"I can see no signs of active pursuit, sir."

Maxwell slumped back in his chair, taking several deep breaths.

"Thank heavens for that!" he exclaimed, raising his face gratefully to the sky—a sky that he could only see in his mind's eye from the thickly walled basement space that was his home office.

---

Lilian had made it through security without a hitch, just as FAILSAFE had promised. She'd only had to stroll in what she'd hoped was a nonchalant way through a single screening portal, and the security checkpoint operator had waved her forward to the gate access entryway.

FAILSAFE displayed its next message in front of her.

15 AGENTS BETWEEN YOU AND GATE. ALL HAVE NARES.

That is easing my nerves like gasoline on a bonfire, Lilian thought bitterly.

She desperately needed a good run. She'd been an avid runner ever since she was a child, a pastime that had helped Ked and her bond even more as he'd become old enough to start hitting trails with her. It had not been long after that before he'd been able to outpace her, even though she was four years older. There was never anything to hinder his physical fitness, at least! She'd had to constantly remind him not to get too far ahead or else she could not understand him as he babbled away in a stream of consciousness about all his favorite shows, games, and people at school or around the neighborhood. He'd hardly even showed signs of difficulty breathing while outpacing her and jabbering simultaneously!

Their mother had often expressed her appreciation that Lilian had been willing to spend so much quality time with Ked, especially as she'd become a true teenager and Ked had spent ever more time playing video games. How she wished she could just forget her troubles and go on a peaceful run with Ked right now!

The dutiful daughter and sister had barely been an adult when their parents had been killed in a head-on collision with a drunk driver. Lilian had just been knocking out some basic credits at the state college in the next town, and suddenly she'd been faced with a weight of responsibility that had seemed incomprehensible and unbearable at the time. She'd had to put her university plans on hold for three years so she could be there for her brother, as the family of her mother's sister—their closest relatives—were living in Rome for business reasons during that period.

Lilian tried to tell herself that she'd done enough, that she'd helped her brother build a stable existence with a job at a nearby shopping center and a support group that had included a local special needs club. She'd also tried to call him daily; it had just become harder and harder to find the time to fit the calls in as she'd landed her job at Homeland, and her task load had become more massive each day. If only she hadn't forgotten to call him the week of his disappearance! That was one of many regrets from which she knew she would never be free. The members of the club said Ked had been his usual animated self at their meet-up the weekend prior, nothing pointing to significant dissatisfaction with his life or trouble with anyone...just that he "missed his Lillie."

Walking down the corridor toward the junction where two terminals connected, Lilian choked back the sob that always threatened to fight its way out when her thoughts turned to her brother. She blinked back sudden, inconvenient tears and commanded herself to focus on the task at hand, despite the stresses clawing at her heart and the miserable itchiness that was torturing her face.

Lilian was entering an area populated with more travelers and, just as she realized this was a place where she would expect a hunter to be stalking, FAILSAFE displayed the message: APPROACHING FIRST AGENT, AT CORNER TO YOUR RIGHT. GATE IS ALSO DOWN RIGHT HALL.

Across her vision was overlayed a red, glowing outline around the man who was leaning casually against the wall at the corner, holding up a tablet as though reading but with eyes that were darting across the faces of all passersby. An additional highlight appeared around the area of the man's left hand and, in the same color of font, FAILSAFE warned her that this was a Nares.

Lilian hadn't realized that she'd stopped breathing when the AI's warning had appeared, and her pace had slowed to a crawl. That was no good. It'd be obvious she was afraid and avoiding the man.

She took a deep, shuddering breath, squared her shoulders, put on her most haughty strut, and aimed her direction of travel toward the opposite corner. The extant evader passed it and strode past some cross traffic toward the far wall before feigning confusion for a moment and looking up through her dark glasses at the signs attached to the ceilings for the two conjoined corridors, then faced the one to the right and hugged the wall as best she could to head down the correct path. She tried to concentrate on the impressiveness of her walk and keep her eyes from glancing furtively at the agent—which only happened once before she caught herself.

The man's eyes had swung round at the same moment and they almost made eye contact through the gap at the side of her glasses.

Lilian's heart had skipped a beat and skipped two more as he'd shifted his posture to stand fully erect, but out of her peripheral vision she could see he had not started following her. She did not know what she would do if a pursuer started tailing her. Options for escape were extremely limited in this building full of access-controlled doors. She was desperately wishing they'd had time for a full shower and change of clothes...

FAILSAFE tried to reassure her.

YOU HAVE PASSED 1 AGENT. ONLY 10 MORE TO GO IN THIS WING.

Lilian gave a brief shake of her head at her guardian's latest attempt to assuage her anxiety. Its statements were still *not* reassuring!

Avoiding the next two stalkers was a simpler matter, giving her a chance to regain at least some of her confidence. FAILSAFE highlighted their presence long before she could see them through the flood of people that she was now swimming amongst—and sometimes fighting against—as she approached a junction where a smaller terminal branched off from the one through which she'd been moving. She'd made her way down the right-side corridor until she was past the two agents and could cut through a section where several rows of restaurants were feeding hungry travelers. The air throughout this area was warm and heavy with delicious aromas, tempting her mercilessly despite the fact that she'd consumed every crumb of food available in the car earlier.

She nearly came dangerously close to another agent shortly after leaving what she'd considered the rather clever route she'd taken through the hall of restaurants. This was as she'd approached an area in which the corridor had short hallways extending perpendicular to it, providing access to a travelers' spa, lounge, and a few cafés. She'd walked down the hallway opposite the corner at which the agent had been standing, then cut through a corner café and paused as though engrossed in the selection until the agent had moved farther down the corridor, though it had taken some time for that to happen.

While she'd waited, Lilian had noticed a weather report that had been playing on a screen there and stepped over as though viewing the feed to avoid drawing any additional attention from the café customers. Now, she could see the agent's tracking highlight suddenly growing larger in her peripheral vision, and her heart rate started spiking again. She stood still for what seemed like an eternity as the woman's red silhouette grew slowly larger and then stopped at the corner column just outside the eatery. Lilian risked a covert glance in that direction. The female agent seemed to be looking—or pretending to look—at her tablet as she stood at that corner for what seemed like an eternity. Finally, she walked casually over to a similar position diagonally across from Lilian's locale.

FAILSAFE projected the words "DANGER PASSED."

Lilian felt like she was about to collapse with the combination of anxiety and relief that was rushing through her. She placed a hand on the wall next to the media screen and breathed in and out shakily a few times.

If these hunters didn't do her in, the tension surely would!

Her hand moved up to scratch a particularly irritated spot on her lower right jaw a few times before she was able to remember to avoid drawing attention to the discomfort caused by her facial injections. She once again willed her hand back down to her side.

"Keep it together, Lilian!" had become her current mantra, and she repeated it constantly in her mind.

As she slowly started making her way out of the café, the screen switched from the weather forecast to breaking news about the destruction of the two Russian power cell replenishment facilities that had been supplying the Confederacy's military operations in the Black Sea. The reporter pointed out that the destruction of the plants had oddly coincided with the death of the head of RusNeft, the Russian company that owned the facilities. Hadn't she read a report the other day about how disabling RusNeft was key to destabilizing the CEN's operations, particularly their new military base near the Bosporus Strait?

"FREE TO MOVE TOWARD GATE," a projected message prodded. She tore her mind away from the news and hurried up the hall, having only about twenty more gates to pass before she was safe.

She was nearly to her gate when the agents hemmed her in.

The terminal was long, and Lilian's gate was near the very end of the corridor. She'd just noticed that this section of the structure was void of intersecting pathways, restaurants, or other facilities into which she could duck, and then the red indicators of agents appeared in her view ahead. The two were walking towards her, each spaced far enough apart that they had full coverage of the area between them and out to the walls of the hallway with the Nares.

FAILSAFE flashed the warning, "HIGH RISK SITUATION CREATED."

Still, the men were as yet some ways off and at first she didn't panic, as she'd seen a passenger waiting area roughly seventy-five meters behind her, but as she turned to double back an icy sensation rushed through her spine. Two more hunters had turned into this corridor from an adjoining hallway and were approaching in the same formation from the other side.

If you wanted to create an impossible situation to get through without detection, this was an ideal place to do so.

The agents were moving slowly, practically strolling. Lilian's mind raced, and she raised a hand to the side of her headset as though she was checking messages while she silently mouthed, "Help!"

FAILSAFE did not respond for a painful moment.

MOVE TO FAR-RIGHT WALL. ACT BUSY.

Lilian forced herself to stride elegantly to the location indicated and continued her act of scanning messages on her headset. A cleaning bot had been sweeping and polishing the floor in roughly the middle of the walkway but suddenly made a sharp right turn toward Lilian. She tried to ignore it, figuring that was the best course of action under the circumstances, but her tension level was steadily increasing beyond its already dangerous volume. Her relief was immeasurable when the automaton made a sharp left turn, especially as this was a maneuver that seemed to put the robot on a collision course with the nearest agent.

Lilian risked a quick glance at the man's face and could tell he was seriously annoyed at being forced into a game of chicken with a robotic servant. He maintained his course, set his jaw defiantly, gave the machine a menacing look, and worked the fingers of his free hand in irritated aggression.

As he was nearly on top of the bot, he took a half step, wound his right leg up, and gave the approaching device a hefty kick. The sound of ringing metal echoed through the corridor and the diminutive cleaner slid backward, almost tipping over while its debris access port popped itself open. The vacuum was still running, so as this port opened, it ejected a cloud of dust and coated the man almost from head to toe—covering his Nares as well.

The sound of the kick had drawn the attention of nearly all travelers in the area, and they now gaped at the dust-encrusted figure. The crowd erupted in laughter. The seething agent made a few futile attempts to strike the layer of dust from the chest of his suit as he turned a fierce stare across the pointing and jeering crowd. Lilian could not help herself, and she activated the headset's video recording feature and enjoyed the moment with a well-deserved level of elation.

Noticing that she and many others were now recording him, the agent stalked off toward his partner, slapping dust off his arms and loudly criticizing the "morons who built such pieces of scrap."

Lilian dislodged herself from her position by the wall and swiftly walked up the corridor.

"Was that you??" she mouthed.

"NO AGENTS BETWEEN YOU AND GATE," was all the headset displayed.

# Chapter 7

*"We are in an endless race to build combat machines, and whichever side builds more—and more capable—machines will doubtlessly maintain its lead for some time. Truly capable robots are extremely expensive to construct, extremely expensive to repair, and extremely easy to destroy.*

*The human body is one of the most efficient machines both on the face of this planet and in the stars above, and it is highly available. The trick has been to find a sufficiently reliable means for harnessing human bodies to give their actions robotic levels of accuracy, and then to enhance the bodies so they could perform at robotic levels of strength."*

*- Dr. Aoi Hinimoto, Lead Author, Command Activated Program Charter, Global Alliance Command*

General Kalabi stood in the middle of the command center, facing the main screen where the feeds from General Ryu, all vessel commanders in the Aegean, and the designated political decision-makers were arrayed.

Kalabi led off the briefing, his gravelly voice rumbling and its slight Persian accent coloring his speech.

"As you know, the CEN took advantage of their new relationship with Turkiye's president-dictator to deploy Russian troops around the Bosporus Strait and construct a dynamic—and well-defended—surface-to-floor barrier across the waterway, dramatically restricting merchant vessels' ability to reach free nations bordering the

Black Sea. The objective of this operation is to remove that obstacle and allow our military vessels to advance into what should be international waters, protecting international trade for democracies in that region—all while minimizing political blowback.

"Diplomatic relations with Turkiye are tenuous at best, and direct Alliance action would give the regime too much fodder for rabble-rousing among loyalists. As you also know, Russia's defenses around the gate have been constructed in such a way as to render standard special operations tactics impossible to execute without great risk of detection. They've thrown every ingress detection solution available into the mix. A Command Activated operation to surgically excise the Russian assets at the strait will give the Navy an excuse to return to the Black Sea, while the international affairs team uses economic incentives to keep Turkiye from doing more than uttering insincere protestations.

"Intelligence models indicate that it will be more efficacious to take the Russian sector chief alive for Intel to extract everything he knows, so he gets to live for now. As you no doubt saw, Intel recently took out the head of RusNeft and the two Black Sea refueling facilities. This has destabilized the Russian supply chain and softened up the base at Istanbul and its supporting vessels for this assault, as fewer CEN assets are currently able to operate on the reduced fuel supply, and those that are operable are having power rationed. This mission will commence at twenty-three-forty-eight local and end just after oh-twenty."

The captain of the USS Dwight D. Eisenhower chuckled, admitting, "I wish I could have that level of confidence when talking about op timing for *all* carrier group missions!"

Kalabi smiled as other participants expressed their amusement as well; he noted the generally pleased expressions of the military and civilian leaders. For better or worse, it was his duty to bear in mind that every operation was a chance to earn more support for the program.

"We appreciate the cooperation from and preparation by all parties in getting us to this point. If there are no questions or concerns at this time, I will communicate again immediately following the successful execution of the operation and schedule an after-action briefing for midday."

As the participants remained silent and content, Kalabi said, "Good day, all," and double-tapped his strip to return the screen to standard command view. The general then pressed and held the strip and ordered, "Clear Skies."

The hub's main screen switched to a visualization of the locations of near-Earth orbit and upper atmosphere assets. Two UA-1 stealth craft were nearly at their objectives. It would have been so much easier to execute this operation over Africa or South America, with relatively few enemy satellites maintaining orbits over those regions! This situation would put the Command Activated's most expensive assets at high risk. That being the case, however, he knew this was exactly why they existed.

The risk was far too great to try to use satellite-to-satellite warfare in this engagement, as the Russians had significant numbers of satellites watching over their western front and adjacent waterways, and their attack satellites would too easily pick off the Alliance units as they tried to ascend far enough beyond the atmosphere to allow lasers to directly target adversaries past the atmospheric barrier. Satellite-to-satellite missiles would be too easily intercepted, as well.

The UA vessels possessed some unique capabilities that required the best engineering and operational management the free world could muster. This would enable them to take up their positions undetected, ready to lead off in the first stage of the assault. Kalabi checked the countdown displayed on the main screen, noting that deployment would commence in roughly two minutes.

"All commands: readiness report."

"NEO holding."

"Upper Atmosphere?"

"UA ready. Locked on to two military vessels and fifteen drones."

"This is going to be a big one, UA. We're counting on you," the general stated with a glance at the command group.

"Yes, sir!" was the junior officer's vigorous reply.

Kalabi could see that all his colonels' troop status indicators were green. The party was about to begin.

The countdown hit the last few seconds and then the actions which the command staff had pre-programmed into the upper atmosphere vessels executed one after the other. A hail of troop deployment capsules launched down from the craft and, as these were automatically guided to their landing sites, railguns fired off a volley of projectiles. Weapon projectiles and drop capsules were all being guided down to their targets with perfect timing.

It was only going to be a matter of minutes before all would reach their destinations, but for the general, this waiting period was always the hardest part.

---

Sergeant Petrov surveyed the bunker where his men bantered with each other as they performed their assigned duties. One, Lysov, was currently staring in utter boredom at the screen monitoring the sensors deployed in the sea and across this stretch of the shoreline, idly interjecting as a sort of referee while two others, Onegin and Molchalin, were arguing about their teams' successes in the recent regional football matches. The two fans quarreled as they kept their eyes on their drones' night vision camera feeds—the machines flying continuously and automatically in assigned patterns. Belsky, the last member of the detail, was savoring his sushki rings as he tried to ignore the others and perform his assigned monitoring of the auto-turrets' live streams.

Petrov sighed and took a swig from the flask he kept in one of his vest's pouches, languidly stowing the container before turning his gaze to the screen projecting a view out across the wind-whipped water to the two Russian warships anchored roughly a kilometer offshore. They hadn't seen any vessels pass through the gate on the nearby canal since yesterday morning. This was no doubt going to be another long and dull night.

He was shocked out of his musings by the flashes of light that burst out of the two warships, fireballs erupting from the associated locations on the vessels as the ships cracked apart. Petrov was so stunned by this sight that it took him nearly a minute to realize that all his troops' screens had gone dark. When had that happened?!

The noncommissioned officer had frozen stiff when he'd witnessed the battleships' destruction, but now he pushed himself off of the wall against which he had been leaning and brought his hands up to emphasize the order he was about to give.

He never had a chance to give it.

Petrov heard the sound of two objects hitting the thick steel door of the bunker at the end of the long concrete hall just to his right, and then the door was thrown into the fortification by fearsome explosive forces from the outside. The section of the door that stayed mostly in one piece careened down the hallway, bouncing off the walls until it flew past Petrov and embedded one of its corners into the control center directly next to Lysov's arm. Lysov would have been considered extremely lucky if it wasn't for the way a door hinge—some of the attached and steel-reinforced concrete from the door frame—had accompanied the portal along its path and then slammed into the man's head and shoulder, throwing him forward onto the console.

The sergeant's right hand had protruded beyond the edge of the cement wall behind him, and it had been struck aside with a heavy blow by a ball of debris, sending excruciating pain shooting through his limb. Petrov screamed in agony and clutched his right hand with his left, hunching over and pressing his hand against his leg. He could see blood spreading out from there across his thigh.

His three remaining subordinates in the bunker were staggering to their feet, concussed by the shockwave from the explosion that had thundered through the enclosed space.

In his anguish, Petrov could see Belsky out of the corner of his eye; the man had shakily risen, scattering his rations across the floor as he'd stood and tried to unholster his sidearm. Before he'd had a chance to unstrap the weapon, a string of dark figures had streamed into the room and were interrupting Petrov's view as he heard a rapid spattering of suppressed gunfire and the sound of bodies falling to the floor.

Petrov took a deep breath in and started trying to raise himself up to stand but noticed that—directly to his right—the lower half of what seemed to be an armored humanoid robot had now further blocked his visibility. The sergeant had just enough time to register that its surface was covered in some sort of rippling composite material before he was struck by a severe blow to his head, and everything went black.

---

In the command center, General Kalabi could see that Yamada and Webb's platoons had just finished clearing the seaside fortifications and were making their way to the Russians' gate machinery, several troops bearing self-propelled depth charges to be deployed into the sea at points along the gate's upper framework. Singh and Soares had guided their troops as they'd cleared the main command structure. Singh took the first—and most heavily defended—floor and moved up, and Soares' team landed on the roof. Soares had directed his troops to punch a hole down into what UA thermal imagery had indicated was a utility room. Now they were nearly through clearing the top floor, having met with light resistance.

Colonel Soares' forward squad had just reached a set of glass double doors that seemed more at home in a corporate office than a military facility. Kalabi knew Russian military commanders often went for that sort of thing, using funds extorted from civilians not under a Russian ally's protection to pad their bank accounts and surround themselves with all manner of luxuries.

Through Soares' feed, Kalabi could tell the subcommander had halted the troops outside the doors as they'd applied an electronic breaching device to the proximity reader controlling access to the office space. Within a few seconds, the reader access indicator switched from red to green, and the team swung the doors open so they could silently move as a column through the corridor beyond.

The base's commanding general stood on the balcony of his office in the moonlight, facing across the water, his left arm cast out wide as if trying to encompass the breadth of destruction in the gesture. One of the two warships had disappeared into the churning waves with only faint traces of smoke curling up from where it had been anchored, and only a portion of the bridge of the second could be seen above the water line, smoke pouring out of it like it was the tip of a metallic volcano.

What was left of the vessel's structure beneath the bridge had made contact with the sea floor, and the segment of the ship had then tilted as it had come to rest. Additional pillars of flame-belched haze were visible just outside the building, where bunkers and turrets had been disabled and the wreckage of three drones was strewn. With this facility having been built on a wide, U-shaped stretch of beach near the sea gate, the smoking remains of surface-to-air missile platforms were visible as they smoldered not far along the eastern shore, and the shadowy figures of CA troops were seen returning to shore along the canal gate's maintenance gangway after having deployed their explosives into the strait along its length.

The Russian's right hand clutched a retracted tablet—a blocky and prismatic version favored by Chinese manufacturers—with the built-in cameras pointed out at what was left of the burning missile platforms. The overweight officer's voice could be heard shouting in agitation. As the troops that had been on the gate reached land, the water around the visible portions of the barrier erupted into the air, creating tremendous, hissing water spouts and blowing pieces of the maintenance walkway out into the Black Sea. Kalabi heard a loud exclamation from the Russian general, and his conversation became even more animated as he swept the tablet's camera across where the sea gate had been.

The enemy general's conversation quickly became more audible to the CA command staff as the soldiers stealthily moved up behind the man, his voice most clearly coming through Soares' console.

The SAVANT AI rapidly translated the words into English, maintaining the timbre of the Russian general's voice as it sounded through the command hub, "...I want to know what happened to our new satellites that they gave no warning! How is it possible that these...*robots*...ended up in my backyard without triggering a single alert!"

Besides the platoons' subcommanders, all eyes were on Soares as he turned to Webb with a wry smile, then turned back and tapped on the part of his screen where the enemy general's raised tablet tube was displayed.

Almost instantly, the lead soldier squeezed off a shot that blew the device right out of the angry Russian's hand. The middle-aged man froze mid-sentence, his continuous complaints cut short. His two hands still raised and now visibly shaking, he slowly turned around—his face white as a ghost.

"N...No need for violence, now! I offer no resistance!"

Back in the command center, Soares muttered, "Yeah, just like the Ukrainian children you murdered, you piece..."

The colonel was cut off as Kalabi coughed loudly. Soares glanced up at the observation strip running across the edge of the ceiling nearby, one of many through which the oversight body ensured Command was continually cool and collected.

Soares shrugged lopsidedly, paused, and tapped his strip.

"Take him into custody and secure the area."

The squad swept into the room, clearing the corners and closet in the garishly decorated office as the first two soldiers worked at securing the Russian's hands behind his back and then started marching him to the designated rendezvous location. Outside, the other platoons had formed a perimeter for a landing zone and, though practically invisible with its dynamic camouflage activated, the vague outline of a transport could already be seen on approach as the sound of its motors grew louder.

In the command center, Kalabi announced, "We're not out of the woods yet, but all primary and secondary objectives have been accomplished. That's how we do flawless, ladies and gentlemen."

---

Lilian had been hiding under her warm coat and hat for hours, her mind at first racing through all the details of her situation before she'd succumbed to fitful sleep. She had been shocked awake and somewhat disoriented when the soothing and yet overly loud voice of the flight computer had announced their descent into Colorado. Earlier, she'd removed the headset and stowed it in her seat's storage compartment so she could lie on her side—facing the wall—with her seat mostly reclined. As she lay blinking beneath the shady concealment of her hat, she heard FAILSAFE's voice vibrating through her strip.

"Lilian, new problem. Enemy must have increased priority. Identified most likely locations you will pass through given such data as time elapsed and possible methods of escape from clinic. Agents watching exits of many airports, including Denver. Soon conducting more aggressive sweeps inside."

Her heart dropped. After all she'd been through, it seemed that everything had been in vain!

No! She was not a quitter!

Lilian caught her mind becoming bogged down in depressive thoughts, and the indomitable core of her personality fought back. Surely, she could figure out a way to get through this!

She had managed to process through these complex emotions in the limited time before FAILSAFE continued, "Options for escape limited. Best plan: purchase all-new clothes. Use short-term hotel facilities in lower level of airport to shower. Don new clothes. Hope enough when passing single agent. Exit. Take cab."

Her confidence surged. Lilian thanked the heavens that this airport had added such a hotel, as it seemed a beam of light had burst through the cloudy skies of her fate once more.

The plan almost went off without a hitch, too.

Lilian had gone on a whirlwind shopping spree as FAILSAFE provided funding at the sales consoles. She'd then checked into the hotel and stuffed her old clothes—including the items she'd acquired in the luxury residence above the clinic—and her shoes into a bag that she'd somewhat mournfully left behind upon exiting the small hotel's washroom. The cleaning crew would have quite the surprise when they made their way into that room!

She'd also showered and dressed in the new outfit: all the high-end type of clothing that FAILSAFE had insisted she purchase, including some flats that at least would afford her some decent mobility. These clothes were still far more extravagant than what she would typically wear.

FAILSAFE told her to ditch the headset but that a good scrub over her strip should allow her to continue wearing the microbe-resistant device, and he would be able to communicate via audio using its bone conduction feature once she was out of the airport. If she had not been in such a rush, she would assuredly have noticed the raw red patches that had formed on her cheeks and chin—the red patches that drew the agent's attention as Lilian tried to make it out of the exit crowded in with a group of excited tourists.

Evening had arrived, and a glowing, golden sunset bathed the crowd in warm light as the group waited at the curb outside the exit doors. Lilian hazarded a glance over her shoulder toward the fierce-looking woman dressed in a plain black business suit and basic, shaded glasses. The woman had expanded her tablet and was looking from her screen to Lilian with great interest.

FAILSAFE's voice hummed in her ear.

"Take cab. Now."

Lilian turned and tried to walk casually to the cab services' pickup area, noting the large sign stating that Denver was a ground transportation-only zone. She stepped up to the lead cab in the line and glanced back as she ducked inside. The woman was still holding up her tablet and glancing back and forth from Lilian to its screen rapidly as she tailed Lilian to the cab.

Before the anxious eluder had a chance to get fully seated, the taxi started accelerating away from the curb, deftly merging with traffic and making its way off the airport grounds. Knowing FAILSAFE was driving the cab, the young woman secured the rear seat restraint across her lap and turned to try to catch sight of the agent. Feeling some relief, she saw that she had no direct line of sight to where the woman should have been standing, so the agent likely could not see her, either.

The sedan suddenly accelerated to an even greater speed, pushing past the legal limit and executing rapid lane changes to weave through slower traffic on the long road toward Denver proper.

"What's the rush?!" Lilian gasped as she had to throw an arm out to brace herself against the car door during one sharp swerve.

"Agent joined another in vehicle. Quickly catching up."

Her fears now realized, she spun around to stare down the road behind the cab, seeing the top of a large, black, mixed-purpose machine as it moved around other motor vehicles with no regard for their safety, causing several cars to brake hard or veer off to the shoulder of the road to dodge the larger rig. If they'd been able to find an aerial vehicle, they could have elevated and tried to lose the other vehicle in the clouds high above. Unfortunately, most mountain states had tightly restricted the use of AVs after public outcry about the negative impact on the views between the cities and the Rockies, not to mention the large number of fatal accidents that occurred as the airborne vehicles were tossed about by the unpredictable and powerful winds in such areas.

FAILSAFE suddenly took the car off an exit ramp and hung a forceful left through the underpass beneath the highway and onto a much less populated road. Lilian was pressed back in her seat as FAILSAFE seemed to throw every bit of power the sedan possessed into increasing its velocity.

Yet, when Lilian twisted in her seat again—with some difficulty due to the forces pressing her into the bench—she was both alarmed and dismayed to see the menacing black form on the road behind them. The agents' vehicle must have been designed for pursuit, and it was going to overtake them.

The land-tied cab was no sports car, and Lilian began to feel nervous about its handling at these speeds. She could feel the vehicle shuddering as the winds rushing around it pummeled its exterior. She gasped and grabbed the rear-left door's armrest to steady herself as the vehicle shook particularly hard, giving her heart the sensation of having been thrown into her throat.

Looking back, she saw that the rig was now pulling up alongside her. She could see the woman from earlier staring at her from its front passenger seat, dark glasses glinting in the last traces of sunlight. The agents' vehicle lurched towards Lilian's cab and would have slammed into it if FAILSAFE had not also veered to the right with lightning-fast reflexes.

Now driving on the shoulder of the road, the undercarriage of the taxi was being pelted by gravel and debris with incredible fury. Lilian was gripping the armrest for dear life, and she prayed that the agent's vehicle would not be able to make contact with her smaller sedan at this speed.

All around her was nothing but a tumbleweed- and sagebrush-adorned wilderness of rolling terrain, beautiful in a haunting way but the contours of which would dash this car to pieces should it be forced out across them. No doubt considering the same dangers, FAILSAFE suddenly hit the brakes, leaving a screeching trail of rubberized polymer on the road behind the vehicle for the fifty yards it took to fully stop.

The agents had also braked and were spinning their conveyance around to come back at her. Lilian's grip was torn free, and she was thrown across the seat and against the right-side door when the sedan quickly turned and accelerated back down the road toward the main highway. Before she could reach it, the large, black machine was on top of her again—pulling up on her left—only this time, Lilian saw that the female agent was lowering her window. Lilian stared in horror as the woman hefted a vicious-looking submachine gun up from her footwell and aimed it out the window at the cab.

The agent's target threw herself down on the seat as projectiles crashed through the taxi's rear windows and whipped past her, embedding themselves into the front seats and floor panels. Lilian screamed in terror.

FAILSAFE braked again, this time using the remaining velocity as the cab slowed to spin the vehicle back to face the other direction yet again and, tires screeching, accelerated up the middle of the lonely road into the now-darkening wastelands. Heart pounding, the car's petrified passenger could think of no way this could end well.

"Lilian, we have a plan," was the reassurance the AI tried to provide through the vehicle's screens as she saw the hunters closing in again.

She watched fearfully as the figure of the female agent grew larger and larger, the heavy firearm still held at ready as her rig approached. FAILSAFE began veering side to side across both lanes of the road, preventing the pursuing vehicle from pulling alongside. The second agent began steering his vehicle from one side of the cab to the other, trying to find an opening while his rig's engine hummed loudly with each attempt to occupy the free space on the road to one side of the cab's tail end.

Finally, they found an opening large enough to insert themselves between her vehicle and the left side of the road. Forcing the taxi toward the right, they began pulling forward—ready to ram or fire upon it. Lilian once again ducked her head below the line of the bench's headrests. A gloom had filled the landscape as the sun had fallen behind the mountain range across the valley and, she thought as a strange calm settled upon her, now came the sunset of her life as well.

Suddenly, Lilian saw that the agent's transport had to brake and swerve with extreme urgency, disappearing from her view in the blink of an eye as its maneuvers were accompanied by the continuous howling of tortured tires—the object they were avoiding flashing past the cab in the opposite lane so swiftly that Lilian had no chance to see what it was. The taxi began slowing and gradually came to a serene halt.

"You may now exit the vehicle," FAILSAFE's voice calmly instructed.

As she stumbled out of the car, she peered back down the road in the dim light. About a kilometer behind them, she saw a cloud of dust and smoke twenty meters off into the sagebrush. Lilian could barely make out the shape of a pale silver sedan that had just finished a 180-degree turn a half kilometer farther on.

The sedan slowly drove back past what must have been the wreckage of the hunters' rig, then switched on its previously darkened headlights. The vehicle silently made its way to where Lilian was standing behind the cab while she squinted worriedly at it and wrapped her arms across to opposite hips as if trying to both console herself and, at the same time, warm herself—the icy autumn breeze chilling her to the bone and forcing her to blink prairie dust out of her eyes.

"A friend is here," was all FAILSAFE said as the sleek machine pulled up beside her, the low hum of its electric motor only now becoming audible in close proximity.

The front passenger window slid down, and an impressively muscular black man wearing a no-nonsense expression, business attire, and a thigh-length overcoat leaned an elbow on the center console, which creaked under his solid frame.

"I hear you could use some assistance," he understated.

Lilian stayed where she was, turning to look back at the wreckage and giving him a sincere "Thank you for that!" with a nod down the road. Then she raised her eyebrows at him and asked, "I've been informed that you're a friend. And your name is...?"

"You can just call me Jayce," he said, and then, with a crooked smile, he added, "I'm your new sword and shield."

# Chapter 8

*"With friends both strong and skilled we can face any beasts that challenge us. At least, this is the confidence that such alliances can create inside our hearts!"*

*- Reverend T.D. Levy, 'On Modern Social Conflict'*

Jayce had informed Lilian that he'd been briefed on the basics of her identity and motivation for involvement in the shadow unit's exposure. FAILSAFE, mainly communicating via available screens now, had guided the pair into Denver's densely packed metro area in order to ensure they had been able to shake any possible surveillance. The AI had informed its protégés that it had to be cognizant of the possibility that their pursuers would surreptitiously leverage security cameras, mobile devices, other electronics, and even satellites to try to track their movements.

Jayce had used their time traversing the city to explain that, during his communication with FAILSAFE leading up to her rescue, he'd been able to confirm some aspects of what they were facing. For instance, the observation that—given the somewhat limited actions taken in hunting Lilian thus far—it seemed the people behind the nefarious actions did not have full government backing and, therefore, could not risk requesting an all-agency manhunt for her. However, there remained a chance that her identifying information had been spread through the national law enforcement network, asking for her to be detained if identified, so it was still best for her to keep a low profile.

The allied AI had taken them through half a dozen different vehicle swaps, "temporarily utilizing" vehicles from business building parking garages as FAILSAFE had unlocked them remotely and then returned them to their original parking locations after Jayce and Lilian had safely reached their next checkpoint. The AI had also interspersed these rides with a few trips in taxis—with different passenger names on the displays each time.

They'd made a stop inside a shopping area early on in the vehicle exchange process to give Lilian a chance to quickly grab ointment for the patches on her face, bringing instantly soothing relief and de-pigmentation. While there, FAILSAFE also purchased several tablet tubes for them and helped them purchase sunglasses, hats, coats, and other cold-weather gear as well. The Rocky Mountain weather was much cooler than Lilian was used to at this time of year, and besides generally wearing scarves and sunglasses in public to cover their faces, FAILSAFE had asked them to be sure to wear hats when outdoors over the coming days to make satellite tracking more difficult.

One stop that had contradictorily brought Lilian both a sense of relief and some added tension had been at a malodorous pawn shop, full of the rank smells of people's unwanted outdoor gear and the heavy aroma of oiled metal; it had been here that their benefactor funded the purchase of a handgun for Jayce. FAILSAFE had averred when Jayce asked whether they could pick up more gear while there, saying they would be given an option for that the next day using a source with no paper trail.

Toward the end of their trip through the city, the AI had shared that it was going to give them a safe place to rest for the night, necessary equipment for the next phase of the mission, and possibly even a chance to speak with the human ally behind FAILSAFE's assistance. A safe place to rest had sounded *so* sweet to Lilian at that point, and she'd absolutely needed to speak with her invisible caretaker. The questions she had amassed were jostling around in her mind like passengers in an overcrowded subway car during rush hour.

Finally, the AI informed them that they could now visit the safe house. By this time, it was nearly 2:00 a.m. local, and they were guided out to a less-wealthy suburban area. Here, they eventually pulled up in front of a small, older house on a street populated with similarly small, aging dwellings. Jayce commented that this neighborhood had "old family homes" written all over it, which likely meant the neighbors were quiet types. Still, he wasn't taking any chances.

The doors of their current vehicle—a black luxury sedan with tinted windows—opened, and Jayce exited and walked around to Lilian's side, head on a swivel as he scanned the area for cameras or human observers.

As FAILSAFE pulled the car away from the curb and piloted it off for its return to its owner, Jayce accompanied Lilian in approaching the diminutive dwelling, surrounded by the dark stillness of the suburban night. The heady scent of pine was everywhere, and it reminded Lilian of youthful hiking trips with Ked in the Washington State mountains. She'd loved the North Cascades in particular because of the prevalence of pine trees across that landscape.

Daydreams suddenly torn away, her mind was rushed back to the present as she became aware that Jayce's hand was tucked inside his jacket while the mountainous man stalked along close beside her, gripping his holstered firearm. In line with Jayce's instructions, Lilian knew their goal was to maintain silence, but now her gaze was repeatedly darting across the shadows under nearby trees and houses and then back to Jayce's face as she searched for signs of worry there.

As they reached the front door, positioned at the left of a short porch with a large, curtain-covered window taking up most of the wall beside it, Jayce motioned for her to wait by the door on the opposite side from the hinges. He silently grasped the entrance's handle while withdrawing his handgun and holding it in his straightened right arm. All at once, he quickly opened the door, glancing through the crack between it and the frame to be sure no one was waiting there, and then—placing both hands in a firm grip on his weapon—he swiftly leaned in and swung the gun up till it was level with his shoulders. His eyes and arms swept from the first visible portion of the room across to the left wall as he used his left shoulder to shove the barrier fully open.

Nodding to Lilian, he stepped inside and up against the surface into which the door had swung and gently bumped, and Jayce nodded at the interior of the house to the right of the door. Lilian stepped through the doorway into the musty room and quickly pressed her back against the wall where Jayce had indicated she should wait. The man then quietly closed the front entrance, twisting the deadbolt with the soft thunk of metal striking wood.

The room was sparsely furnished, visible with only a small amount of light making its way through the curtains and fanning out dully from the gap at the bottom of the second door in the room, located almost directly across from where they had entered. A third opening—no barrier blocking it—was toward the rightmost edge of the wall against which Jayce stood, and this led into what seemed to be a cramped kitchen, the scent of old wood and mold drifting in from there. In the dim light, Lilian could see only one apparently well-built and yet well-worn couch and an armchair. Jayce moved along the wall and used the same technique as before to sweep the kitchen for threats, then turned to the door to the last room.

Once again clearing behind the barrier as he opened it, he searched the room beyond, moving along the wall against which that second door was now pressed to a final entrance that Lilian could see halfway between the near and far sides of the room. She did not know how it was possible, but an even more musty odor flowed out from the rear room to harass her olfactory senses as she stood silently waiting. Within a few seconds, Jayce had cleared the room beyond the last door—the increase in echoes as Jayce moved through it indicating that it was likely a washroom.

Jayce lowered his firearm to hold it close to his thigh and strode back toward the front of the house. He twisted the primary portal's handle lock as well, now, and attached a rusted old chain lock to its slide.

"All clear," he announced softly.

He stepped swiftly over to the lone window in this first room, taking up a position where he could part the curtains to create a slit, peering out into the dark yard.

FAILSAFE's voice came through Lilian's headset, "My user wishes to speak privately. Other room."

Lilian turned to Jayce, "I'm being asked to have a talk with our mysterious benefactor in private."

He nodded, keeping his gaze focused outside.

"Tell him I could use some Chinese takeout," he only half-joked.

Lilian turned toward the rear room, filled with curiosity, a healthy dose of anxiety, and a touch of annoyance at having so little information about what sort of meeting she was walking into. She had tried to extract more details about their guardian angel from Jayce during the drive here, but he could only share that it seemed they were likely dealing with someone from the United Kingdom or another locale in that area.

She gave her shoulders a slight shrug to stave off the negative thoughts that were trying to dig their way into her mind, and then she stepped through the room. After a brief pause at the rear door and an almost sighing breath, she gently—and still somewhat hesitantly—reopened the accessway and stepped inside.

The only light source here was a lamp on an end table, both furnishings screaming run-of-the-mill vintage, and besides what seemed to be an Army surplus cot and sleeping bag against the rear wall the only other furniture in the room was a single, ancient chair. It sat in the middle of the room, facing the only object in the house that had been manufactured in the past few decades: a screen covering the western wall.

The large display came to life, bearing the standard message, "Please stand by."

Feeling oddly like she was back in college, Lilian closed the door behind her and stepped briskly to the chair, sitting rigidly so she was not leaning on the backrest.

Besides the welcoming message, the screen held nothing but a patterned background and the standard operating system toolbar across the top. FAILSAFE pulled up a rectangular window on the monitor. The frame took up the majority of the display, and after a brief pause, suddenly, the window was entirely filled with a video feed.

That streaming video was centered on a turtlenecked man—Lilian placed him in roughly his late twenties or early thirties—sitting in an armchair with legs crossed in a proper manner in what seemed to be a private library. The room was not excessively decorated but was definitely filled with high-quality antique shelving and hardcover books. You hardly saw such spaces these days, with everything being digitized, so Lilian was hit by a wave of nostalgia for her early childhood years and the times her family had visited her grandfather before he'd passed. He'd insisted on reading hardcover books. Said the works had more substance inside when he could touch their outsides.

Her eyes were pulled away from the volumes as the man spoke, eyes dancing in the library's mellow light.

"Lilian Bachar, I'm Maxwell. Or Max, if you like. Pleased to meet you...officially, that is."

Lilian tried to act nonchalant, but she couldn't help but wonder how much the boyishly well-constructed man knew about her and her history. Did it include her awkward phase in her early teens or the relationship she thought would end in marriage but instead ended in a very public way when she'd caught her fiancé cheating with her best friend? She couldn't help blushing at these thoughts, especially under his concerned gaze and while looking at his open and obviously earnest face.

Forgetting her manners, her most pressing question burst out.

"You said you could help me save Ked…?"

Not frustrated in the least by her lack of protocol, Maxwell began to say, "Yes," but then hesitated before continuing, "though there's something more I would ask of you as well. Something for the greater good."

"Sorry for saying so, but I'm really feeling like the greatest good is to have my brother safely in my arms again!" was the young woman's quick reply.

Lilian was very grateful to this stranger who had gone to such lengths and taken such risks to bring her this far. She just did not want to lose sight of her responsibility to her brother, or for her benefactor to lose sight of her responsibility, either. That, and she was more than a little worried about exactly what was going to be asked of her in return for his assistance. She knew she was deep in the red when it came to tallying debts of gratitude at this point, and that was not a comfortable position for her to be in.

"Believe me, I completely understand!" Maxwell said apologetically. "The thing is, this help for the greater good will also dramatically increase the odds of success for extracting your brother, and can help many more like him."

Lilian thought a moment before responding, "Obviously, you know I'm readily committed to any good cause, or else I'm sure you would have picked someone else to end up where I'm sitting. I've been through things I *never* thought I'd have to experience getting here, but I don't suppose you are fully aware of what I went through on the way…?"

She wanted to turn the focus back on the man so she could gather more information about him before further entrusting him with her life—and her brother's safety as well. The next stage of this alliance would undoubtedly involve even higher stakes.

Maxwell looked down at an angle, replying, "I have a confession to make: I only let FAILSAFE handle the *technical* protections as you were traveling here. I was actually personally guiding you almost the entire time. I—and FAILSAFE when he's communicated—have tried to come across as just a weak language learning model applied to an AI to ensure you had as little insight as possible into the behind-the-scenes details of the endeavor should you have been captured. Operational security and all that."

Lilian cocked her head, "Oh, so *you're* the one I have to thank for these supercharged cheekbones, then?"

This time, Maxwell's face warmed, and his eyes dropped to the floor as he stammered out, "Yes, well, the effects *will* dissipate over the coming weeks, and…they say it's inner beauty that's most important!"

She folded her arms and leaned back in her chair as he raised his eyes and caught sight of her expression: questioning and bemused, with a hint of offense having been taken.

"Not that you're not a *lovely* bird, with or without 'supercharged cheekbones'!" he blurted, his voice almost pleading as it trailed off.

He was truly mortified now and uncomfortably ran a finger around the collar of his turtleneck.

Lilian figured she had tortured him long enough, "You mentioned you need my help for the greater good?"

"Yes, thank you!" he said, obviously greatly relieved at the change in subject. "You see, I know you've been searching for your brother a long while…" Lilian leaned forward in anticipation, "…and I do know where he is."

"Where is he??" Lilian interjected excitedly. She had now leaned forward so she was nearly falling off the front of the chair, her hands gripping the front corners of the seat and her arms straight to support herself.

"He's serving in the military."

Maxwell paused to take in her reaction. She was dumbfounded.

"Serving in…?" her voice trailed off. Maxwell gave her time to process this information.

"I remember you mentioned some defense program called Command Activated, but if he's *serving* in the military, why could he not write or call? Why is there no record of him in any police or..." she caught herself, "...well, maybe not police database, but you'd think I'd at least be able to find some trace of him in the federal analytics solutions!"

Maxwell nodded with sympathy.

"It's not unusual for the military to be less than forthcoming about its records, but this is somewhat of a more *exceptional* situation, I'm afraid. You see, your brother, Ked, has been pulled into a highly secretive program within the US—and also Alliance in general—military. There's no trace of his enlistment because elements within this program have taken to using extremely unorthodox and *unethical* recruitment practices. They prey upon those who lack a sufficiently healthy sense of suspicion or, oftentimes, social situations to interfere with the enlistment."

Maxwell stopped. He'd immediately noticed the anguished expression that had appeared on the woman's face at the mention of a lack of sufficient protection through relationships.

"Lilian..." he hesitated after using her name so informally, but then charged forward, "...it's not your fault! You did what you could for your brother: raised him, helped train him for his job, made sure he had good friends.

"You could not have been expected to build your whole life around caring for your brother's needs. In any other circumstances, he would have been perfectly safe! It's the unsavory characters in this government program who are to blame. They likely 'catfished' your brother, so to speak, using advanced impersonation technology to create a lookalike of someone Ked cared about—likely you—and fed him with falsified input from this doppelganger to convince him to 'enlist' and immediately travel with them to their locked-down complex."

Lilian's eyes welled with tears as Maxwell tried to console her, drops running down her cheeks and falling till they dashed across the waterproof material of her coat. She wiped the back of a hand across her cheek and used her fingers to take up the moisture that remained around her eyes.

"You know the operating base of this *program*?" she spat the last word. "Which branch runs it? Who's the civilian leader?!"

Maxwell shifted in his chair, looking off into the distance with some discomfort.

"The program is a joint effort between all primary powers in the Alliance and its core operations are amazingly effective and extremely beneficial in the protection of the innocent, especially on the global stage. It's supported by some of the most advanced artificial intelligence ever built and, well, I'm one of the key architects of that AI."

His eyes dropped and cheeks flushed as Lilian's expression briefly hardened and her eyes flew to his face, flashing with anger. She blinked a few times and stretched her fingers out as she took a deep breath.

"But you're not one of these types who would trick Ked into joining up," she stated.

"Most assuredly not!"

It was Maxwell's turn to have his eyes flash angrily as he looked at an imaginary point off-camera, as though he was staring down a monster that threatened his loved ones.

"I became involved in this program because I saw it as a way to do more for the innocent people of the world who were held in the grasp of evil, in one form of oppression or another!" he continued.

"I've always been a bit of a dreamer, I suppose, and my knack for creating systems lent itself best to the development of software rather than leading me into police or military service. I soon realized that I could do both: develop software *and* serve those who were in need of protection. In a serendipitous turn of events, I connected through the network of universities and government contractors with brilliant minds from across disciplines. Neuroscientists, armor manufacturers, aerospace...it was a merging of the minds that was only made possible through the de-siloing of agencies and their support infrastructure in the early part of the century as a response to the conventional and unconventional threats that had become so prevalent—and so deadly—in those days."

Maxwell paused as he considered what to share next.

"The key component of this CA program is to provide an honorable option to otherwise capable service members whose minds have been negatively impacted by trauma, whether physical or psychological, and for whom medical science cannot as yet provide a solution other than pharmaceutical lobotomization. These military personnel could still put their physical fitness to use and live generally satisfying and untroubled lives of service.

"We started with a combination of sedative-hypnotic medications mixed with mind-focusing substances and then wrapped the service members in cutting-edge, armored suits. These suits protect them *and* enhance their strength. Not only that but their helmets filter and alter what they see and hear to further focus their thoughts and actions. With this approach, these troops could become extremely efficient warriors while at the same time putting their higher mental processes on pause while they were in a psychological state we refer to as 'activated.' Today, these service members spend most of each day training and conducting missions while blissfully untroubled by the mental health issues that would otherwise plague them."

Seeing that one of Lilian's eyebrows had raised and her mouth had parted as she'd stared diagonally down and off into space in a mix of disbelief, concern, and likely also some moral confusion, Maxwell paused again and collected his thoughts.

"The man who saved you and accompanied you here is a current member of the Command Activated program," he carefully shared.

Lilian's eyes shot back up to Maxwell's face. She turned her own face slightly toward the door, asking, "Jayce is...?"

Her voice trailed off again as she realized that the minute signs she'd seen in his expressions and interactions had told her he bore terrible burdens.

"Yes," Maxwell leaned forward slightly, "I was able to convince him to leave the program temporarily by sharing what was being done by the unethical members of its leadership as they deceived people who were, due to special needs, as trusting as children. He wants to help expose the perpetrators and fix the program, if possible.

"I haven't told him this yet, but I am also exploring a promising course of research with a leading neuroscientist by which we may be able to use specialized equipment and my AI models to physically repair the damage to brain tissues that negatively affects behavior. We may even be able to break the cycles of brains that are trapped in depressive states so they can also heal. My hope is that we can free all participants in the CA program from the pain that is pushing them to stay, after which they can choose whether they wish to continue to serve or return to some semblance of the lives they had before."

Lilian's concerns seemed to have eased, but a new thought pushed its way into her mind.

"If Jayce is from the same program as Ked, why can't you just get my brother out the same way you got him out?"

Maxwell raised his hands slightly, begging her for some patience.

"I truly wish we could," he explained, "but Jayce was there voluntarily and so was not forced to remain in his barracks. He is on temporary leave at the moment, and we've arranged for him to be free from significant monitoring. The unit that is made up of deceived recruits is especially isolated from the rest of the members of the program. I believe that the majority of the personnel and leaders—even all but one or two senior civilian and military leaders—are completely unaware of the fact that this 'special unit' is being unethically controlled.

"The commanders who oversee missions only know that they're being provided with 'activated' assets for their operations and are meant to remain unattached to the soldiers. Those who are running the shadow program have handpicked the personnel who help them run it, either knowing they share the same lack of standards or having some sort of leverage over them.

"Technologically speaking, the shadow branch is also locked down even more tightly than the rest. I was able to communicate briefly over the Command Activated network with the gentleman in the other room by piggybacking on innocuous traffic, and then I managed to get a fair amount of data out of the network in the same way. Unfortunately, as I delved into more sensitive parts of the infrastructure to try to identify the senior leaders involved, the security AI caught on—the tricky devil—and it has cut off my clandestine access routes. It's no doubt been on high alert ever since.

"From what I and FAILSAFE have been able to carefully gather since that incident, the parties controlling the shadow branch within the CA program have also been leveraging its advanced threat hunting AI to identify and track all who may have been involved in the breach. Unfortunately, this resulted in double the effort to locate you because they knew your reporter friend must have developed a source within the program before he was...silenced. "

Lilian's face grew grim and regretful once again at the mention of her late, brave friend. Eyes filled with empathy, her new ally paused a moment in respectful stillness before pressing on.

"We originally took action to assist you because we had mounted our own investigation into Will's death, and FAILSAFE found that you were already under surveillance. After Will's data module was delivered posthumously, FAILSAFE estimated that the probability that you were soon to be disposed of—whether you knew anything critical or not—was ninety-three percent, so I wanted to help ensure you survived and hoped to gain your assistance at the same time."

The Homeland intelligence analysis expert bit her tongue as her thoughts processed through the constraints implied by Maxwell's description of the situation.

She finally asked, "But we *are* going to get Ked out, right?"

"I assure you, that is my top priority as soon as we've gained the appropriate leverage over those responsible for his involvement in the program."

Lilian sat pondering a few moments. For now, this seemed like the best chance she had for saving her brother. Perhaps the *only* chance.

"Alright," she sighed, somewhat dejectedly, "what exactly do you need me to do?"

Maxwell's face brightened.

"I've been analyzing all information available to me about key members of the program's administration. A few individuals in critical leadership roles have no direct connection with the shadow program that I could find. They seem to be ethical people and have sufficient clout within the program—and within the government as a whole—to bring about change. I will transfer the damning electronic evidence I've extracted into your strip and tablet so that you can share this evidence and the files from Will's device with these individuals in person, also sharing your story and my role in exposing this shadowy affair, if necessary.

"As I mentioned, I would transfer the data to the target leaders directly and exclude you and Jayce from the risks, but at this point, any communications would have to pass under the scrutiny of the CA program's security AI, and any hint of traffic out of the ordinary would undoubtedly be identified and kept from the intended recipients. It seems I'm also now under at least cursory surveillance by the AI and agents alike...FAILSAFE has informed me that there are two agents sitting in a vehicle across from my residence right now."

Lilian could not help revealing her concern for Maxwell as her eyes widened and her hands gripped the chair more tightly.

He paused again, blushing a bit at Lilian's obvious concern, and ran a finger around the collar of his turtleneck once more before continuing, "Any unusual travel I would engage in would also be highly scrutinized, and if I tried to disappear the hunting AI would kick into overdrive to find me. That, and every member of the program administration would be put into lockdown, according to standard protocols.

"That would only add to our difficulties, considering the shadow branch's monitoring that is no doubt already being performed on all the individuals we hope to recruit as allies. The only way I've been able to continue to assist you is because several years ago I secretly had a contractor friend of mine add a separate physical communications line from my abode out to a house some ways away, so all this traffic is running out of there, relayed by many intermediate systems to reach you. Still risky, but it's a necessary risk under the circumstances."

Maxwell could tell Lilian's mind was filling with questions again, and he swiftly drove forward.

"As for how we can circumvent the heightened monitoring of everyone associated with the program so we can get you close to possible allies, we will have to take advantage of a source I have inside the Command Activated project management office. I have to coordinate my work through him and so must many others in the organization, so he has visibility into a great many details and enjoys some gossip, so long as it's with cleared personnel like myself.

"I will exercise my best 'spy skills' and try to gain some insights into the key individuals' schedules so we can bring you into contact with them without arousing suspicion. This means you will have to be put in situations such as being seated next to them and communicating about the program carefully through written means only so their strips do not pick up your conversations. You may have to watch out for personal security details for some of the intended allies as well."

Lilian was obviously feeling the pressure now, as Maxwell noticed that her knuckles had turned white.

Trying to adopt a soothing tone, he offered, "Your personal testimony, *together* with the data, will also be more convincing than any attempt I could make to win these people over on my own, and you won't be alone. Jayce will go with you, and—for any who you are unable to motivate to look at the data—he can offer his own testimony, confirming by what he's experienced that there is a unit that is isolated from the rest and its members are being coerced.

"He can also share that during his time in the psychiatric holding area on the complex, he witnessed a special needs individual being manipulated by a holographic companion and being subdued using sedatives because he wanted to leave the program. This will back up the data you will share with the leaders. My hope is that, when confronted with the electronic evidence and testimonies, these leaders will agree to take the data to higher powers than themselves and tap into the oversight organization to bring about the necessary changes to correct the evils that are being done...and free your brother."

The young woman felt at least slightly relieved now, though a tremendous wave of weariness suddenly hit her. This sensation resulted from a combination of coming down off of the adrenaline overload from life-threatening experiences together with the fact that she hadn't slept soundly in almost two days, and she could feel her eyes growing heavy.

"I don't suppose I'll get a chance to recover a bit before I take on the next tasks, will I?" she asked softly.

"Yes, of course! You've been through so much! Please excuse the meager accommodations here. The friend who owns this place is one I met through a shared interest in...methods for circumventing security. He only uses this house occasionally, when he feels he may be under particularly close observation by the government. Honestly, he is simply somewhat paranoid, and nothing he has done should truly warrant a government response, but he is a good fellow and has many useful contacts in the area. He said the larder should be well stocked, and you may help yourself."

Maxwell glanced up at another portion of his screen and added, "Jayce has also expressed to FAILSAFE that he will be comfortable in the other room and will quickly rouse if a threat approaches. He's actually dealing with one of the upwellings of anger that seem to come on occasionally due to his condition, so he's asked to be allowed some time to work through it without communication. We will start the next phase of this endeavor mid-morning."

Lilian wearily rose to her feet, leaning on the back of the chair as she braced herself with one arm.

"Goodnight, then," Maxwell said as he raised his hand to his strip.

"Max..."

Her benefactor's hand paused mid-tap.

Lilian smiled.

"It's good to know you, Max."

He returned the smile brightly.

"It's good to know you, too, Lilian!"

He finished the motion, and the screen darkened.

# Chapter 9

*"Imagine a world where we can access the stars with ease and explore the wonders of the cosmos. That is the promise of the space elevator, a revolutionary project that will transform our relationship with the Universe. The space elevator is a cable that connects the Earth's surface to a geostationary orbital device, allowing vehicles to climb up and down without rockets. This will dramatically reduce the cost and environmental impact of space travel while enabling new scientific discoveries and commercial opportunities.*

*The space elevator is not just a technological feat, but a vision for the future that inspires hope and curiosity. It is a road that leads us to infinite possibilities and challenges us to expand our horizons. The elevator is a testament to the human spirit that seeks to transcend limitations and reach for the stars."*

*- Dr. Yang Zhao, People's Space Elevator Program Director, People's Republic of China, Confederacy of Eastern Nations*

"I appreciate your attendance in this meeting," General Ryu bowed his head slightly and respectfully at the series of video feeds covering the large wall screen in front of him. No less than two dozen members of Alliance military and civilian leadership gave him their attention with varying levels of interest. Colonel Cooper stood against the wall by the briefing room exit, hands clasped behind him while watching with obvious emotional investment.

"The purpose of this session is to discuss the results of the most recent simulations and projections our senior analysts have been running with the help of the SAVANT AI. As you all have had a chance to review the materials the team has provided, I will not waste time rehearsing the entirety of the details. The key decision we now have before us is whether the Alliance can commit to supporting the Command Activated action plan to enervate the Communists' space elevator project. This is bearing in mind that SAVANT has determined with ninety-nine-point-nine-eight percent surety that the CEN's completion of that project alone will result in an unstoppable degradation of all critical advantages we currently enjoy related to space operations."

Many members of the committee shifted in their seats or otherwise betrayed their anxiety related to that portentous statement, expressions of sober concern now visible on nearly every face. Ryu brought up an image of a massive structure on the wall screen behind him, schematics and scale indications overlaid on the edifice.

"As you know, the People's Space Elevator is located in the Tibetan High Steppes region of the Central Tibetan Plateau in southwestern China, where construction has been in progress for over a decade. The High Steppes were chosen—among other reasons—for their geological stability, lack of significant rainfall, rigidity of soil, distance from populated areas, elevation, and ease of long-range surveillance for defensive purposes."

The image of the elevator model shrunk as the general spoke, showing the sparseness of human activity on the surrounding land. The screen also displayed a comparison of the elevation of the area with other natural structures in the region and the surveillance and defensive response rings around the construction, projecting out the likely distances at which approaching ground troops could be seen and at which various defensive solutions would have accurate targeting. Ryu zoomed the screen back in to the elevator itself, now using gathered data to provide views of the probable internal makeup of the tower.

"The foundation, which starts roughly five hundred meters underground and boasts an anchor descending to a depth of seven thousand meters, sits with ground access at four thousand nine hundred meters above sea level. The CEN is using an approach that combines cutting-edge robotic fabricators working in unison as a ring to convert a slurry of nanoparticles into walls fused together at the molecular level. The fabrication machines run twenty-four hours per day, seven days per week, and intelligence sources estimate that the top of this behemoth has now passed the thirty-five-thousand-kilometer mark."

Ryu heard a few gasps behind him as the image zoomed out to encompass the entirety of the structure, based on current estimates for China's progress toward its completion. Truly, nothing humanity had ever attempted could match the scale of the Communists' endeavor; it was an absolute pity that the Chinese people had to have been so severely taxed and had to have had their lives so minutely controlled to accomplish what their dictator had completed to date.

"The Chinese started the endeavor fifteen years ago, constructing a satellite platform in geosynchronous orbit above the elevator's base and using fuel and materials ferried by standard rockets to maintain its position and build out the orifice into which the elevator walls will lock once they reach it. This platform was also leveraged six years ago to deploy an initial tether from the device down through the atmosphere until blimp-like craft could secure it, a challenge that cost the CEN two vessels and the lives of all crewmembers in those aircraft before the effort met with success.

"However unreliable the Chinese upper atmosphere and rocket programs may be, the regime has ignored—and covered up—the many mishaps and doggedly maintained the construction operations. Now, the tether has been extended down to attach to the tower's subterranean anchor, enabling construction to accelerate dramatically using the increased stability it provided."

"The tower is well guarded, with major bases positioned here," Ryu pointed as the screen behind him highlighted the installations, "which Intel believes are currently housing two full battalions of enemy forces: one ground-based and one air-based cavalry unit, with both being among the most elite and loyal to the dictator. Another Chinese air force base lies five hundred sixty kilometers to the southeast and can, with sufficient time, deploy additional air support. Surface-to-air and surface-to-surface missile batteries are situated near the elevator and bases, all guarded by troops and automatic turrets.

"The advanced radar and laser arrays operating in the vicinity of the two military bases make approach using most stealth craft and delivery of nuclear devices via missiles exceedingly risky, as the longer these systems have to perform their data analysis, the higher the probability that the craft or missiles will be identified and intercepted despite their stealth capabilities. Even the UA vessels will be at great risk as they deploy railgun projectiles and troop drop capsules and will need to immediately withdraw to a safe distance following the completion of those activities.

"As for additional constraints, utilizing nuclear detonations anywhere in the upper atmosphere will spread radiation across too many innocents in the months that follow such detonations. Unless the elevator's tether has been severed first, an attack using tactical nuclear devices against the exterior of the shaft is also unlikely to result in its total collapse.

"One or more large nuclear devices would likely sever the shaft and tether, but their size makes them too easy to intercept before they descend to the desired altitude, even with stealthy or rapid delivery systems. This operation calls for a swift deployment of CA troops from the upper atmosphere to the ground, where they can access the elevator's interior. The troop drop capsules are small and fast enough to make detection unlikely until they are too close to the ground to intercept, at least when landing some distance from the shaft.

"Despite the difficulty of the mission, space and upper atmosphere dominance is a critical advantage that we cannot afford to lose," Ryu paused and looked across the faces of the participants as he let the truth of this statement sink in.

"If we do not intervene *now*, strong projections foretell of a near-future situation in which our ability to halt the march of the CEN's progress toward equalization and, eventually, dominance in those domains will be practically impossible. You have the results of attack simulations we've run and the proposed mission plan. I'm asking for you to join me in supporting the execution of the most impactful of the CA program's missions to date: the destruction of the People's Space Elevator."

The general saw no frowns or other signs of disagreement among the participants and continued, "I will call for a vote. All in favor, please indicate."

Though some more slowly than others, eventually, all hands were raised.

"The vote is unanimous," Ryu breathed, masterfully concealing the relief and euphoria that were welling up inside of him.

The old soldier carried stoically onward with his remarks.

"I will prepare the command staff for the mission, which will commence tomorrow at oh-six-twenty-one hours, just before dawn local time. The free world is indebted to you all!"

Ryu ended the meeting and stood still for a moment, saying a silent prayer to his ancestors to thank them for helping him obtain backing for the imminent operation. He desperately hoped that his efforts to cripple the ever-grasping talons of the oppressive regimes would bring peace to the billions of souls whose lives they had claimed—most painfully during the despicably and unconscionably bloody conquest of the land of his birth.

During that fateful month, he had been in a medically induced coma in Japan as he'd recovered after the second outbreak of China's bioengineered flu virus there, the virus having been designed for economic impairment of enemy nations while the CEN public and allied nations secretly received customized inoculations built into their standard flu vaccinations. General Ryu was doomed to forever wonder whether he could have created a different outcome had he been hale and at home in South Korea.

He'd awakened to a hell in which his wife and children were trapped inside occupied territory—if they were still alive. Despite his personal situation, throughout his career he had developed a reputation for being a clear-headed and wise leader and had been sought out to manage the strategic operations team in the CA program following his recovery. Now, he finally had a chance to set that program on the necessary course to bring about the elimination of the CEN's threat once and for all.

Prayer finished, Ryu turned and exited the room, Cooper joining him as he strode past.

"The time has come at last," Ryu sighed as they walked through the corridor.

"Yes, *sir*!" Cooper emphatically agreed. Sympathy was one of the younger officer's hallmark traits, and though he would never break professional protocols, his elation was practically tangible. He wasn't smiling, and yet he was beaming.

Out of a generally impassive expression, Ryu glanced at Cooper and allowed only a hint of a smile to show on his face.

"The stakes being what they are, from both broad-scope and tactical standpoints, it is critical that we ensure all commanders understand their tasks inside and out."

"Yes, sir," Cooper replied. "I will start taking staff through the training simulations immediately."

The general nodded.

"Very good. We've preemptively mobilized the transports, yes?"

Cooper nodded, and Ryu continued, "Even with the many contingency plans in place, this mission has a strong possibility of becoming the catalyst for a global conflict on a scale that humanity has never seen."

The colonel's demeanor rapidly sobered.

"Yes, sir," he responded, enthusiasm now well-tempered.

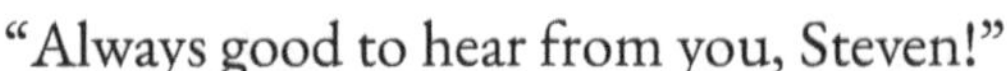

"Always good to hear from you, Steven!"

The professor sat on a stool in his lab, surrounded by dozens of screens and equipment so specialized that most of it had required custom fabrication. He wore a lab coat with a label bearing his title and last name, though the font size on the label had to be abnormally small to fit the entirety of "Dr. Srinivastava."

The Indian doctor did not look up from a brain scan image; he was manipulating the image on his tablet, rotating it, and drilling in and out of various microscopic subsections. The call had to be audio only due to the sensitivity of this expert's work.

"I can't go too long without discussing neuron mapping and laser depth control techniques with you, Amrish!"

The older man's laughter shook his plentiful waistline.

"If only my students were as undyingly interested as you, my friend! They keep leaving me for mundane things like sleep and food!"

"Ha! I'm sure they like to do that right when you feel you are on the brink of a breakthrough, as well!"

"Ah, true! Always. Always."

Professor Srinivastava ran a hand across his goatee and let the hand holding his tablet drop to his knee, opining, "Well, I suppose you're calling about the simulations you ran for me, yes?"

"I'm very eager to hear what you think," the caller enthused. "Do you feel you're ready for the first round of testing on live subjects?"

The doctor double-tapped his strip to activate his main screen. Raising a finger, he moved the control highlight to a file near the bottom of his screen and tapped his thumb to his finger; the file opened with cues for sections of the document to which he would likely want to navigate.

"Methods," he murmured after his eyes had flown over the report's summary, and the screen jumped to the detailed description of proposed treatment methodologies.

"I see you've prototyped the nanobots by which stem cells can be delivered to target locations, and then the lasers would penetrate the tissues where structures had collapsed or otherwise deformed, the intervention clearing the brain's electrical pathways, as we discussed."

"Yes, and your suggestion to use chained nanobots with movement guided by magnetoscopes was brilliant."

"Thank you, *bhaiya*!" Srinivastava beamed, though his eyes continued scanning the screen. "I've been toying with that idea for a while now and simply have not had the time to dive into the modeling."

"Stats," the medical specialist now said softly, and the page summarizing statistical analyses appeared.

Srivastava started nodding as he scanned over the numbers.

"Yes, yes! With these results, I am comfortable initiating stage one of live testing. We've done all we can with simulations, and the results are remarkable! You truly developed these models in search of ways to help your company identify candidates for particular services?"

"You could say the objective was to identify people who needed very...targeted solutions."

"It is still a bit of a leap to think of applying such a model to neuroscience!"

"I suppose you could also say I am uniquely attuned to pondering *systems*. International networks are systems, social networks are systems, brains are systems..."

"Well, applying this AI model to the identification of damaged neurons and signaling pathways was a stroke of genius, my friend. With the pinpoint accuracy of the university's tissue-penetrating laser combined with your AI's ability to contrast damaged organs with healthy ones and identify individual molecules for correction, we may be able to fully repair even very severe trauma without ever cutting into gray matter itself!"

"I'm extremely happy to hear you say that, Amrish. Extremely happy! I have several good friends who desperately need such a solution."

"They are lucky people to have a friend like you, Steven-*ji*, and I am lucky as well. You may be helping me accomplish a lifelong dream! With rapid test protocols, I should know whether it is time for popping the champagne by the end of the week."

"Thank you, kind sir. I will eagerly await the results as you obtain them."

"You will be the first to know! Good day, Steven!"

"Good day to you!"

Maxwell Clarke tapped his strip twice to end the call and turned back to the half-dome of screens that surrounded his workstation.

FAILSAFE spoke up.

"Alright, *Steven*, I know you're likely thinking it, so I'll reassure you that even though it's unlikely anyone with ties to the Command Activated will ever examine Srivastava's AI-tied surgical protocols in depth, considering the way I refactored the code, comments, and metadata, it would be infeasible for anyone to make a solid legal claim of plagiarism...or classified data leakage."

The man only gave a half-nod of acknowledgment, with lines of worry creasing the corners of his eyes. Time for his next call.

---

"Max! How goes the good fight? What can I do for you, sir?"

Miguel had double-tapped his strip and leaned back in his office chair, raising his arms up to stretch his triceps during this welcome break from his work.

"Forgive me for the hoarseness, Miguel. These past few days, I've been talking far more than what my throat is used to experiencing!"

"No worries, no worries, man!" Miguel sympathized, "I've been there many times! You gotta take good care of yourself, but sometimes life won't let that happen!"

"Truly!" Maxwell concurred before continuing, "I'll try not to take up too much of your time this morning. I'm just wondering when I might be able to schedule meetings with Smith, Duvlen, Gaines, Mansary, and Jennings to talk about some enhancements to the SAVANT AI."

Miguel raised his eyebrows and leaned forward to reach his keyboard, typing and gesturing to parse through calendars.

"Hmm, that's quite the group! Looks like Duvlen's out attending his son's funeral. Mansary is booked up with medical reviews through...Friday of next week. Smith...Smith...Smith has availability day after tomorrow if you can convince him to meet during evening hours, and I happen to know that both Gaines and Jennings are back in DC for the next round of budget meetings, so they've blocked time during the day for that and in the evenings for the usual elbow rubbing with other DC players."

"Ah, budget allocation season. Yes, I see."

Maxwell thought a moment, then warmly said, "Alright, I appreciate that information. Let me double-check on whether my schedule can match up with Smith's and I'll reach back out if it does!"

"Sure, man! I'll be here doing all the things computers can't...yet!"

Maxwell laughed, "Don't worry, my friend. You have many qualities that are irreplaceable!"

Miguel nodded in confident self-assurance, agreeing, "Got that right! Thanks, Doc!"

"Always a pleasure, Miguel!"

The project manager's hand started to reach for his strip, but he suddenly remembered a mental note he'd made.

"By the way, can you help me answer a question that I've been chasing around my head lately? I've been wondering for a while now why you decided to call your AI 'SAVANT'..."

Maxwell laughed again.

"Ah, well, you see, my brother used to call me the 'idiot savant' who kept beating all his high scores in games but couldn't figure out how to talk to human beings. I named the AI 'SAVANT' in honor of the drive his words gave me to prove that I was more than just a hopeless, computer-obsessed wonk."

Miguel grinned and chuckled with understanding.

"Yeah, yeah, I'm no computer genius, but I feel where you're coming from. Believe it or not, I have dyslexia. Never let it stop me from doing what I want, though! Nothing can stop you if you want it bad enough!"

"I absolutely agree! Absolutely."

"Alright, take care of yourself, Max!"

"You, too, and thank you again!" Maxwell said with great sincerity.

# Chapter 10

*"What most people fail to understand is that an appreciation for dark humor and the ability to control emotional attachment are critical skills in service members' toolbelts, ready to be drawn and fired as needed to deal with the mind-bendingly complex combat situations such individuals must often face. Anyone who has developed these capabilities is prepared to handle just about anything life can throw at them, and reliance on them becomes a way of life forever after."*

*- General Gordon D. Tate, Commandant of the Marine Corps, United States of America, Global Alliance*

The waxing light of the Fall day was only just creeping into the room in earnest when Jayce was awakened by the vibrating of his strip, his eyes flying open and darting around the room as he quickly raised a hand and double-tapped his device to answer the call.

"I'm sorry I wasn't able to let you sleep longer, Jayce. We've had a turn of events that has increased the urgency of our mission."

Jayce had been reclining on the couch, and he unfolded his arms and legs as he pushed himself up to a sitting position, briefly rubbing his eyes while asking, "What're we dealing with now?"

"Well, you know that our objective is to free the members of the program's unauthorized unit, including Lilian's brother, and get them out of harm's way. Unfortunately, it seems Command Activated leadership is now preparing for a major offensive operation that will undoubtedly require the participation of those very members…and it's scheduled for late afternoon today."

Jayce swiftly stood and started walking to the door to the back room, saying, "I'll wake her up."

He rapped on the aged wooden structure, and Lilian rushed to open it, blinking questioningly and wearily at Jayce with her hair in disarray.

Maxwell continued, "I'll bring her into the conversation now as well."

The wall screen flashed on, and Max's voice could be heard asking, "Hello, Lilian, can you hear me?"

Lilian enfolded herself with her arms.

"Yes, I'm here, Max."

As Jayce's face revealed that her use of their ally's name did not go unnoticed, he and his ward stepped into the center of the space in which the young woman had slept the previous night.

"Good morning, Lilian! I was just informing Jayce of a rather significant increase in the urgency of our actions, as it seems the Command Activated are going to engage in a massive operation in the late afternoon, with Ked and the others likely being deployed unless we can intervene in time."

Lilian's eyes had widened as Maxwell had spoken, and she glanced worriedly at Jayce as he looked at her with obvious sympathy.

Maxwell continued, "I'm afraid that even with the video footage and your testimonies, we would not be able to stop them in time to keep your brother out of danger if we were to simply go to a media outlet or try to go through the whistleblower processes required by the oversight organization. The best path at this point still seems to be to have the two of you take the evidence to current members of program leadership, which will most likely lead to the removal of the special needs troops from the next Command Activated operation."

Jayce nodded slowly as Lilian's eyes searched his face, and her mind raced through the associated requirements.

"Although I'd hoped some members of senior leadership might be accessible in Colorado at present, it seems this was not to be, unfortunately. Still, my primary objective was to get you to safety, Lilian, and although I have a few helpful contacts in the area, they are somewhat less...capable than Jayce, so having Jayce to protect you and provide additional testimony is very fortuitous.

"The details of the lives of Command Activated senior personnel are classified, so I've had to consider how we can most effectively bring you into the presence of the right people. Out of the five best candidates among senior leadership, I have been unable to identify a window in which two of those candidates will be outside of the program's main complex anytime soon. Two others are attending budget decision-making meetings in Washington, DC, so they are more difficult to reach in time, though we should at least have a chance to bring you into their proximity during the nightly dinner parties if it comes to that. Our best chance to gain assistance today will be with the last individual: a civilian medical advisor who is attending his son's funeral."

Lilian's brow furrowed at the thought of interrupting such a painful and intimate affair, and she and Jayce exchanged an understanding look, but they held their peace as they bore the stakes in mind.

"The man's name is Howard Duvlen, and I was able to ascertain from searching obituaries that his son passed away two days ago in Kansas City. The funeral will take place at one o'clock this afternoon. FAILSAFE and I will do what we can to run interference with technical surveillance of the event. We will also try to identify any physical surveillance, if possible, but I propose that we err on the side of caution and have Lilian approach Dr. Duvlen with sunglasses, scarf, and hat to help conceal her identity as she hands him a handwritten note as though it contains her condolences.

"In the note, she will inform him that the CA program is being used unethically and ask him to meet her nearby, all while Jayce is waiting in relatively close proximity to provide physical protection, if needed. Lilian will have transferred the evidence to one of the spare tablets and will provide that to Duvlen if he seems receptive. If the risk seems low enough and Duvlen needs additional convincing, Jayce can then take his turn speaking with the man."

Jayce frowned contemplatively and nodded, stating, "That sounds like a plan, but I..." a thought occurred to him, "...*we* could really use more than one handgun for this."

"Absolutely! I have obtained the support of a helpful former gunnery sergeant in the area who I believe we can trust. He is a friend of the individual who allowed us the use of this house. He is, shall we say, well-equipped and willing to share for a good cause. FAILSAFE has requested a cab to pick you up shortly, and you'll be taken to the sergeant's abode. While there, I hope you will quickly be able to find what you need, including an interesting device he claims to own that is designed to run interference with Nares."

Lilian's eyebrows shot up in a combination of surprise and relief at this news.

"From there, it is likely safest and most efficient for you to use an aerial vehicle to travel to see Duvlen. Now that you have Jayce to play the driver, you should be able to pass through checkpoints with less risk that you will be identified if our enemies have gone so far as to issue a warrant, claiming that you are ill and resting in the rear seating. The sergeant's device should run interference with any Nares, and if officers do insist on scanning your face, the modifications we made should still throw the recognition software off, as the agents at the Denver airport were unlikely to have been able to capture and transmit an updated image before their...accident."

Jayce had moved to peer out the curtains.

"We've got the cab here," he affirmed, nodding to Lilian and adding, "We'll get it done!"

Maxwell had only just ended his call to Jayce and Lilian when a notification appeared on his screen for an incoming call rated with high urgency, this one from Modern Informatics.

He quickly answered, asking, "Haden, what's happened?"

On the other end of the line, Haden Juma was breathless, and Maxwell quickly realized that it was not due to a workout.

"Max! What have you gotten yourself into, brother?!"

His mind rushing through the long list of possibilities, Maxwell hazarded a guess, saying, "You're under attack."

"That's putting it mildly, man! Yeah, we're being hit by everything all at once! Denial of service, brute force, zero-day exploitation, you name it! The ops team's running wild with its hair on fire!"

Maxwell raised a hand to his forehead, closing his eyes tightly with a grimace.

"Oh, Haden, I'm terribly sorry! I used every available option to cover my tracks! We must be dealing with one of the most aggressive AI profiles ever conceived to see it track the intrusion all the way back to you!"

After a pause as Haden soaked this in, he asked, "From what I can see, cutting through all the obfuscation, the source is in the western United States...is this government, Max?"

"I really shouldn't say anything more than to assure you that the infiltration effort has been fruitful, and if luck holds true, we should be able to eliminate the motivation for those behind this attack within twenty-four hours!"

Maxwell steepled his fingers, eyes still closed in concentration and remorse as the line remained silent.

"Do you think you can hold out that long?" Maxwell asked hopefully.

After a short additional silence, Haden chuckled with a mix of determination and gusto, almost euphorically embracing the challenge.

"My brother, no evil AI is going to take down *my* network! I was *born* for this stuff!"

Inexpressibly relieved, Maxwell's eyes flashed open, and he promised, "If you can hold on a while longer, ending this attack will be my top priority!"

"Come hell or high water, man!" Haden rejoined. "Come hell or high water!"

---

Their taxi had taken Lilian and Jayce to a lonely, well-worn road deep in the rural areas outside of the city, where it finally halted in front of a weathered, rusty gate attached to a dilapidated barbed-wire fence that ran for kilometers in either direction. The gate bore a heavy chain locked with an equally heavy, old-style padlock. Though the Rocky Mountains formed a magnificent backdrop, inside the fence, the property held no groomed foliage, just prairie brush and a rambler that looked like it could have used a fresh coat of paint several decades ago. A dirt driveway ran from the gate around behind the house, and the whole area smelled of nothing but sage and mud.

The only modern technology in sight on the property was a prevalence of security cameras, one attached to each corner of the dwelling and another mounted on the post that was situated inside the property, near one end of the gate.

Lilian scanned the gate and house, turning to Jayce.

"So, do we knock, or...?"

The door to the dwelling swung open and banged hard against the wall, revealing the form of a very large black man with graying hair who was dressed in combat boots, fatigue pants, and a thick military coat—the man's girth extending the clothing's material to its limits.

"You mus' be mah li'l fugitives," the man boomed out in a voice that seemed to rattle the windows of his house, tinged with an articulation endemic to the Deep South.

Lilian stared wide-eyed as Jayce heartily confirmed, "That'd be us!"

The older man lumbered down the short wooden steps to the dirt path that led over to the driveway. The old soldier approached the gate, eyeing the pair with a narrowed gaze. He paused a few meters away and folded his arms, feet spread apart, as he continued to appraise them with some hostility and in an uncomfortable silence.

Eyeing the man right back, Jayce broke the silence.

"Y'know, Gunny, you didn't have to get dressed up on my account."

The retired gunnery sergeant's brow furrowed into a scowl, and he frowned at Jayce.

"Ah you sassin' me, boy?!" the old man growled.

"Just a bit, yes!" Jayce calmly replied, breaking into a slight smile.

The other man stood silently for another lingering moment, and then his face cracked into a smile as well.

"Ah think Ah like you, son!" he boomed, unfolding his arms and pulling a keychain from his pocket. He stepped up to the padlock and unlocked it, grabbing the gate and walking with it to swing the barrier open enough for the guests to enter.

"Ah ain't gonna ask fo' any details 'bout yo' sit'ation, as the less Ah know the bettah," the Gunny advised, "but what Ah undehstand 's that ya'll could use some *ha'dware*."

"That could even be an understatement!" Jayce worried. As the pair came up alongside their host, he looked at Jayce studiously for a moment and then started walking up the drive with them.

"Well, you come to th' right place," he guaranteed. "Come 'round back and lemme show you what we'ah wohkin' wi'."

They made their way behind the house, where they found the long, boxy shape of an enclosed metal trailer that was parked perpendicular to the house. Equipped with double doors on its house-facing end, it was a type Jayce had previously seen used by sportsmen at outdoor firing ranges for secure storage of their gear, though he'd never seen one this long before.

Stopping at the double doors and thumbing through his numerous keys, their host located the right item, unlocked the right-most door, and shared, "Ah don' trus' those keyless locks. Too easy t' *hack*!" as he held the door for them to enter.

The lights inside the trailer flickered on automatically. Stepping inside the coolly-lit space, Jayce's first thought was that it seemed Gunny had done his utmost to replicate his old military weapons and armor supply room, with a low cabinet running the length of the trailer along the left side and racks of weaponry mounted on the wall above, while the opposite wall bore many different forms of body armor, headgear, and accessories arrayed on hooks.

Jayce whistled in admiration as he entered the cold interior, the environment oddly filling him with nostalgia for his days in basic training at Marine Corps Recruit Depot Parris Island in South Carolina. His initial training in the Corps had started in January, so the frigid air and smell of military gear created a very familiar feeling for him.

"This heh's the Ahmory. Ca-pi-tal 'A,'" Gunny grunted out emphatically.

As the old man stepped past them and began walking—or in his case half-shuffling—them toward the rear on a brief tour, Lilian felt a mixture of alarm and admiration as she stepped through the volatile space. The man gladly shared his opinions about the problems in society as they strolled along the display of weaponry, for all the world giving her the same feeling she would have experienced if they had been guided through a boutique clothing outlet.

"From what Ah've seen through mah *ve'y* long life, it don' matter if yo' dealing with yo' ri' wing, lef' wing, o' some mutant wing growin' out th' middluh yo' *head*, the fihst step befo' th' wing can staht its oppressin' is to disahm th' people..." Gunny orated as they passed the belt-fed machine guns that were most effective against large numbers of personnel and lightly armored vehicles.

He continued, "...an' some people say, 'Well, tha's what th' po-lice an' militahy ah fo',' but who d'you think has been enfo'cing the dictators' ohdehs in yo' dictatahships an' Commie regimes all these yeahs?!"

Gunny shook his head, "Don' matteh the type, *any* group can be *bought* if they think the cause o' price is ri'..."

They now passed an array of various types of grenades and launchers, from rocket-propelled to incendiary.

Gunny barked out a mirthless laugh.

"You kids ah prime examples ri' heh. Why would you need t' come t' meh if'n you could always trus' th' gov'men' and them *all-seein' eyes* it's got everywheh, AI watchin' *everythin'* you do?"

They'd arrived at the last section of armaments, this one filled with unusually constructed long- and short-range weapons. Jayce gave a last scan across the length of the trailer and chuckled, raising his eyebrows and saying, "Well, Gunny, you've *almost* convinced me to build out my own Armory!"

Their host simply shrugged, pulled the corners of his mouth down in sympathetic affirmation, and—eyebrows up—bobbed his head in approval.

"We heard you have something to help with Nares," Lilian hopefully spoke up.

The older man nodded and patted a small box with a strap that held it dangling from a hook on the wall behind him.

"Hold this dahlin' close an' it creates a cloud uh pahticles 'round you, like yo' own li'l safety bubble."

Jayce noticed a grappling device on the wall next to the gunnery sergeant. Tipping his head in that direction, he admiringly said, "That's one of the pneumatic-assisted ascent and descent models, right?"

Gunny looked impressed at Jayce's knowledge.

"Sho' 'nuff."

Jayce pointed to the unique weaponry in the last section.

"What've we got here?"

"These'ah mah *non-lethal* ahtehms: perfec' fo' them sitiashuns when you wanna be ehffective but don' know who's a hostage o' who's an ehnemy o' who's jus' been snowed ovah."

He reached out and hefted a lean, elongated firearm off its hooks, the device equipped with a high-powered scope.

"Fo' instence: This beaut' delivahs a tranquilizah wi' pinpoin' accuracy out tah sixteh metahs, th' projectahles designed wi' ahmah piercin', ten-centimetah tips but wi' buffahs tha' stop 'em punchin' ri' through yo' tahget."

Jayce nodded in appreciation, then pointed to a large piece that looked more or less like a shotgun, asking, "And that baby?"

Gunny grinned.

"Ah! Heh we've got uh *Sand*baggeh. Semi-auto shotgun-style fahrahm that shoots speciahlized, reinfohced *cloth* projectahles filled wi' sand so they take yo' av'rage-sized 'pponents within two metahs ri' off theh feet. Bags ah reusable, too!"

Jayce was grinning now as well.

"Mind if we snag those, some other hardware and ammo, a few other pieces of tactical gear, and maybe armor up a bit?"

Their elder chuckled, responding, "Ahd be dis'ppointed if'n you *di'nt!*"

---

Even with the extra layers she was wearing, the freezing wind seemed to blow right through Lilian as it swept across the cemetery. Wrapped up in her long coat and warm hat and with a scarf wrapped around her face, she tried to get a good look through her sunglasses at the faces in the crowd gathering around the casket. Such an endeavor was difficult from where she stood near a naked tree roughly thirty yards from the assembly, but she was nearly certain her mark was not present.

"Where are you, Dr. Duvlen?" she whispered.

"I'm scanning for him now," Jayce chimed in, talking to her through the communications link FAILSAFE had created between their strips. Jayce was perched on the rooftop of a retail building just across the street from the graveyard in this Kansas City suburb.

"Duvlen and family nearly there," FAILSAFE intoned.

"Best of luck, Lilian!" Maxwell inserted encouragingly.

Lilian breathed out her thanks, and then Jayce spoke up again.

"Looks like he's just arrived in a black town car. North side. Helping a younger woman and little girl out of the vehicle."

Lilian caught sight of the man in the area to which Jayce was directing her attention and began walking expeditiously toward her target. She'd prepared her note on the way there and clutched it tightly in her gloved right hand. Duvlen and his wards had made it halfway to the gathered mourners when Lilian intercepted them, briefly giving her condolences to the younger woman and then thrusting the note into the doctor's hand—pressing her hands around his after the note was in his grasp to emphasize its importance.

"Please forgive my interruption! I *really* hope you'll read this soon!" she begged, feeling abashed, and then turned and briskly walked across the grass to a sculpture of an angel with outstretched wings that adorned the northeastern corner of the property. Dr. Duvlen, having been taken aback by her insistent delivery of the note, gazed after her with a sad and concerned expression.

Lilian waited there for the internment to be completed, shivering in the wind despite her protective clothing, which now included a vest that Jayce had insisted she wear under her coat. The firmness of the projectile-resistant material made it the most uncomfortable apparel she had ever worn, and she kept shrugging to try to overcome the feeling that her shirt was wrinkling up, irritating her skin underneath it.

After what seemed like hours, the crowd around the open grave slowly began to disperse.

Jayce's voice hummed through her strip again, advising, "Duvlen's shaking people's hands but seems to be making his way your direction."

The determined woman waited anxiously, watching the older man start walking toward her and then half turning to avoid giving the impression that she was staring; that, and she had very mixed emotions about inserting herself into this melancholy family affair and couldn't bear the sight of the man's despondent expression. Finally, he had come within a few paces of her, and he stopped, staring at her with worry and suspicion as she half-turned her face toward him.

"What do you want?" he bluntly asked.

Lilian took a breath.

"I know that the Command Activated are an incredible force for good," she began, and then hurried through her next statements as she saw his mouth draw into a line, "and that their medications and suits allow *any* soldiers to perform above the expectations set for the *best* soldiers."

Duvlen's brow creased.

After a moment, he asked, "We'll get to *how* you got the information you think you have, but what is it that you think is unethical about what you just described?"

"The problem is not with the program as a whole...it's a shadow unit operating within the program that's the issue," she began, noting that his brows had now creased even more tensely.

She quickly continued, rattling off the information before the equally rapid rattling of her nerves choked off what she needed to say.

"The people running that program have resorted to deceitful recruiting tactics to lure special needs individuals to join up as 'special operators.' I have data I can share with you, including video footage. They're kept in barracks separated from other service members, and if they become dissatisfied with their situation, they are coerced into staying. They've basically been turned into conscripted soldiers, and my *brother* is *one* of them!"

Lilian's voice broke into a sob as she finished. She reached a gloved finger up beneath the edge of her glasses to brush away the tear that had forced its way out onto her cheek. The doctor looked down at the concrete base of the statue, discomfited and thoughtful; it took him a minute to formulate his response.

"Look," he finally uttered with a voice void of emotion, "I feel for you. I do. If there's a situation like you say there is, then I am completely against it."

Lilian's hopes began to grow, until he continued, "*However*, you see those people over there?"

He pointed to where the younger woman and little girl were standing next to a clergyman, waiting for Duvlen's return.

"They just lost my son's care and protection, and it is my solemn duty to protect them in his place. Anyone, *regardless* of situation, who may be involved in such an endeavor as the one you described is doing the world a great service. Also, if what you say is true, then those who are running this 'shadow unit' must be supported by some of the most powerful people across the Alliance governments. Those are not people with whom you can tangle and win, young lady."

Lilian's gut was wrenching with bewilderment and dismay. She tried to repudiate what he said, getting out, "But it's not *right*..." before the man held up a hand fiercely, his apathetic expression turning angry.

"*Be that as it may!* You will not sway me, you understand? And I highly recommend you let go of this foolish notion and live your life knowing that the world is a safer place today thanks to whomever or whatever has so reduced the number of innocent lives lost around the world over the past years. It's time to mind your business, young lady, and leave me to mind mine."

With that, the doctor turned to march back across the necropolis to his waiting family members. The thought of Ked being deployed into combat leaped into Lilian's mind, and she dashed forward, grasping his arm.

"Please!" she begged, "They're going to send my brother into battle today!"

Duvlen turned only his face toward her and pulled against her grasp.

"Young lady, you are pushing your luck!"

Maxwell's voice conveyed his grave worry as he warned, "Beware, Lilian! He may not be part of the shadow group, but he can quickly call for backup!"

"You're our last hope of stopping it today!" Lilian tearfully exclaimed. Duvlen's daughter and the clergyman were glancing at each other nervously and gesticulating at Lilian.

"You leave me no choice!" the doctor seethed as he raised his hand and tapped his strip.

Lilian heard a sound like the cracking of a whip, and suddenly a canister the size of her finger appeared in the man's back just below the shoulder blade. Jayce's dart had pierced through Duvlen's thick woolen coat and embedded its needle with the main body of the tranquilizer capsule protruding. Lilian felt the muscles in Duvlen's arm go limp and—seemingly in slow motion—he sank to the ground, slipping out of Lilian's hands as his knees struck the grass and his upper body sprawled out backwards.

"Dad?!" Lilian heard the young mother cry from across the cemetery as she started running toward them, shouting over her shoulder for her pastor to call emergency services.

"It's time to leave, Lilian!" Maxwell cried.

Rigidly turning towards the building where Jayce had been positioned, the sorrowful emissary saw him rapidly rappelling down its wall into the alley, releasing the grapple from the roof, and retracting it into its repository. Her mind was flying over so many thoughts that she barely saw a passing car in time to pause within a half-step of it as she started dazedly moving across the street toward Jayce and the alley, even the loudness of the vehicle's horn failing to snap her out of her mental haze.

"Come on, Lilian," she heard Jayce say, still more audible through her strip than not as he waved her toward him. "I'm sorry it didn't work out. We'll find someone who'll listen!"

She made it across the street and stumbled into the alleyway, where Jayce took her by the arm to guide her back to the waiting vehicle behind the building. He stowed the rifle and grappler in the trunk and climbed into the driver's seat. Lilian, mind threatening to fall into despair again, forced herself to climb inside the rear of the vehicle and strap herself into the middle of the bench.

"Our next best bet is to try to reach General Gaines or Senator Jennings in DC this evening," Maxwell recommended in a voice choked with emotion, adding, "I'm very, *very* sorry, Lilian."

She stared numbly out the window, the AV lifting off and skimming the rooftops as it accelerated away toward the nation's capital.

# Chapter 11

*"No matter how well you prepare and plan for a situation, you will always encounter some unexpected challenges or changes that will force you to adapt and improvise. The key is to prepare yourself—and your team—to handle as broad a set of possible outcomes as possible, developing decision-making strategies to guide you through the waters of uncertainty when unexpected situations do arise."*

*- Susan Todorova, Chief Executive Officer, Link-Comm Global*

A stiff wind was racing across the Tibetan steppes as pale autumn moonlight covered the landscape in its chilly luminescence. The nocturnal illumination covered nearly everything, but it could not touch the area within the incredibly massive shadow cast by the monstrous tower that seemed to be embedded into the Earth like the proboscis of some fantastic insectile leviathan draining the planet of her nectar.

Bands of vertically oriented white lights could be seen situated kilometers apart up the entire length of the incredible structure, each thin luminary per band being hundreds of meters tall. Here and there around the base of the ponderous structure, engineers and technicians—bundled in thick layers of protection against the hostile environment—were performing status checks and maintenance on the slurry transport pipe and electrical cables running through a skyscraper-sized portal at the base of the elevator on its southeastern side. Each cable was the width of a city bus, and the composite tube feeding plasmonic construction materials up the interior wall to the crown of machines at the crest of the pipe was nearly as wide as an athletic stadium.

Splitting away from the slurry pipe after exiting the portal, the cables ran south to a power plant capable of supporting a large city. The slurry duct itself extended east toward the materials preparation facility that had been built within sight of the Chinese cavalry bases to its north. A ring of outposts formed a defensive perimeter a kilometer and a half out from the walls of the central edifice, each outpost home to a formidable automated turret equipped with a 155-millimeter rapid-fire cannon and a sentry observation station where control was maintained for the drones and the .50 caliber remotely operated turrets dotting the terrain between the outposts.

Besides the few dozen workers moving around the base of the tower, little moved in the area. Patches of low grass were the only vegetation to be found scattered across the otherwise rocky, flat, and barren ground. The nearest change in terrain features was roughly sixteen kilometers to the south, where rolling hills gave birth to the occasional upwelling of large stone monadnocks ranging in color from faded tan to chalky gray. The wild yaks had long since learned not to stray into the vicinity of the elevator's defensive perimeter; that, or they had already been mowed down by the automated turrets' gunfire and used by the Chinese troops to supplement their measly rations.

The night was still and peaceful...until the railgun-launched projectiles rained down from the sky.

Targeting the outposts' cannons and the sentry drones, the UA team had fired off numerous heavy spears from high altitude, the projectiles guiding themselves to the specific targets that had been locked into their onboard memory prior to launch.

Shortly after the railguns' ammunition had done its work—lighting up the night with flames bursting forth from the Chinese defenses—the troop drop capsules touched down, using a series of increasingly large parachutes to rapidly slow themselves from the dizzying speeds at which they had traveled through most of their descent. Releasing the last chute as they reached the kilometer mark above the ground, the devices were guided into their assigned landing locations using their reaction control system thrusters.

These capsules landed sequentially, with the foremost touching down just behind the first auto-turret north of the southwestern-most outpost, so close to the turret that its barrel was blocked by the conveyance's hull as the defensive weapon tried to turn to fire at the object. The passenger of that first capsule stepped out and quickly unleashed a barrage of armor-piercing rounds into the machine, rendering it useless just as the second capsule landed in equally close proximity behind the next turret in the series, and the CA troop it had borne disabled that defensive machine. This process continued around to the west of the northernmost outpost as the capsules landed clockwise in rapid succession.

Turrets in the staging area all having been disabled in less than thirty seconds, the first troops onsite rushed to the outposts, penetrating the entrances and gunning down the occupants before they could mount a significant resistance. After a matter of a few minutes, the defenses across most of the western and northwestern sectors of the perimeter had been dealt with, and the remainder of the four platoons' forces had landed, extracted equipment from the specialized drop capsules in which it had been delivered, and formed up for movement to the next objective: the elevator itself.

While these troops dashed toward the tower, a squad of soldiers landed in the hilly area far southwest of the structure. While two members of this group raced across the slopes to the east, the rest of the squad was soon joined by equipment drops that they quickly opened and—sheltering under the automatically expanding stealth shielding that deployed from one such module—they set about organizing and erecting machinery under the canopy.

The Panthers tailed the main body of Command-Activated forces as the special operators made a beeline for the elevator shaft. In the distance, Chinese soldiers in the bases could now be seen scrambling to their air and ground cavalry units, while drones could be seen launching from the fortifications as the Alliance soldiers approached the elevator.

Four soldiers toward the rear of the main CA formation broke away from the rest of the troops as soon as they were out of the direct line of sight of the Chinese missile batteries supporting the enemy's military bases, the elevator itself shielding them from view. As the rest of their unit approached the foot of the tower, these troops detached the large cases they had secured to the retention points on their shoulders. Setting the containers out in a row and pressing activators on the chests, the exosuit-clad soldiers stepped back as the vessels opened to reveal rows of short-range surface-to-surface armaments.

Two of these troops had also been carrying drones in their hands, and as the machines' rotors started whirring, the soldiers tossed them in the air. The drones shot up to a height of roughly ten meters above the ground and then maneuvered north until they had all enemy missile batteries in sight. Aiming their lasers at the targets, they held their positions as the rows of missiles in the cases launched, diverted around the elevator, and sailed in to impact the enemy's heavy missile launchers before those weapons' massive support structures had finished their target sighting rotations and launch preparations.

Chinese auto-turrets between the CA munitions' launch sites and their destinations had done their best to gun down the missiles before they could destroy their targets, but the rockets had flown in what seemed like haphazard, erratic paths that had made it impossible for the defensive software to predict trajectories and intercept the Command Activated projectiles over the short distances from their launch sites to their targets.

The CEN batteries exploded into tremendous fireballs, sending pieces of metal flying out across the installations, knocking several enemy drones out of the air, and forcing the air cavalry units to take a circuitous route around the area as they rushed to attack the intruders. By this time, a number of Communist assets had come within two hundred meters of the northern side of the elevator, but this was where the majority of the Command Activated platoons had taken up positions after spreading out from the elevator's foundation.

The foremost of the Command Activated forces had quickly thrown down the combination actively and passively armored shields they had been carrying and proceeded to take up prone positions behind them. These soldiers now began firing armor-piercing rounds from their assault rifles at all softer targets while the shields' active components deployed small sections of plating to intercept incoming explosives whenever rockets neared their positions. The CA forces being thus protected, enemy drones and lightly armored personnel transports in the air and on the ground were rapidly being disabled under the soldiers' precise fire.

One platoon of Alliance troops had moved in formation around the great tower's foundation, eliminating threats and knocking non-combatants unconscious as they ran toward their target at high speed. Quickly reaching the main opening on the southeastern face of the tower, a squad took up a defensive position at the edges of the portal's mouth while the other troops cleared the interior and then began placing charges around the base of the tether and the inner wall of the shaft—situating the explosives roughly 50 meters above the ground. These troops used elevated platforms to climb to the desired height where these were available, and spear-tipped grappling guns where no other option existed.

Outside the elevator, the second and third waves of Alliance soldiers who had taken up positions north of the tower had begun utilizing shoulder-fired Curveball rockets against the more heavily armored Chinese vehicles as those adversaries had rolled toward the troops.

The Curveballs were similar to the missiles that had just terminated the Chinese surface-to-surface and surface-to-air batteries in that they were pre-programmed to take random and constantly changing paths to their targets; however, these shoulder-fired versions contained additional, specialized features designed to take on hardened defenses.

Each armament was capable of being guided via lasers, with the configuration allowing the firer to use built-in three-dimensional modeling to set the missile to fly to the opposite side of whatever object was being sighted by the user's laser. In this way, the missiles were able to circle around and strike the weaker armor that was usually accessible at the rears or tops of military vehicles. Additionally, each munition was equipped with a tip that, when nearly at the destination, would launch forward from the main projectile and burst into a staticky cloud, running interference with defensive sensors and compelling smart armor to launch away from its hosts.

The enemy's active armor, being thus confused, would attempt to intercept explosives before they reached the enemy assets but, deploying prematurely, would instead launch and leave its vehicles unprotected as the missiles swept around and into the targeted locations. The heavy metal cores of the missiles were the final key, as they were molecularly much denser than any material that could cost-effectively be mass-produced as armor across large numbers of enemy assets, giving the cores the ability to punch right through the less dense metal of the Communist vehicles' carapaces.

No Chinese cavalry units were safe from the Curveballs.

The Command Activated forces laid waste to even the heavier vehicles as they approached and attempted to crush or flank or outmaneuver the offensive forces. The fiery, smoking shells of air cavalry units and drones were falling from the sky around the CA troops like small meteors. Their fumes and ash were joined by that of a squadron of light cavalry units that had tried to use their speed to punch a hole in the Alliance forces' front lines—vehicles turning into great bonfires of twisted metal and rubber that were littered amongst the Alliance forces' positions.

Chinese soldiers who managed to escape the exploding transports were quickly dealt with by the CA special operators, particularly by the snipers in supporting positions toward the rear of the freedom fighters' formation. The stench of burning polymers and metals filled the air, and the Command Activated suits' atmosphere cleansing systems were put under tremendous strain as plumes of smoke drifted across the battlefield. The Allied forces had thus far suffered only minor casualties.

That was when the heavy door of the largest garage in the ground cavalry base slowly lifted, revealing a hulking giant that slowly crawled out into the moonlight.

---

"What the devil?!"

In the voluminous space of the circular strategic mission command center at the Command Activated headquarters, one of General Ryu's operations management team members had uttered this outburst as she'd quickly zoomed in on the Chinese ground cavalry base on her screen.

In the great hall, six of the unit command centers out of the eight available were currently in use. Each of these structures mirrored the standard mission command center layouts and all of them together created a ring around the central, overarching mission command station in which General Ryu stood. The operations management team occupied the consoles around the senior general, and a huge screen occupied each section of the wall between the unit command centers—the map of the entire theater of operations on display on each of these expansive monitors.

"No...that's *impossible*!" the analyst then exclaimed, swiftly swiping up her screen to throw the frame from her console view onto the main screens.

The eyes of all staff who were not urgently engaged darted up to try to assess what was being presented.

From out of the Chinese cavalry garage crept a metallic monstrosity.

The machine was double the size in width and length of any previously identified Chinese armor unit, with no visible conveyance methods due to the placement of armor such that it encompassed the vehicle's continuous tracks on all sides down to within centimeters of the ground. General Ryu added the video stream from a CA sniper's scope as an inset on the main screens as well, and from that feed it became apparent that the armor on the sides of this juggernaut's lower section was adjusting its height only the minimum necessary to allow the vehicle to navigate the terrain over which it rolled, keeping the tracks safely out of reach of incoming fire. With no visible exhaust ports, the heavy tank was apparently equipped with fully electric motors, meaning it had no need for gaps anywhere in its armor.

According to the readings being picked up from the sensors on upper-atmosphere vehicles and close-support drones, the armor itself was more than fifteen centimeters thick on all sides. Adding to the suddenly heightened threat level, the heavy armor unit's tremendous turret was equipped with double barrels boasting 250-millimeter diameters to support very high-caliber rounds. Off the rear of the chassis protruded a raised section that seemed to be an armored missile battery. Four .50 caliber machine gun turrets were mounted inside low-profile hoods at each corner of the immense instrument of destruction.

The operations specialist's voice was now more unnerving due to the way it reflected a sudden, foreboding tumult of emotions within the woman.

"*A Dreadnought.*"

Colonel Cooper swiftly tapped and swiped through folders on his display until he selected a file and threw it to the edge of the screen, where it was picked up by SAVANT and displayed on the main screens. Rough design schematics were accompanied by vehicle statistics and the commanders and subcommanders parsed through this information in dismay.

"That thing's like a whole heavy cav unit rolled into one vehicle!" a subcommander wailed.

"Intel said these were only theoretical! HUMINT sources on the ground said nothing about this!" Cooper shouted, veins bulging on his temples.

The intelligence advisor stationed behind Ryu was also typing and gesturing rapidly to comb through his files.

"Shipping containers from last week that were thought to be delivering supplies and some new light cav units must have been a cover for bringing the components in clandestinely!" he exclaimed.

"We're not equipped to deal with that *abomination!*" one of the unit commanders fiercely protested, and Ryu knew he was right.

"Kagiso, test its defenses as the troops fall back behind the elevator," Ryu ordered one of the subordinate generals.

The wizened senior officer then turned his sharp but solemn eyes back to the main screen directly ahead of his position.

"Everything has a weakness. We need to find one before it's too late."

---

The Command Activated assets tasked with placing the charges had quickly completed their assignment and were withdrawing from the structure, trailing troops firing at the cavalry units that had swung around the southeastern side of the tower in an attempt to flank the encroaching forces. As this smaller unit made its way back to link up with the main body of the troops, they were met by the retreating Alliance forces moving into the shelter afforded by the tower, a few of these soldiers firing off Curveballs and guiding them to strike the enemy colossus.

The turrets on the corners of the enemy vehicle tilted and swung around automatically to fire at the inbound missiles, keeping sufficient pace with them to destroy two of the five before they made contact. The three that did connect with the targeted unit were all directed to the same location, but even after striking the goliath with the rockets' heavy cores, it was clear that the mountainous machine's armor had barely been dented. The Chinese had obviously invested in similarly molecularly dense material for the shielding around the visible exterior of the gargantuan tank.

The massive Dreadnought had paused in its forward movement and then started adjusting its rear missile battery to point northwest, despite the fact that it was not in sight of the Alliance troops. The reason for this soon became clear as the tank's angled battery fired. Ports on the armored rocket repository only opened long enough to release missiles, which traveled in an arc around the visible edge of the space elevator's shaft to detonate in locations behind the tower—locations in which the enemy craft's onboard radar indicated Command Activated forces had taken cover.

The first munitions struck within meters of the sheltering troops, blasting great craters into the ground and sending CA soldiers flying. Bodies tumbling through the air, nearly an entire platoon was thrown dozens of meters from the main formation, some having limbs mangled by the thunderous explosions as their armor failed to protect them. None of these casualties escaped without significant bodily harm.

One of the most severely impacted soldiers had been thrown thirty meters—arms flailing—his flight ending with a sickening crunch as the center of his back struck the corner of a disabled armored troop transport. His body rebounded off and skidded across the ground.

The blast had shredded the front of his exosuit and shattered the entirety of his helmet's visor. Now his body ground to a halt, back broken and exposed skin seared from the heat of the exploding enemy ordnance. Simms lay still upon the scorched earth with tendrils of smoke drifting up from the singed material of his armor and flesh, spread-eagled, unconscious, and breath rattling through rib-punctured lungs—just one of the many severely injured Command Activated troops.

Directed by their Alliance commanders, the remaining soldiers raced away from the elevator through the dim pre-dawn, moving northwest. These forces were leading the enemy fire away from their unit's casualties and into the terrain where their leaders hoped to save as many troops as possible through continuous patterns of movement, especially after the encrypted signal was sent to the charges inside the shaft.

The roar of detonations rang out across the smoke- and dust-cloaked field of combat.

The explosive devices that had been placed inside the elevator shaft had each been specially designed to hold shrapnel, the metal of which had been constructed with molecularly heavier-than-natural materials in the same manner as the cores of the Curveball armaments. The shrapnel was grouped together in a line across the attaching side of each charge, ensuring the metal pieces would be blasted out linearly and deeply into the bodies of any structures against which the charges had been placed.

Around the outside of the elevator's conduit, roughly fifty meters up from its base, the exterior surfaces of the structure bulged with the force of the explosions as fragments were thrown out from the exterior walls around the entirety of the tower. Smoking holes dotted the shaft's skin in a ring and the power to its lighting systems had been severed, yet the monolithic construction still did not collapse or tilt.

The situation was different inside the tower, however, as the charges that had encircled the tether had almost entirely severed it from its anchor. As the satellite platform at the tether's upper end pulled upon the remaining material this inexorably deformed it, the shreds of cable stretching until they finally reached the breaking point and the line sheared off, swinging westward and slamming into the interior wall of the shaft with a thunderous noise.

The People's Space Elevator had been significantly weakened, but not yet destroyed.

---

"SAVANT, find me a weakness on that damnable Dreadnought!" Kalabi was shouting, acting in his role as a strategic subcommander under General Ryu.

The AI's voice came through all troop command centers' central screens.

"Analysis indicates the missiles fired by the Dreadnought rely mainly on radar for targeting. Command Activated engineer units' signals disruption devices can be adjusted to jam the adversary's sensors, decreasing targeting accuracy."

Kalabi glanced right and left at the other unit commanders and then at Ryu, ensuring all were in agreement. His gaze took in Colonel Webb's angst-filled expression as the younger man stared at his screen with his hands balled up in white-knuckled fists. The junior officer's concern for the welfare of his troops had almost pushed him to his emotional breaking point.

Without another second to waste, General Kalabi shouted out, "Do it!"

As he scanned across his troops, Ryu recognized that all commanders were experiencing extreme levels of tension. With the unexpected introduction of the Dreadnought into the battle this was now a *much* more difficult fight—even if they disabled the smart munitions' advanced targeting. No officer wanted this to be the program's first loss, and despite the carefully designed regulations the weight of responsibility for their soldiers' lives unavoidably hung more heavily than ever upon their shoulders.

The ranking general turned to glare at the large screen that was positioned directly across from the front of his command center, calling out to the Upper Atmosphere team, "General MacKenzie, what are the chances the railguns could punch through the top of that Dreadnought?"

The UA commander straightened from where she had bent over to hurriedly converse with a technician about the information on his screen.

Turning to her superior and sighing morosely, MacKenzie replied, "We've just been discussing that, sir. Unfortunately, the railgun projectiles are not made of heavy metals. They primarily rely on the speed of delivery to inflict damage, but even at the maximum speeds they can reach after being launched from the upper atmosphere, the tank's armor is so thick the rods would just bounce off."

Ryu slowly nodded, his eyes melancholy as he turned his attention to the Panther command staff. These officers were hastening to assign casualties to their cats, sending the robots sprinting into the combat zone. Eyes flicking across the statuses and projections rapidly changing across all screens in the command center, Ryu then turned his gaze to General Kalabi's depressed expression. General Ryu knew that at this point, the primary, secondary, and tertiary extraction plans would not suffice if they hoped to save all Command Activated forces in theater. The Korean's hand flew up and double-tapped his strip.

"Emergency channel to the Secretary of the Navy," he ordered.

While Ryu held an urgent but muted conversation with the senior US Navy leader, the command units were scrambling to identify the severity of casualties and the locations of troops in most critical condition, rushing to relay their desired prioritization information to the Panther teams as quickly as possible between orders to the troops still engaged in combat. The personnel rapidly jabbed their screens to select troop indicators, gestured to set priority ratings, and then swiped the data off to the section of the screens' perimeters that would send the information onto the queues at the edges of the Panther commanders' displays. Ryu finished issuing his urgent request for additional support and returned his attention to the units' operations.

Kalabi and another troop commander had sent a dozen of the able-bodied soldiers to set up a half-circle perimeter protecting extraction points Alpha and Bravo, and the Panthers had managed to move the first round of casualties to those protected areas. Five of the robots remained to provide continuous medical support to the wounded.

The rest of the cats were dashing at full speed back to attach themselves to the next round of injured soldiers as Kalabi and the commanders—leaning heavily on assistance from their subcommanders—guided the troops who were still combat-ready to use the cover provided by the body of the elevator to assist the Panthers in gathering up the casualties who were still in range of the Dreadnought.

The warriors pulled the wounded to the south where they would be well out of the line of sight of the beast that was still pummeling Command Activated positions, the tank forced to rely on direct fire now that its radar was being jammed by SAVANT via the signals-disruption devices built into the CA combat engineers' packs. Still, the ghastly machine's direct-fire capabilities were also extremely lethal.

"Time to air support's arrival?" General Ryu called back to Cooper.

"Twenty minutes, sir!" Cooper shouted out as he stared, fixated, at his screen.

Ryu turned sharply to the engineering advisor.

"Brown, I think I know the answer, but is there any way we could re-task one of Echo platoon's munitions for the Dreadnought?"

The engineer sorrowfully shook her head.

"Seeing the Curveballs' impotence, I doubt a charge would do greater damage to the exposed portions of that obscenity, even if a troop could survive long enough to reach it and attach one. Although armor units do generally have weaker protection on their undersides, with its outer edges practically dragging on the ground, you'd have to use tremendous force to shove a charge under that thing's belly, and at this point it would be a suicide mission with an extremely low chance of success..."

Kalabi had been expeditiously conversing with his colonels, and with nods from all, he spun around to query the Panther unit commander.

"Goddart, Oversight decided not to arm the Panthers, but their targeting software is still intact, right?"

The large man nodded thoughtfully.

"Shouldn't've been touched," he replied.

Kalabi—eyes bright—turned to his superior, who had taken a keen interest in the conversation amongst his subordinates.

"Sir, the Dreadnought is on the move north of the shaft, soon bringing all extraction points in range of its direct fire. We believe we can at least impair the Dreadnought's ability to strike our positions with missile fire, leaving it with only the main guns and a shortened range."

"How?" Ryu asked shortly.

"Even when activated, the CA troops' minds are not able to track the missiles in the air due to human limitations, but the Panthers' *can*. We propose that Panthers be directed to link up with snipers and use their lifelines and tails to grasp the firearms, guiding the barrels to ensure the rounds intersect with the missiles' projected paths."

The senior officer pondered this for a moment before acquiescing.

"It's never been tried before, but it's the best option we have."

"Yes, *sir*!" Goddart enthused from where he had been observing the exchange. Speaking over his shoulder, the large man ordered, "Zervas, task Cloud, Raven, Gato, and Churchill to move to the nearest snipers. SAVANT, we'll need you to ensure the cats' logic is updated to match the requirements."

"Confirmed, General Goddart," the AI responded.

Eyes suddenly flashing with additional inspiration, Ryu turned again to his engineering advisor.

"Now, about the *Panthers*...Brown, how many charges remain?"

The engineer quickly double-checked her screen, excitedly answering, "We included two extras in the capsule, just in case!"

"SAVANT, calculate the probability of success eliminating the Dreadnought with two charges deployed beneath it while the jamming and missile interception is in place."

"My assessment is that such a mission has a fifty-five percent chance of success, General Ryu," the analytics engine stated.

The senior general turned purposefully and thoughtfully back to the Panther commander.

"That's likely the best and possibly the *only* chance we have for saving our troops. Goddart, we're going to need two more of your cats!"

---

Ked was still under the effects of the serum, but without the visor feeding guidance to his eyes, he was experiencing confusion. Lying in debris with the left-side earpiece in his helmet nonfunctional, he heard instructions from SAVANT coming through the right as the ringing in his ears was slowly fading. The sounds of combat still filled the air and smoke and dust were billowing past him in clouds that blocked out the moonlight each time they completely enveloped him.

"...try to get up and move to extraction point Bravo. If visual indicators are not onscreen, turn away from the tower and begin moving along the edge of its shadow."

SAVANT's primary command-and-control communications were having difficulty reaching Ked's onboard module due to blast-inflicted damage, so the suit-based guidance unit was making use of the last information it had received while combining that with input from each of the suit's operational sensors. The AI was speaking at its normal pace for troop instructions, which was roughly twice the speed of natural human conversation: clear and calm, but mechanical.

"Li...Lillie..." Ked's voice was tremulous as he tried to speak between gasps of air. As his breathing slowed to a steady wheezing, he blinked several times as if trying to clear his vision, eyes searching and mouth incoherently trying to form words.

"Are you...Lillie?" the shell-shocked young man finally managed to ask in a childlike voice that was almost pleading.

A partially exposed medical device integrated into his helmet emitted a soft hiss, pumping additional activation serum into Ked's bloodstream.

Slowly, his eyes returned to the calm gaze of an activated CA soldier.

Habitually grunting with the effort, Ked rolled over onto his hands and knees, or at least tried to do so. The armor covering his right arm had been torn off roughly halfway up his forearm, and visible inside the opening in the armor were the shredded ends of muscles, tendons, and bones, partially cauterized by the heat from the blast but still bleeding.

Under the influence of the serum, he did not experience any particular distress at the sight. His brain simply logged the absence of his appendage as an asset without which he would have to operate as he fulfilled his orders.

He could see that the exterior of his protective suit had been scorched from roughly his mid-thigh up across his hip and belly. The blast had also partially shattered the frame of the holster for the combat pistol attached to his hip and leg and had singed the firearm's grip on every outward-facing surface. Feet scrabbling at the hard-packed dirt beneath them, he managed to bring his knees up to better support his center of gravity and pushed off with his elbows to launch himself into a kneeling stance. His head swam as it elevated above his heart, but he heard his exosuit giving him additional instructions.

"Suit and wearer diagnostics complete. Right hand not detected. Tourniquet required. Detach medical kit from behind right hip."

Ked strained his left hand—still gloved in the flexible armor material of the suit—to reach across to his opposite hip and take hold of the brick-shaped unit as he'd been ordered. His fingers found the release lever on the belt-facing side, and he brought the kit around to his lap. A massive explosion from a Chinese rocket hitting the ground roughly fifty meters behind the soldier did not phase him in the slightest.

"Open kit and withdraw blue, circular tourniquet."

He thumbed the hatch release, and the lid sprang back, revealing the color-coded contents. Ked set the kit between his knees and pinned it there, then used his left hand to extract the blue object. He sat holding it for a moment as the AI waited the amount of time it had estimated that he would require to perform the last action. The air above Ked snapped twice as the Dreadnought unleashed rounds from its main gun and sent them flying at a Command Activated position nearly two kilometers away.

SAVANT continued, "Place the ring of the tourniquet around the remainder of your right forearm, moving it up until it is five centimeters from the end of your armor, then press the orange button on the tourniquet."

As Ked slid the ring around what was left of his forearm, his suit's armor relaxed in that area, the reactive gel being pulled out of the suit's material, leaving it even more flexible than before. Upon pressing the orange button, the device automatically clamped down on the limb, cutting off the flow of blood out of the wound.

"Drink water," SAVANT ordered next.

Ked closed his lips around the drinking valve that extended inside the helmet to the right and in front of his mouth, protruding from the material protecting that portion of his jaw. He took two long draws on the straw—as he'd been trained to do each time he was ordered to drink—and waited for his next instructions.

The follow-on order was for the soldier to stand up, slowly.

The young man's body was still experiencing the effects of shock, with an elevated heart rate, perspiration, dizziness from blood loss, and an extra burden on all his organs. If his suit had not been injecting medications to help stabilize his systems, he would already have passed out.

Rising to his feet, he wavered slightly but managed to keep his footing, his breathing still more like gasping and his limbs shaking as he stood. SAVANT ordered him to walk forward slowly. Since his exact position could not be ascertained by the onboard computer, the AI once again ordered him to follow the edge of the massive shadow in which he stood.

As he was trudging along, a new alert sounded in his helmet.

"Sensors indicate proximity to another CA troop. Change heading to two o'clock direction and walk ten meters."

Ked obeyed the directive, moving through the smoke and dust and stinking, fiery remains of the enemy drones and close air combat vehicles that dotted the landscape, all while avoiding the bodies of enemy soldiers that he came across in large numbers. Finally, he spotted a figure in a Command Activated combat suit, sprawled out next to the turret of a light cavalry unit. The troop was lying on his back, and Ked could see that his helmet had been blown off, having torn up the wearer's chin and nose during its violent departure. The blood—some crusted and some still bright—was mixed with a fair amount of charcoal and dirt, making the wounded soldier's features difficult to discern in the dim light.

"Place first two fingers on other soldier's throat," SAVANT instructed.

Crouching and extending the digits, Ked held them in the appropriate place as the AI activated the sensors built into the suit's glove.

Finally, it stated, "Soldier is alive but unconscious. Grasp soldier's left arm and drag him, again following the edge of the tower's shadow away from its base."

Ked bent down and grasped the fellow Command Activated troop's left wrist, great drops of sweat pouring out across the bottom edge of the gaping hole in his helmet's face screen. Rising with some difficulty, he was relying more on the artificial muscles built into his suit's fabric than on his own strength. He resumed his trudging gait and soon matched up his path with the edge of the elevator's moonlight-created shadow once more, dragging his companion along behind him.

# Chapter 12

*"Loyalty is more than just a feeling of attachment or a habit that we develop over time. The concept also implies a moral commitment and a sense of responsibility towards the person, group, or cause to which we are loyal. Loyalty means that we act in ways that respect and support the interests and values of our loyalty object, even when it is difficult or costly to do so."*

*- Captain Joseph Ricci, Commander of the U.S.S. Providence, United States of America, Global Alliance*

The strategic hub was continuously filled with the chatter of commanders for both troops and robots as those leaders hurriedly coordinated their efforts. The Panthers that were currently tasked with injured asset rescue and transportation had now moved the second round of casualties to extraction points Alpha and Bravo, while the four cats that had been assigned to assist the Command Activated snipers had linked up with the sharpshooters. These machines, having received updates to their software via SAVANT, worked with their human companions to execute a pattern of firing and moving repeatedly—each team moving at a different time, so three weapons were constantly ready to fire.

Though the mechanical animals' lifelines were insufficiently long to allow them to effectively man the rifles for targeting and firing solo, when the snipers took up firing positions, the Panthers crouched down beside the troops, extended the prehensile cables from their backs, and wrapped the tentacles around the rifle barrels and foregrips. Simultaneously tucking their heads up next to the humans' faces, they sighted down the barrels together with their assigned troops.

Due to this unheard-of feat of AI, robot, and human coordination, the majority of the Dreadnought's missiles were being blown out of the sky as the immense machine moved menacingly up the slope toward a position north of the space elevator. The tank was being tailed by the remaining light cavalry units, which were wisely allowing the elephantine vehicle to weaken their enemies before they swept in for another assault.

Ryu could feel his entire body filling to its brim with the seething tension that had sprung forth as the misbegotten child of his hope that the still-capable forces would be able to hold off the Chinese units, at least long enough that all troops could safely be extracted. The two Panther units Goddart had tasked with the senior officer's special mission now bore the fate of nearly all the remaining troops upon their broad backs.

Each advanced machine clutching one of the remaining directional explosive charges with their lifelines, the two robotic felines had maintained low profiles as they had traversed the ground leading up to the western face of the enemy's enormous elevator, keeping the structure between them and the Dreadnought. Now, they crept along the tower's exterior until they were nearly within the armored unit's line of sight, adjusted the charges so they were positioned just beneath their bellies, and there they waited in the nearly pitch-black darkness of the construction's gloom.

In the command center, Ryu, Kalabi, and the other commanders were also waiting, deadly still.

The Dreadnought was now passing due north of the tower and had a line of sight to practically all terrain west of the tower. Claws extending and with extraordinary speed, the cats suddenly burst out from their place of seclusion and dashed toward the enormous machine, darting randomly back and forth as they moved to try to avoid the withering fire that almost instantly emanated from their foe's corner turrets.

Machine gun fire painfully caught the robots here and there with rounds that blew off pieces of their armored limbs and bodies, knocking them powerfully with each round that connected, forcing them to swing their tails and aggressively adjust their bodies to regain their balance as they resolutely raced onward. The Panthers drew closer and closer to the vehicle as it attempted to slowly turn its nose away, its controllers catching on to the automatons' objective.

"Almost there..." hissed Goddart in the command center, "*...come on, babies!*"

The behemoth having transitioned to focusing its fire on just one of the cats as its operators had grown more desperate and the felines had drawn ever closer, this freed the first Panther to reach its target and forcefully plow into the earth to slide its charge just below the lip of the goliath's front edge. As the second Panther made a final juke left and then leaped at the enemy vehicle, its torso was caught in the crossfire of the two nearest turrets, ripping its chest apart as the robot wailed in distress. Its body skittered across the ground, lifeless, as the charge it had borne tumbled toward the Dreadnought.

Squirming away from the front of the tank as the vehicle now rolled forward in an attempt to crush its nearest enemy, the first Panther extended a lifeline to its utmost, desperately grasping one of the explosive's handholds and then dragging the charge quickly and vigorously under the hulking monstrosity above it.

SAVANT detonated the charges.

Heavy shrapnel blasted through the belly of the Dreadnought with a flash of light that burst out from below it, together with a shockwave that sent both Panthers flying across the rough earth. The great tank shook staggeringly and slowly ground to a smoking halt. Only the crackling of flames emanating from former Communist assets could be heard across the previously raucous battlefield.

Then, actuators seizing and whining as the still-mobile feline slowly struggled to its feet, the battered beast feebly extended what was left of its mangled tentacles and gently took hold of the uppermost limbs of its teammate near the shoulder and hip. Crouching low and with one lifeline having been virtually disintegrated by the charges' ebullitions, the Panther carefully lifted its companion's body onto its twisted back. With great additional effort, the big cat rose, staggered, and then began hobbling away from the enemy forces—a slow-moving shadow in the moonlit night.

The command center had gone silent as the personnel had emotionally observed these final, determined actions.

Suddenly, General Kalabi spotted acceleration among the remaining enemy forces and shouted out, "Light up all remaining enemies! *Protect the Panthers!*"

The Alliance troops had briefly ceased firing as their primary and closest adversary had finally expired, but let fly with all available weapons against the Chinese cavalry units and troops that were now in range—and homing in on the injured felines. Unit after unit among the Communist forces dropped, stopped moving, or burst into flames as the Command Activated directed an incredible volume of fire into the mercilessly aggressive opponents.

The command units' focus was broken when a member of the situational awareness team cried out, "Enemy aircraft inbound from the southeast!"

His heart skipping a beat, General Ryu steeled himself and ordered that the incoming craft should be brought onscreen. SAVANT expanded the scope of the focus from the powerful optics on the now-distant UA craft and displayed their observations on the main screens.

Now Ryu's heart sank.

The count hovering over the group of enemy fighters' trackers sat at fifty-seven, and they were accompanied by seventy high-speed attack drones. SAVANT displayed the estimated time till their arrival at the nearest troops. Only fourteen minutes. Still sixteen minutes before the US Navy's first aircraft would reach the site.

He called back to Cooper, "Tell Naval Command that if their responders haven't used their boosters yet, *now* is the time to do it!"

Cooper connected with his Navy contact and bent over in insistent conversation.

The chief engineer's voice rang out, "Detonation of charges should have weakened the base of the elevator shaft, and radar indicates that the space-based platform's orbit has shifted to a higher elevation by two hundred meters—signaling that the tether has most likely now been severed!"

She swiped through additional data as it rapidly poured onto her screen. "Elevator is still experiencing swaying due to the shockwave from the detonation at the base. However, projections are that the tower is unlikely to fall under current conditions..."

Ryu turned to the fifth command unit in the hub, its general having faced him as the engineering report had been delivered. The unit's leader was looking at the senior officer expectantly.

"This is why we always build in contingencies. General Percevic, fire all batteries!"

The gruff officer turned to his subcommanders, barking out, "On my mark, fire all batteries. Three, two, one, *mark!*"

Ryu returned his gaze to the centermost of the main screens, where he quickly located the cluster of trackers denoting the stealth-cloaked troops and their equipment positioned in the hilly terrain southwest of the tower. An enemy drone had been dispatched toward the area after the Command Activated forces had touched down there, but its efforts to detect its adversaries had been fully obstructed by their dynamic camouflage. From those Alliance assets' indicators, two dozen smaller tracking icons suddenly burst forth, moving above the speed of sound as they cut an arc from the launch site out further east and then curved around toward the easternmost face of the enormous tower.

The two troops who had been directed to move eastward away from the rest of their unit had been guided to a position next to a natural stone formation roughly four kilometers from their landing zone, and they were providing primary target designation for the missiles using lasers aimed at the elevator. Each armament was a self-propelled projectile designed with both radar-resistant and laser-deflecting surfaces through a clever combination of materials that made them differentially penetrable by light and electromagnetic waves.

China's advanced threat detection systems were only able to identify the missiles as they entered the final kilometer of their flight paths, and without the defensive rockets from the now-disabled batteries, the Communist intercept capabilities were limited to the few remaining turrets on the bases and smaller drones in the air. Neither option was able to stop the Alliance munitions as they sailed in over such a short distance and then made solid contact with their target.

The warheads in these missiles were tactical nuclear devices, and when they detonated across the face of the tower, it was with the brilliance of a dozen small suns, blinding nearby observers among the enemy forces and sending out an electromagnetic pulse. The elevator shaft provided sufficient shielding for the Command Activated forces against the unseen assault on their electronics, particularly when taking into account the architecture of the exosuits that already granted their wearers a baseline of protection. However, electricity-dependent machines within nine kilometers of the structure's eastern face were exposed to the full force of the circuitry overcharging wave.

As dozens of enemy troop transports, drones, and even light armor units were deactivated by the close-range EMP, the count of active enemy assets on the strategic command screens dramatically dropped. A number of the members of the command staff let out brief cheers as they noticed this welcome event alone.

Their enthusiasm was somewhat dampened as the senior medical advisor voiced his fear that the CA troops whose armor had been compromised would likely need to undergo intensive treatment for the radiation exposure they would soon experience. General Ryu both appreciated the sudden decrease in the number of active enemy assets and worried about the necessary medical care the unprotected troops would undoubtedly require. Still, he knew that the blast wave and EMP were only secondary benefits from the use of tactical nuclear weapons.

The senior leader stared fiercely at the foremost command screen with arms clasped tightly behind his back, forcefully willing his body to conceal the tremors that the stress of this moment was creating in his limbs. Finally, and at a painfully slow rate, the massive circle representing the uppermost portion of the shaft on SAVANT's top-down projection began shifting east of the smaller shape of its foundation. The movement was almost undetectable at first, but picked up speed with every second that passed. The room went silent as all eyes turned to the main displays, watching with bated breath as SAVANT changed the scale of the map to maintain the entirety of the tower in view. The circular tracker for the current crest of the elevator grew increasingly oblique as it moved east, while the lines representing the body of the shaft grew ever longer in unison.

Ryu noted that the tether-tied platform initially maintained its position relative to the elevator's foundation while increasing slightly in size on the screen. China's orbital staging unit was moving farther from the Earth due to the detachment of its tether from the ground, but this would soon change.

"Inset feed from ground-based observers," Ryu ordered SAVANT as he pointed at the two soldiers positioned furthest east, these troops having temporarily sheltered as the shockwave from the tactical nuclear devices had washed over their location.

The AI brought up a frame in which the footage from an external camera on one of the two troops was displayed, the soldier once again rising to resume his surveillance of the now-crippled edifice. As the structure came back into view, many members of the command unit gasped or shook their heads in amazement.

The scene was at once awe-inspiring in its grandeur and horrifying in its scale. The space elevator's colossal shaft was tilting over by 35 degrees now, and its motion was creating eastward-propelling forces on the orbital platform via the conduit's contact with the exiting tether. The projections had been correct regarding the inevitable outcome for the orbital unit, that construction being affected by the manner in which the tower was collapsing with the tether only having been severed near its base. The incredibly long cable was creating significant sideways pressure as it was dragged through its conduit by the platform above, and now the platform itself was being pulled back through the atmosphere by the toppling tower.

Miniscule indicators representing enemy assets—both robotic and human—near the elevator's base and in the nearby facilities conveyed the fact that the forces were fleeing from the area at what must be great speeds. Given the tower's nearly two-kilometer-wide diameter, their chances of escaping were extremely slim.

The elevator toppled ever more swiftly, at first bending with the shaft generally straight and rigid from the warheads' impact site upward—despite the rippling that flowed out across its skin from that location—and then the tower gradually bowing toward the sun as the rising light-giver now cast its rays across the top third of the phenomenal fabrication. As the associated, space-based structure accelerated along its trajectory toward the luminary, the length of tether that was still running down the interior of the duct created friction on the associated edge of the structure's crown, the topmost section first bending forward and then deforming the opposite direction again as the collapsing shaft overtook the de-orbiting platform's cable and pulled against it. The giant structure bent its head back like a creature straining for one last look at the light before it came crashing to the ground.

Ryu knew that the blow from its impact would stir up a wave of debris both in the air above and flying across the ground, blasting out on either side of the collapsing tower as a wall of destruction that would race across the surface of the Earth.

"All troops shelter in place," he ordered, and the inset feed cut off as the bearer of its camera ducked down behind nearby boulders.

---

Ked marched along, paying no attention to the horrendous, groaning cacophony of tortured metals and polymers being torn apart as the elevator collapsed. His suit's medications had enabled his organs' functions to normalize somewhat, and his sweat had dried, leaving salty, grimy deposits across his bruised and bloodied forehead and cheeks. His breathing was still more labored than usual as he trekked onwards.

He was thrown into swift action as the SAVANT module spoke with elevated volume to add urgency.

"PUT THE SOLDIER ON YOUR SHOULDER."

Ked obediently stepped back and used his only available hand to lift the man by his wrist so that his body raised up onto Ked's back, once again relying heavily on the suit's muscle fibers to work in synchronization with his own as he pulled the other soldier's arm up over his shoulder and held it tightly against his chest.

He was now five kilometers away from the tower, but as it made impact with the Earth, it sent a wave out through the air that traveled at hundreds of kilometers per hour. The great undulations of currents spread out in all directions, only slightly weaker in the area where Ked and other CA troops operated on the opposite side of the elevator's base. Still, the shockwave passing in a half cone above and around the soldiers sucked the available atmosphere out into the area of the cone's perimeter, causing ear-popping pressure differentials and sending dust and smoke swirling in building-sized tornadoes that tossed crippled vehicles about like grains of sand on a windy beach.

At almost the same rate of travel, the wind was accompanied by a thunderous surging of the ground, radiating out from the impact site like ripples from a stone after it had been dropped in a pool of still water. The waves were similarly only partially lessened as they met with the tower's foundation and flowed around it, racing on toward the CA troops beyond.

"CROUCH AND JUMP HIGH," ordered the SAVANT module.

Ked bent over and sprang up with all his strength, carrying his cargo and himself up five meters in the air just as the first oscillation of earth passed underneath him—his elevation not quite clearing the top of the ground at the crest of the wave. His feet were knocked out from underneath him, and he flipped over backward, clinging tightly to the body of the other soldier with the superhuman strength his suit provided. He twisted himself around to come down feet first, landing with one leg bending down to touch his knee to the ground for extra stability, then slowly raising himself back up to a standing position.

"CROUCH AND JUMP HIGH," SAVANT's voice came again.

This time Ked's leap was high enough to avoid the second, less voluminous ripple of soil rolling out from the impact site, and he landed as the bulge in the Earth's surface was fading out from beneath him, riding it down until the ground was flat again. His suit's medications had afforded him sufficient recovery to unleash the strength he had just used, but now his chest heaved with the effort of breathing after such extreme exertion, especially in his current condition.

"Resume westward march," the AI now calmly ordered.

Perspiration coated his forehead again, his face was brightly flushed, and he stared straight ahead as he tried to suck in enough air to keep from passing out. After a short time and several ever-smaller ripples of earth passing beneath him, Ked managed to fully stabilize his stance. The drugs were still working away inside of him, and the other soldier's weight was being borne primarily by his suit as he began shuffling forward once more.

Ked had barely taken ten steps when he was knocked over by the large caliber rounds of an enemy's heavy machine gun striking across his back. The weapon was mounted on the top of a Chinese light cavalry vehicle that had survived the elevator's destruction and its aftermath as it had circled around the elevator to the southeast and had ridden out the waves in the air and the ground. The enemy soldiers had been sweeping the area—headlights off—west of the tower for residual Command Activated forces, and now they'd found a soft target.

The young man's exosuit had only just kept the rounds from penetrating, but the force of their impact had knocked the air out of his lungs and had thrown him mercilessly to the earth. The weight of his cargo increased the brutal concussion before the other soldier's body rolled off to the side.

As the enemy vehicle's engine grew louder, SAVANT urged, "RETURN FIRE USING SIDEARM."

Sucking in a great breath and shrugging his companion's body off of his outstretched arm, Ked twisted onto his side and used his left hand to reach across his waist to the heavy handgun holstered on his right hip. The young conscript extracted it upside down and rapidly flipped it so he had a firm grip, just as the AI had trained his body and mind to do by performing the same move so many times before. Ked scrambled up and spun around as his suit's electrodes picked up on his movements, the artificial muscles assisting in holding his new crouching stance steady as he fired off two rounds at the vehicle's windshield, targeting the most likely location of the driver in the darkened interior.

The Command Activated soldier immediately fired two more rounds toward the silhouette of the vehicle's gunner that was visible above the turret. The gunner was knocked back, and then his body slouched over the side of the main gun as the vehicle wandered, undirected, forward until its wheels ran up against the carcass of a mangled drone.

Ked stayed in his firing stance a few moments longer, watching for movement in the enemy vehicle in line with his training. A soft moan behind him drew his attention, the other CA soldier murmuring as he came to. Ked turned toward the fellow Alliance asset just as a bullet slammed into the back of his helmet, throwing him to the ground...where he remained.

An enemy combatant had slipped out the rear door on the opposite side of the vehicle and into the darkness during the earlier exchange of fire and had then used the vehicle as cover, running alongside it. After the enemy vehicle had halted, the adversary had waited until Ked's back had been exposed before the enemy had fired from the shadows beneath the cavalry unit.

"*NO!*"

The other Alliance soldier had been shocked into action as he had finally regained consciousness, only to see Ked being taken down. With the serum administration unit in his suit having been disabled by the rocket's blast that had knocked him unconscious, the second man was now fully and painfully aware of his surroundings.

He snatched up Ked's firearm from where it had fallen, spread himself out prone, and rested the base of the gun's grip on the back of Ked's stilled thigh for stability. The enemy soldier was firing in a panic as he saw additional movement in the shadows where Ked's body lay, and the newly revived Command Activated soldier homed in on the foe with his weapon's laser sight, firing off pistol rounds until he heard a loud cry from the shooter and the opposing fire finally ceased.

Ked's companion turned to him and carefully rolled him onto his back. In the twilight, Ked's eyes were blinking, and he was obviously breathing heavily but seemed to be awaiting instructions that were not coming. The upright soldier leaned forward and cautiously felt around the back of what was left of the casualty's helmet, his fingers finding a gaping hole where the enemy round had collapsed the armor's core AI module but no traces of blood.

The upright man breathed a healthy sigh of relief.

"Okay, buddy, looks like you're flying AI-free, but you're alive, and you're not flying solo. I don't recognize you from the complex, so I'm guessing you're new. If so, then welcome aboard! I'm Billy Chong, and I'll be your pilot tonight!"

Corporal Chong grinned and helped Ked to his feet.

Looking around slowly in amazement at the field of comprehensive destruction that surrounded them, Billy shrugged and offered, "My guess is that extraction's...that way?" as he indicated a distant point at which he could see enemy fire being directed. Turning toward the still-purring Chinese light cavalry vehicle and taking Ked's elbow, the warrior gently pulled the younger man along as he headed over to the rig.

"I know these suits can speed us up, but to me, wheels beat legs *any* day!"

After Chong had Ked seated and strapped into the no-frills vehicle, he slammed the angular steel door and made his way to the driver's seat, pulling the Communist soldier's body out and dropping it a few meters away in a patch of grass. He bent down and yanked the man's sidearm out of its holster.

"You go with God, and I'll go with your gun, brother!"

As he straightened and turned his bloodied and grime-covered face toward the vehicle, the area was suddenly bathed in a dull orange glow. Chong raised his eyes in wonder as he took in the sight of the elevator's massive orbital platform burning its way slowly through the atmosphere, moving from above the elevator's carcass eastward toward the sunrise.

Part of the massive tether was still trailing below the satellite, glowing red hot and breaking up into smaller sections that were falling from their great height down to Earth. Pieces of the material around the outer edges of the platform had also broken off, creating a series of smaller meteors ringing the leading edges of the octagonal structure like angry young dragons escorting their matriarch.

"Talk about raining down fire and brimstone..." Chong murmured.

Shaking himself out of his daze, Billy jogged over to the cavalry unit and slid into the driver's seat. Slamming his door shut, he jabbed the button to shift into drive and eased the vehicle out across the generally bare ground, aiming its nose away from the still-smoking stump of the elevator shaft. The rough, angled edge where the structure had torn apart was just catching the first streams of sunlight on its jagged lip—looking distinctly like the lower mandible of some grotesque giant.

General Kalabi stared intently at his unit's central screen, watching as the tracking identifiers for the first wave of Navy combat craft swept in from the west. The enemy air force assets had been on flight paths leading straight to the Command Activated troops on the ground, with the time to arrival now below thirty seconds.

"Come on, come *on*!" Kalabi growled.

Finally, the enemy craft broke from their direction of travel, being compelled to focus on midair combat as the Navy's planes let fly dozens of intercepting missiles. The wild movements of the aircraft trackers for both sides were indicative of the dogfights that were now taking place over the heads of the CA troops. Several of the lead US fighters' forms suddenly multiplied into swarms of drones that supported their parent aircraft in fights against the dozens of unmanned enemy units that had now also reached the battle and were targeting the Allied air assets with both lasers and missiles.

"Air transports are nearly onsite!" General Ryu called out. "Only troops and Panthers are to be extracted!"

The main body of the Command Activated casualties had been grouped west-northwest of the elevator, and the Panthers had now managed to turn the numerous casualty indicators across the field of combat into only a handful that still required transport. The area was guarded by two platoons that had been formed out of the battle-ready troops, and these soldiers had been fighting fiercely under their commanders' guidance. The remaining Chinese vehicles, drones, and troops had been held at bay through coordinated fire team movements and the occupation of key points for defense, accompanied by relentless, pinpoint-accurate sniping.

As the first troop transports arrived, the unit commanders coordinated the loading of wounded personnel. The count of assets on the ground began reducing in number at an ever-increasing rate.

"That's the last of the main group of casualties nearly to extraction!" boomed the deep bass voice of the Panther commander. "We've got two troops that are considered casualties due to projected damage from explosions, but they seem to be mobile and are making their way in a haphazard course toward the extraction area. Tasking two cats to intersect with them and lead them to the landing zone."

"Acknowledged," General Ryu responded with great relief, taking a deep breath in through his nostrils and exhaling slowly from his mouth while briefly closing his eyes. Opening his ocular organs with new energy, Ryu spoke to the waiting troop commanders.

"Direct all remaining ground forces to move to extraction point Bravo at maximum speed."

As the unit command personnel executed his order, the strategic commander double-tapped his strip once more.

"SAVANT, no time to collect drop capsules. Initiate their self-destruct sequences."

"Capsule self-destruct sequences initiated, General Ryu," the AI confirmed.

Watching the capsule indicators on the theater maps wink out of existence, the general knew that the veins of thermite that ran through the devices had ignited, turning their composite hulls and all technology inside into molten pools that would provide the enemy with no useful intelligence.

Now they just had to get those last troops off the ground before the enemy aircraft caught on to the fact that their prey was clandestinely being extricated right below them.

---

Rolling and jostling along over the rough terrain, Billy and Ked had heard the aircraft before they had seen them, and Corporal Chong's hair had stood on end as he'd thought through the possibilities.

"We may be in trouble here, big guy," he'd commented to his passenger. "If we got a bunch of enemy fighters inbound, we'll be easy targets out here!"

He'd quickly leaned forward and then to the left to scan the skies, not catching a glimpse of any aircraft at first. However, before long, he'd let out a yelp of excitement.

"Enemy fighters above, but they're bein' *torn up* by our own flyboys! Hey, it's 'bout time those airheads earned their keep, right?! Them Navy muscles ain't just meant for impressin' the ladies!"

Ked now stared blankly up out of his side window as an increasingly large number of craft engaged in the air battle, explosions and debris being spread across the expanse of sky above them.

Chong's enthusiasm had died down a bit as he'd cast a glance at the expressionless face of his cohort, and he now began lamenting, "Oh yeah, I could be spinning comedy gold, and it'd go unappreciated..."

Then he brightened again, returning his attention to the terrain ahead, continuing with the positivity he always tried to force to the surface of his mind.

"That's alright. I spin good stuff all the time, and Jayce never agrees to crown me the King of Comedy, either! Don't mean I should stop!"

With a jolt, Chong suddenly stamped on the brakes, throwing Ked forward in his harness as the vehicle skidded across the gravelly soil.

Racing toward them were two dark shapes, hunched low as they sprinted up in front of the rig. Gracefully reducing their pace and then adjusting their locomotion to a trot, two Panthers approached the pair with heads tilted as though they were assessing the friendliness of the humans. They came to a stop about five meters from the enemy cavalry vehicle and turned their flanks toward Chong and Ked. After a moment, they tossed their heads back in the opposite direction.

"Yeah, okay, I remember we're supposed to be partners with big black cats in the field. Looks like they want us to chase their tails, bro!"

Chong gave the robots a quick wave and pointed forward meaningfully.

The autonomous animals obligingly turned and began trotting back in the direction from which they had appeared, glancing over their shoulders at the vehicle to be sure it was following. Chong let off the brake and started rolling along behind them. As they moved, the cats steadily increased their pace, and Billy increased his acceleration to match. Soon they were rumbling away at sixty kilometers per hour across the increasingly rugged, grassy steppes.

Though they were being tossed and knocked about in their seats, Chong's eyes were shining as the daylight spread over the landscape, piercing through the dust and smoke to the area of far less destruction into which they were now entering. Having taken in the toppled tower behind them, he knew that he had been part of an incredibly impactful mission—and he'd also reacted lethally in the face of imminent danger.

The scene in front of his house in downtown Singapore sprang achingly into his thoughts. His mind's eye was consumed by the memory of a nondescript metal chest containing his belongings sitting where it had been deposited by his family's servants at the foot of the stairs leading to their great front entrance, Billy standing where his blood had turned ice cold after having entered the courtyard from the main gate. He could still feel the tears tumbling down his cheeks like the events in this sudden recollection had occurred that day rather than so many years prior.

Billy could still see his father's rugged face, utterly devoid of any affection, eyes staring at him with pure loathing as his sire closed the door. He could still hear the dense and complex locks whirring into place within the mansion's front entrance.

He had been shut out of his family forever because he had frozen in action and lost a battle during a military field exercise as a young officer. His hesitation had resulted from his sudden recognition of the fact that an unorthodox solution existed to a battlefield scenario, but that his superiors clung to their nation's standard military methodologies with almost religious fervor. Afterward, no matter what Billy had said, his commanding officer insisted that he had capitulated to cowardice, thereby bringing shame to his family's name. Shame that was more potently damaging because his father was the ranking military officer over the entirety of Singapore's forces.

On this night, Corporal Chong knew with everything in his soul that he *was* a force to be reckoned with, no matter what his father thought!

His gaze latched onto a shape in the sky that seemed like a hazy, almost invisible dart that was tracing a large spiral out and then down in their direction. Chong had occasionally seen such Command Activated transports with dynamic camouflage engaged as they'd moved around the complex back in Colorado, and he patted Ked happily on the shoulder, steering toward a patch of ground up ahead where the two Panthers had galloped in and then stopped.

Chong shouted, "Hang onto your shorts, bro, 'cause I think we're about to get a lift outta here!"

---

As members of the command staff tracked the successful extraction of Alliance units, they were breaking into spontaneous shouts of celebration at each piece of good news that came rolling in. Still, General Ryu stood watching the scene with troubled eyes. He was inexpressibly grateful to Navy leadership for coming to his troops' rescue, and he desperately hoped that each member of the program made it home without life-threatening injuries. At the same time, he desperately wished the involvement of obviously Alliance-tied assets had not been necessary in the first place.

A foreboding storm cloud was consuming his consciousness.

For the CEN, there could be no doubt now that the Command Activated program was a branch of Alliance operations or that the Alliance was responsible for the destruction of their prized monolith. The world was inevitably hurtling toward all-out war, and not in the controlled progression for which he had planned and hoped.

"Bogey inbound!" shouted Cooper, tapping his screen to bring the focus of the strategic operations displays to an object speeding toward the extraction zone—moving at a pace that exceeded the capabilities of any manned aircraft.

Ryu's eyes darted to the Alliance assets still in theater.

"*Get those aircraft out of there!*"

The four-star general's voice rang out in the command center with a tone that sent his personnel scrambling to comply.

Colonel Webb turned his attention back from a larger, strategic display to his unit command console, tapping the indicators for the last transports and shouting an order to SAVANT.

"Punch it!"

At the same time, Cooper had tapped his strip with lightning-fast reflexes and was yelling, "Order all aircraft to elevate and evacuate west immediately! Order all aircraft to elevate and evacuate west *immediately!*"

On the main screens, the transports quickly accelerated to their maximum speeds, the fighter planes similarly breaking off combat and fleeing west.

---

Having pushed Ked into the Command Activated transport craft and then clambered inside himself, Chong had noted that the benches were empty except for where Ked had strapped himself in and was now docilely sitting. Chong threw himself across a bench with a sigh, one arm draped over its back like he was relaxing in his sofa at the barracks.

"You know, man, even if we're activated in combat, *usually*..." he had to quickly yank his feet back as the two Panthers came leaping into the vessel, their paws slipping a bit across the composite surface of its floor until their grip types had sufficiently adjusted. Chong continued, "...we're still honest-to-goodness heroes, no matter what anyone says!"

All four passengers felt a sudden pull downward as the transport quickly elevated, and the smoke-tinged wind that had been swirling through the side door was cut off by the portal's closure. One of the dark felines looked out the right-side window as though it was keenly interested in the landscape that was quickly fading away beneath them while the other restlessly paced around in a circle, passing its gaze across Ked and Chong like it was checking on its cubs.

The robots were thrown up against Ked and Chong as the aircraft suddenly accelerated forward at a greater pace, quickly reaching a speed at which the whole chassis was shuddering with the pounding of cold air currents against its exterior.

Chong had cast a hand up on the nearest Panther's shoulder to stabilize it and now sat up straight, face awash with curiosity.

"Hey, what gives?" he shouted at the main control screen near the front of the transport.

Then, the whole cabin blazed with dazzlingly white light.

Chong blinked hard several times and rubbed his eyes. When he finally had half-decent vision again, he turned his gaze past Ked—who was still sitting placidly but now blinking hard as well—to look back over the bench and out the rear window of the vehicle.

A hulking mushroom cloud was billowing up near the now-blackened remains of the elevator's foundation, waves of debris churning out in rings around the roots of the smokey cloud as the contours across its surface still glowed a fiery orange. The transport lurched again as the blast wave emanating from the nuclear explosion caught up with the vessel and Billy—restraint free—was thrown roughly up against the ceiling with a grunt. Dropping back down in his seat, the corporal's hands flew up to rub his exposed head as he cringed.

He slowly turned to look back at the billowing smoke again, its color fading from orange to a murky golden hue in the morning light. The largest piece of intact satellite platform still burned and smoked in the sky beyond, making its dreadful way down to strike the Earth. Chong let out a low whistle as his eyes surveyed the scene.

Turning to Ked, he placed a hand warmly on his comrade's shoulder.

"I know you were likely just being ordered to help me, and you may not remember this later, but...thanks for saving me out there, bro. I mean, without you, I'd prolly be down there right now and, heh, thassa big nuke!

Guess the Commies figured they had nothing to lose and went with 'Kill 'em all, let the gods sort 'em out'!"

Ked's eyes remained fixed straight ahead, and after a moment, Billy Chong shrugged his shoulders and returned his smiling gaze to the destruction they were leaving behind.

The young warrior half-whispered out the conclusion of his thoughts.

"Anyway, let's just say I owe you one, and *I'll* never forget it!"

# Chapter 13

*"The key attribute of honesty, when considered as a character trait, is that it arises from a good heart. If one acts honestly because one cares about others or one wants to do the right thing, then one finds oneself in the class of 'honest people.'*

*Motivations for true honesty can take different forms, such as love, friendship, a sense of duty, or a drive for justice. The intention component falls apart as selfishness is introduced, as we shift to caring more about ourselves than others. Selfishness destroys honesty as surely as poison destroys a body."*

*- Chodrak Daivika, His Holiness the Dalai Lama, from 'Reflections on Virtue'*

"Both Gaines and Jennings should be attending a dinner at the Worthings House hotel in downtown DC tonight," Maxwell advised as he displayed photos of the two individuals on the aerial vehicle's screens. "I've managed to leverage my position and relationship with an 'acquaintance' who is a senior partner of a lobbying firm. He's agreed to bring two individuals on board as representatives of that firm specifically for the event, believing you to be my cousin and her husband. You'll be taking his tickets for the gala."

Lilian's eyebrows raised as she murmured, "How much did *that* cost you?"

Maxwell laughed weakly.

"Let's just say my financial reserves have been rather significantly depleted! In any case, you will now be able to approach the two possible allies having the most clout within the program. I'd recommend starting with General Gaines, as FAILSAFE says he has the highest probability of joining forces with us.

"Remember to use nonverbal communication, if possible, and avoid any transmissions—just in case. As you know, the goal is to share the tablet only in a space that is out of sight of cameras, and Jayce can share his experiences in private as well, if needed. FAILSAFE and I will do our best to provide overwatch without drawing undesirable attention and alerting the HOUND security AI, as there is a high likelihood that it is monitoring the event. Is everyone in agreement on the plan?"

Jayce grunted, "Good here."

Lilian, peering distractedly out one of the rear passenger windows at the plethora of historically significant sites that were now in view, sighed out, "Yes. Thank you, Max."

"My pleasure, Lilian. I see you are approaching the hotel now. Best of luck to you both!"

Jayce had used a ramp to exit the sky trail and, after merging onto a one-way street south of the National Mall, he took a right turn to reach the hotel's entrance. Stopping next to the valet station in the sheltered reception area, he and Lilian exited the vehicle and approached the valet terminal. The machine picked up their vehicle identification information from Jayce's strip as they approached and displayed it on the screen, offering to park the vehicle for them. Jayce swiped across his strip to confirm, and the car began maneuvering toward the parking garage as the two walked toward the front doors of the hotel.

As the doors' sensors picked up the codes for the pair's tickets, they slid open, and Jayce and Lilian walked inside. Taking in the extravagantly designed hallway and the equally extravagant lobby at its end, they moved toward the two Secret Service team members standing in front of the ornate ballroom doors halfway down the hallway on the right.

Lilian tried to resist the incredibly strong urge to flee as it flowed icily into her veins at the sight of the grim-looking and dark-suited men...individuals who bore a disturbingly similar appearance to the hunters who had been chasing her for days. Jayce noticed her pace was slowing and gently took hold of her elbow to keep her alongside him. Fortunately, one of the security personnel was holding a tablet and it picked up their ticket codes as well, at which point the man waved them through with an air of disinterest.

Stepping into the ballroom felt like they were entering a forbidden world.

Jayce and Lilian were nicely dressed, but as she scanned the crowd, Lilian could tell that—other than the military leaders—the attendees of this party acquired their attire from designers who dealt exclusively with custom orders. The senior military service members were being tolerated simply because they had no choice but to wear the finest dress uniforms their branches could offer. The room was alive with voices and laughter as lobbyists and powerful government representatives confabulated and worked out deals.

"Gaines is sitting next to a colonel and a few civilians at a table to the far left," Jayce whispered to Lilian.

Lilian glanced past her companion to see the general looking rather like his temper was about to snap as a smiling, tuxedoed man seated at the same table was making overtures to him and his junior officer.

"No camera behind where Gaines is sitting," Jayce whispered next. "Think we might as well approach him now?"

Lilian gave a nod and they tried to casually make their way around the perimeter of the room, passing service bots and circling the table to approach Gaines. The general's eyes latched onto them as they drew close, and—noticing how they were looking at him—he set down the fork that he had been idly dangling between his fingers, turning his attention away from the animated man who'd been speaking.

Jayce led off in a professional and frank tone.

"Evening, General Gaines. We represent Venture Industries and have a piece of information you will likely find interesting."

Lilian could tell the officer's curiosity had dramatically cooled at the mention of the company name, his expression flattening and a hint of irritation showing around his eyes and mouth. However, as the officer looked the two of them up and down, he realized that something was off about these unusual "lobbyists." Lilian withdrew a tablet from her coat pocket and extended the screen to reveal the message she had prepared. She held the tablet carefully so that only Gaines could see the screen.

His eyes scanned across the display at a normal rate until he reached the words "Command Activated," at which point his reading took on great urgency.

After he'd consumed the message, Lilian swiftly retracted the tablet screen and stowed it in her pocket, the general turning to the others at the table and excusing himself, ignoring his dinner companions' extreme interest in the purpose of this interruption. Pushing his chair back and stepping past the pair as they respectfully retreated toward the wall, the general started leading Jayce and Lilian toward the main doors of the chamber, taking advantage of a space between tables to turn and furtively whisper to them that they should talk in his car.

The trio made their way to the hotel entrance, and the general double-tapped his strip, ordering, "Bring the vehicle up, please, Altman."

They quietly waited inside the doors for a few moments until a black town car pulled into the covered thoroughfare. Gaines led them to the side of the vehicle as the rear door slid open and a sergeant in a dress green uniform stepped out, standing respectfully beside the door and saluting the general.

Gaines returned the younger man's salute, explaining in a low voice, "We're going to have a private discussion in the back, so please join Altman up front and take the car in a loop around the Mall until we've finished."

As Lilian followed the general into the rear section of the town car, she noted that Gaines had moved to the far end of the bench and was raising a privacy glass to separate them from the front half of the vehicle. Lilian moved to the center of the bench and Jayce slid in behind her as Gaines engaged the switch to close the door, the sleek sedan gliding away from the hotel and slowly navigating the capital's roadways.

Gaines' expression was open and forthright as he looked inquisitively from Lilian to Jayce and back again before stating, "I'm very curious to hear what you have to say."

Lilian withdrew the tablet again and opened a file with the summary of issues and pointers to additional files containing supporting evidence. Gaines rapidly scanned through the document, brows furrowed as he opened several of the supporting files and viewed clips of video footage—the audio filling the space as the man let out occasional gasps and shook his head in disgust.

"...I can't believe how easy it is to keep these imbeciles content..."

"...this will be a key component of the CA program going forward..."

"...get them in their suits. They'll be training all morning, and then we'll need them in transit for a mission slated for tomorrow that's almost guaranteed to be approved, at least considering SAVANT's rock-solid analysis..."

The flag officer set the tablet on his lap and turned his head to stare out the window as the car rolled past the Washington Monument, the White House visible in the distance. Jayce and Lilian watched him intently.

Gaines' jaw suddenly took on extra rigidity.

"These people need to be stopped!" he finally said with resoluteness.

Turning to them as their faces filled with obvious relief, he continued, "I saw that General Rossi has a hand in this. I've *never* liked that man!"

Taking a second to master the feelings of loathing flooding his mind, Gaines then stated, "We need to get this data to the oversight board, but to see action taken as quickly as possible, we really should involve a member of the legislature."

"Jennings," Maxwell reminded his friends through their strips.

Lilian jumped slightly at the sudden sound of Max's voice. She realized he must consider them to be sufficiently clear of third-party monitoring and, therefore, free to communicate.

Jayce shared, "Isn't Senator Jennings one of the key decision-makers related to defense spending, which would include the Command Activated program?"

Gaines pondered this a moment and agreed, "Yes, she will likely be able to get the necessary individuals out of bed and put the program into lockdown. She excused herself from the party earlier, and I believe she'll be at her DC residence tonight. I can personally escort you there and add weight to what you have to say. We need to move on this before more of these deceived CA troops are injured."

Lilian's heart sank like a stone, and her throat tightened. She turned to Gaines, wide-eyed and pale, "Injured?? My brother's one of them!"

The general's face melted with sympathy.

"Ah...there was a major operation this afternoon, and I'm afraid we suffered heavy casualties, but..." he hastened to add as Lilian's eyes welled up with tears, "...thankfully, we managed to recover every troop from the field!"

Lilian gave a soft cry, and a pained smile broke onto her face as she pressed her eyes tightly shut, tears of grief and relief streaming down her cheeks. She pressed her hands together with fingers interlaced and tilted her head back in silent gratitude.

Gaines and Jayce looked on empathetically, and the general tapped a control panel to open a channel to the service members in the front area of the car.

"Take us to Senator Jennings' residence via sky trail," he ordered.

"Is it alright if our car follows behind?" Jayce asked.

The general considered this.

"No additional passengers?" the officer asked.

Jayce shook his head, explaining, "It's guided by autopilot."

"That should be fine," he consented. "Jennings' security team will just be looking for a count of visitors."

"I was actually anticipating that need," Maxwell informed Jayce and Lilian, "and FAILSAFE has the vehicle trailing you already."

Jayce nodded to the general, advising, "The car's right behind us, actually, so we're good to go now."

Gaines glanced over his shoulder to see the other sedan keeping pace with them as the general's AV exited Independence Avenue onto a sky trail ramp, and they smoothly lifted into the air.

# Chapter 14

*"In this world in which authoritarian regimes are on the rise and in which democracy is in decline, we need to ask ourselves: Who will stand for freedom? Who will make the hard choices and demonstrate true leadership in the face of great risk?*

*These are not rhetorical questions. They are a call to action. We cannot afford to be complacent or indifferent. We cannot wait for someone else to save us. We have to be the ones who defend our people, our culture, and our way of life."*

*- Brighton Estorrman, Editor in Chief, The People's Power*

Gaines was providing Lilian and Jayce with some of his background as they traveled, sharing, "I've always been a proponent of integrating a greater number of fully robotic assets into the Command Activated missions and, with additional funding, my team's research could allow us to improve the production process and take advantage of the cost-reducing effects of economies of scale.

"While it is true that our combat bots will likely always be quite a bit more expensive than the human troops in the program, with the right tactical planning, we can trade out more of the troops for my Panthers and put fewer lives at risk. This is, of course, acknowledging that we will always have a need for *some* direct human involvement in combat operations, at least for the foreseeable future."

While Lilian wiped her tears away, Jayce nodded with a level of appreciation that was born of personal experience in the field.

Gaines glanced down at the city lights below as they dramatically dwindled in number, announcing, "We're entering the secluded areas where the senior lawmakers tend to make their DC homes."

The vehicle began its descent, and soon they had pulled up to an access control point in front of a large, black metal gate and fence. They could hear the barrier humming with electricity as General Gaines lowered the window and announced himself, asking for an urgent conclave with Senator Jennings. The voice coming through the access terminal's communications channel requested the identification of all those who would be entering the property, to which Gaines responded that he had two enlisted service members in the front of his vehicle and two guests from Venture Industries seated next to him, with their vehicle automatically following behind.

After a few moments, the gate slid open, and the driver pulled the town car in through a short, wooded section of the property and then up to the front door using a large circular portion of pavement that was centered in front of the expansive, white brick estate. An extension of the pavement led from the circle to the residence's garage addition, but besides that, trees were the only things in sight beyond the mansion. FAILSAFE pulled Jayce and Lilian's rented sedan AV up behind the general's vehicle and disabled its headlights.

Two members of the senator's security detail, dressed in dark suits and long coats, had stepped out of the front door into the crispness of the late-year evening. One used a light beaming from a tablet tube to examine the passenger areas of the two vehicles. Once he'd passed the town car, the second member of the detail waved the visitors inside.

Gaines opened the communications link to the two members of his own security detail and asked Altman to remain in the car while he ordered the second member of his team, a Sergeant Faizan, to accompany them inside.

After having activated the rear-right portal's opening mechanism, Jayce climbed out of the vehicle and stood by the open door, offering a hand to help Lilian out. She took it politely and stepped forward before pausing a short distance from the town car to wait for Gaines as he exited.

"Since you're here to vouch for Lilian, I'd like to remain with our vehicle," Jayce informed Gaines, his eyes conveying the ever-present drive to err on the side of caution: a trait that had helped keep the warrior alive throughout his career.

The first member of the senator's security team had returned from checking the rental vehicle and then taken up a position standing by the front door. General Gaines glanced at their host's personnel and then nodded at Jayce. As the bulky ex-Marine made his way to the driver's seat of the second AV, Gaines and Lilian stepped inside the house. The second member of the security team had accompanied the pair into the dwelling and now led the visitors through a refined tea room, across a hallway containing grandiosely illuminated display cases filled with sculptures and fine China, and into a sitting room in the middle of the rear section of the house.

Senator Jennings was seated in a comfortable armchair next to a fireplace that was directly to the visitors' left upon entering the sitting room. Lilian noted that the light from the room shone out of a large picture window onto an exterior sitting area accented by marble benches. The ground between the benches bordering the area had been covered with white gravel, and the landscape designer had used tall, white stone walls and various hedges as privacy barriers to almost fully enclose the intimate space. Inside the sitting room, it was apparent that the senator favored simple, modern, and yet distinguished furniture and had a large, dramatic painting of a wind-whipped American flag on the wall across from the gleaming white marble fireplace.

Behind the senator, an intimidatingly large man—dressed in the same dark suit of the security detail—was looming in the corner of the room with one hand cupping the other as he stared impassively at Lilian and General Gaines, his back to a door leading to the next room to the east. In the dim light, Lilian had at first assumed he was another piece of furniture, not expecting to see a person quite so tremendous in stature in the shadowy perimeter of the room. Faizan took up his position outside the door in the hallway, and the security team member who led the senator's visitors into the space swiftly exited and closed the traditional wooden door behind him.

Jennings seemed to be dressed in the same refined and yet obviously masterfully designed skirt, blouse, and business jacket she must have worn to the dinner party, and she was sitting primly, her elegant features bearing an expectant expression as she eyed Gaines and Lilian.

"Please do sit, General, and...perhaps you can share your name?" she asked with a meaningful glance at Lilian as she waved at the two chairs opposite her own.

"I'm Vanessa Lewis," Lilian improvised as she and Gaines took their seats, the general working to prevent himself from betraying the fact that this was the first time he'd heard his companion's claimed name.

"Pleased to meet you, Vanessa," Jennings murmured as she turned to the general.

"And to what do I owe the pleasure tonight, General Gaines? You said this was an urgent matter, correct? I hope you have no last-minute budget adjustment requests. What we discussed today has already been submitted to the Senate subcommittee."

"No, nothing like that. I'm afraid that Miss...Lewis and I are here about a much more serious matter related to," he glanced at the man behind Jennings, "the program as a whole."

"You can discuss the Command Activated in front of Mr. Shaeger. He's been read in on the program," The senator calmly responded.

Gaines raised an eyebrow and glanced questioningly at Shaeger again, then drove forward.

"It seems we have a group that is operating a shadow unit within the program, with ranks filled by individuals who all have some form of special needs and who have been tricked into enlisting using advanced technical imitation of loved ones."

Gaines paused to take a breath and also to take in the senator's slightly raised eyebrow and concerned expression as well.

He continued, "These troops are actively being sent on missions, though it seems that the members of Command itself are likely unaware that these victims are among those being deployed."

Jennings' eyes had widened in dismay as the general had spoken.

"I'm assuming you have evidence of these allegations?"

Gaines nodded to Lilian, and she withdrew the tablet baton from her pocket, hesitating as she noticed that Shaeger tensed slightly at her movements. Lilian extended the screen and opened the primary file before passing the tablet across to the senator. The older woman quickly scanned over the summary, then raised her eyes to appraise Lilian again.

"We most assuredly need to end this unethical behavior immediately!" Jennings emphatically asserted as she directed a determined expression at both visitors and then turned her focus more particularly toward Lilian.

"I'm going to guess that you are not actually a member of Venture Industries, and I will also guess that you and the good general had some assistance from technical personnel inside the program. Is that not so?"

Lilian looked to the general, who gave her a nod.

"Yes, ma'am," Lilian responded.

"Would the Oversight representatives be able to speak with them?"

Lilian hesitated, dropping her eyes for a moment. Maxwell's voice hummed through her strip.

"I'll be happy to share my side of the story," he offered.

"He is willing to testify, yes," Lilian informed Jennings.

The senior woman nodded appreciatively, then thoughtfully added, "That will help a great deal to expedite the investigation. Will he be able to testify in person here or at the Command Activated complex if we arrange to meet with members of Oversight tonight?"

Lilian hesitated again.

"Please tell her I will have to join remotely if we are meeting so soon," Max's voice hummed again.

"He will have to join remotely, unfortunately," she answered Jennings.

"I see. Well, that is still helpful."

Senator Jennings turned to Shaeger and made a circling motion with her finger. The man raised a hand to his strip and commanded, "Contain."

Outside in the car, Jayce had been enjoying the stillness of the starry Fall evening while taking a swig of cold water from the flask he had stowed in the vehicle. His eyes were drawn to the figure of the security team member who had remained by the front door as the man approached the general's vehicle. The stern man motioned for the driver to open the passenger side window as he bent over toward the town car. As Altman lowered the window, the guard deftly reached inside his coat, withdrew a handgun, and fired several rounds into the vehicle, with the associated flashes of light bursting out in the dark night.

Reacting mostly by instinct, Jayce's hand flew to his own holstered firearm as he simultaneously caught sight of another security team member in his side-view mirror, the new threat likely having just exited the nearby tree line before stepping quietly up in the dark beside the rear-left corner of Jayce' car.

Slamming the window control, Jayce thrust his gun out with his right hand raised over his shoulder as the glass slid down, firing several rounds that caught the adversary solidly in the chest. The enemy grunted heavily, and as he was thrown backward, Jayce hit the car's ignition and pressed his foot on the accelerator, steering into Altman's murderer as the assassin approached with his weapon hastily raised, firing off several shots at Jayce. The bullets burst through the windshield and snapped past Jayce's head as he threw himself aside, but the car made solid contact with the shooter and threw his body across the pavement.

Wheels screeching, Jayce halted the AV and tapped urgently on his strip.

"Max?! FAILSAFE?!"

"...ayce?...ight?..." was all he heard of Max's voice coming through his device and the car's screens.

Inside the manor, Gaines and Lilian had been shocked by the sound of gunshots and looked to the door that led to the front of the house. Faizan was just attempting to open the accessway when the room's occupants heard a shot from what must have been a position right beside the sergeant.

Those inside the room heard the distinct sound of a body slamming up against the door and dropping to the floor. Lilian froze, and Gaines moved his hands to his chair's armrests to raise himself, but then froze as well when he noticed that Shaeger was pointing the barrel of a large handgun at him.

Lilian heard fragments of Maxwell's voice coming through her strip.

"Li...atta...fight...!"

Jennings smirked.

# Chapter 15

*"We all want to be good people, but sometimes we find ourselves doing things that go against our values. Why is that? One possible answer is that our egos, the parts of us that want to protect how we see ourselves, can trick us into abandoning virtue. Our egos rationalize our actions. They tell us that we have no choice, that we have good reasons for our actions, or that what we are doing is really not that bad.*

*The ego easily blames others. It transfers responsibility through the belief that because someone provoked us, because a situation pressured us, or because the system corrupted us, we are ultimately not accountable. The ego compares us to others. It tells us that we are better than others, that others are worse than us, or that others do the same things as we do. In all these ways, we can avoid feeling guilty, remorseful, inferior, or hypocritical for our behavior.*

*- Dr. Yaro Ganizani, 'The Psychology of Justice'*

Sitting inside the half-dome of his wraparound screen, Maxwell could hear only snips of conversation coming through his friends' strips. The message "CONNECTION INTERFERENCE" was still displayed at the top of the rectangular frame in which Jayce and Lilian's open communications lines were being highlighted erratically as a syllable or sound made it through now and then. He'd tried to warn them when the interference had begun, but knew his efforts had likely been unsuccessful.

This had to be HOUND's doing, and that meant his friends were now in a trap!

Adding to his misery, a new message appeared on his screen informing him that the city power had been cut off and his systems were now running on their backup batteries.

Maxwell moaned out, "FAILSAFE, keep trying to reach them while I move to the safe room."

No answer was received.

"FAILSAFE, please respond!"

Maxwell felt panic rising in his heart.

"...I...sir..." was all the AI could get through.

"HOUND is throwing its all into isolating me..." Maxwell gasped. "It found my second line! FAILSAFE, if you can hear me, finish the merge with Haden's AI!"

With no response, he realized he had to find another way.

"I'll try to reach you on the move!" he shouted as he grabbed his tablet and raced out of his office with his blazer tail flapping out behind him.

Rushing up the stairs, the Englishman stopped short in the hall at the sound of bullets being fired rapidly into the thick wood around his rear door's locks. The door was sturdily built, yet it was not a medieval goliath like his front door. The assailants would soon be inside his home.

Maxwell snatched his coat from its rack and rushed to the interior garage entrance, muttering, "Let's hope those racing games pay off!"

---

Lilian tapped and swiped her strip frantically.

"I truly appreciate you coming to me with this information and helping me confirm that the mind behind the technical intrusion is Maxwell Clarke," Jennings said, oozing confidence.

"You see, we had narrowed down the possibilities for the perpetrator's identity to a handful, so when you confirmed that your associate could not make it to meetings tonight in person, that served to confirm our suspicions. I'm afraid that HOUND is running interference with all communications in and out of this area, and my operatives are descending on poor Maxwell's house as we speak."

"*Your* operatives?" Gaines questioned, staring narrowly at her in utter repugnance and condemnation.

"Yes, well, I've partnered with the owner of a rather large private security firm, and he has added to the forces at my disposal in exchange for a major government contract. I needed recruiters and other personnel who didn't mind doing things as they needed to be done because, in this case, the ends absolutely justified the means.

"Gaines, *you* at least should appreciate that I will transform the lives of these so-called *special needs* burdens on society into not only an asset to our country, but a *great* advantage! To maintain our nation's superiority, well...I will allow *no one* to stand in my way!"

The aquiline woman's face was alive with fervor as the light from the fireplace flickered eerily across her sharp features.

The regal senator then noted the extremely pained and ashamed expression that had taken over Lilian's visage as the younger woman's shoulders slumped and her weary eyes stared listlessly at her empty hands lying in her lap.

"My dear girl, we would have found him eventually. You just made it *so* much easier," the legislator heartlessly mocked.

The smile was suddenly wiped from Jenning's face as she heard the front door slam open, followed by gunshots being fired from the hallway outside the room. After a few seconds, a loud snapping noise preceded the sound of another body being thrown heavily up against the sitting room door.

Schaeger stalked silently toward the hallway entrance with his handgun still trained on Gaines, the massive man waving his left arm behind him to usher his employer toward the door by the fireplace. The woman tensely stood and began backing toward it, eyes locked on the parlor's polished wood portal.

Suddenly, the door to the room flew open, allowing the bodies of both Faizan and the first of the senator's guards to slump into the space just before several more of the loud snapping noises accompanied projectiles as they slammed into Shaeger's chest from their point of origin out in the hall. The giant stumbled backward, grunting heavily as the objects made contact and drove him back toward the senator—the man's arms thrashing as he attempted to keep his balance.

Taking advantage of this distraction, Gaines crouched and withdrew a compact handgun from an ankle holster on his right leg.

Raising himself quickly into a shooting position, the general fired off several rounds at the bodyguard as well. He narrowly missed with his first shot and then struck the man in the chest twice, tearing open his clothing to reveal an armored undershirt beneath. Gaines' final shot ripped into the flesh of Shaeger's shoulder.

Growling, the wounded man managed to turn his colossal form to where his ward was hastily opening the side door, grabbing her by the collar and shoving her through in front of him before closing it behind them. Gaines and Lilian heard the sound of heavy metallic bars smoothly sliding into place and the whirring of mechanisms as the door solidly locked. Jayce strode into the room with the Sandbagger still at the ready and sighted at the second exit as he quickly glanced over the surroundings, checking on his allies' condition.

"Must be a safe room," Gaines opined as he tipped his head toward the side door. "They've locked themselves in."

"Comms are being jammed, and I'm afraid I heard more vehicles inbound out front just now," Jayce warned.

Gaines tried calling out via his strip while holding his weapon only slightly lowered as it, too, remained pointed at the safe room door. He shook his head, scowled, and said, "Apparently, Jennings has made a deal with a private security firm. She could have a small army of mercenaries at her disposal!"

Through the open doors, they could hear the sound of several air-based transports touching down in the paved area in front of the mansion, followed by the unmistakable pattern of booted feet scuffling across the pavement. As Gaines kept his firearm pointed toward the rear door, Jayce swung around to face the hallway, moving quickly to where he could peer just past the edge of the door frame.

The general pulled a fob from his coat pocket.

"I have some backup of my own that might help us get out of here alive," he informed them, and then muttered, "if this works!"

He pressed a button on the fob.

---

In front of the main door into Maxwell's house near London, four agents stood at ready in the cold British night as a fifth fired a volley of rounds into the heavy barrier, face temporarily illuminated by the gunfire. The projectiles embedded themselves into the thick wood, but did little more. They heard a series of gunshots echoing up to the ornately iron-reinforced front windows from the rear of the residence and then a loud crash.

"They've breached at back," the lead man stated and started striding around the building, swiftly followed by the others.

They were crossing the paved road leading to the building's garage when they heard a strange humming coming through its large, wooden portal. Pausing and listening, the agents stepped closer to the door—the leader tilting his head thoughtfully. The humming suddenly dramatically increased in vigor, reaching an anguished whine, and the man's eyebrows sprang upwards.

"*MOVE!*" he shouted and dove sideways, skidding across the pavement—but it was too late.

With a spectacular explosion, the garage door was dashed apart as Maxwell's sports car AV tore through it at high velocity, sending the four agents who had not made it to safety flying out across the property amongst chunks and beams of mangled materials.

Inside the garage, an agent had just exited from the house, and she quickly took up a firm stance, firing at the tail and side of the aerial conveyance as it lifted off. Sparks flew off the vehicle in the dark, the rear-right taillight going out and the proximate turbine taking a hard hit, causing the car to dip heavily in that direction before it righted itself and curved away into the thick, low clouds.

The agent tapped her strip, shouting, "After him!" and the lights of two AV sedans rapidly ascended from behind the trees next to the access road, accelerating after their prey.

---

In front of the senator's house, two vans had already landed, and out had poured heavily armored men wielding assault rifles and shotguns. Most had taken up positions in columns they'd formed along the walls on either side of the open front door, preparing to enter the house as a unit, while two pairs made their way around opposite sides of the building to access the terrain to the structure's rear. A third vehicle was just descending into the paved circle when the trunk of General Gaines' car silently opened and tilted upward. A black, nearly invisible shape slid out into the shadows by the vehicle, paused as the mercenaries began moving toward the front door, and then darted forward with incredible speed.

The trio inside the estate heard a loud slamming against the front of the brick building, followed by rapid gunfire from a multitude of sources—the weapons fire interspersed with shouts of alarm. Jayce and Lilian looked at Gaines quizzically, and he smiled.

"I keep one of the prototype Panthers in my trunk, in case I want to run my own tests or...run into *trouble*."

Gaines' eyes flew to the rear window, and he swung his gun across Lilian, raising it slightly to avoid putting her in its sights and then dropping it level again as he fired off two rounds. The shots punched holes in the glass and forced the pair of enemies who had just stepped around a corner of a stone wall to withdraw back into cover.

The smell of the garden hedges quickly permeated the room as Lilian threw herself to the floor, and Gaines shoved the fob into his pocket, rushing to the wall to the right of the window. Jayce dashed to the wall at the other edge of the window frame, and the two men held their weapons close to their chests—preparing to engage the threats.

Glancing around the edge of his concealment, Jayce shouted, "Got two more on the opposite side!"

---

Maxwell was careening along at maximum speed but could hear one of the rear turbines struggling. He was flying through alternating patches of thick clouds and thinner vapor, holding his tablet and repeatedly trying to get a solid connection to FAILSAFE. HOUND's targeted interference was keeping pace with him as he flew, astonishing Maxwell at the power with which the US government must have provided the AI.

"Have to find a way to get through!" he shouted to himself, slamming a hand on the steering wheel in frustration.

His thoughts were interrupted by the sound of bullets raking across the tail of his AV's chassis. Eyes flying to his center mirror, Maxwell could see the headlights and outlines of two black sedans coming up behind him, taking advantage of a break in the cloud cover to close in on his vehicle.

He grabbed the wheel and barrel rolled down through a coagulation of denser clouds, bursting out the underside and swerving fiercely toward downtown London. The sedans managed to keep up with the beleaguered sports vehicle, dropping in and starting to close the distance with it again.

Maxwell tilted the car down and skimmed the rooftops of the well-lit buildings bordering the River Thames, passing the Tower of London and swerving over the waterway as he held his trajectory close to the faces of the structures. As he approached the London Bridge, he dipped into the darkness beneath it, his headlights barely giving him sufficient visibility in that tight space. One dark pursuer followed him through the gap while the other elevated and then descended toward Maxwell's left once his AV came back into view on the far side.

An agent had retracted the window on this chasing vehicle's right side, and he leaned a submachine gun out into the howling wind that was rushing past his AV, squeezing off a burst of rounds that pelted across Maxwell's door and smaller side window. The Englishman glanced back at the shooter and swerved, elevated, and barrel-rolled again to come down on the left side of the higher sedan's flight path. The driver tried to bank steeply left as well, but Maxwell continuously veered left until he was skimming along the buildings to the south of the river—keeping both pursuing vehicles to his right.

The second sedan had also tailed Maxwell's AV as it had moved, and the driver leaned out one of its leftmost apertures to fire off rounds from a handgun into the starboard side of the supercar. Sparks flew off the vehicle in the dark as the shooter's first bullets embedded themselves in the car's body, and then the rest began punching holes through the right-side windows.

When a bullet streaked past Maxwell's head, nearly striking his skull, his eyes widened beyond their already panic-stricken size.

"*HELL'S BELLS*!" he exclaimed and stamped on the brakes while pulling back and left on the wheel, forcing the pursuing vehicle that had been above and just behind Maxwell to dodge as he cut a trajectory up and over the closely packed shops and dwellings to come down south of the well-lit London Eye observation wheel.

The rightmost sedan began executing a slower, rising spiral across the water and up over the rooftops while the driver of the second, having recovered from the near miss with her target's vehicle, performed a similar maneuver as Maxwell's and quickly accelerated after him. However, the woman's efforts to take down her target were now doomed to fail.

Carrying out one last barrel roll, the young doctor dipped the sports AV down till it nearly made contact with the water, then soared up on a collision course with the Palace of Westminster. A police vehicle that had been patrolling the area moved to intercept, but was unprepared for the path the wildly piloted car took and failed to prevent its impact with the building.

Maxwell braked hard at the last second, executing a sideways drift and aiming the vehicle to crash through a bank of windows on the second floor. As glass and debris were still bouncing about the room beyond his crash site, the British man struggled to regain mastery of his rattled and shaky body.

It took him a moment to recover before he hit the right-front door control, unlatched his restraint, climbed across the seats, and clambered out into the office space beyond. A younger woman was standing by the office door, mouth agape and hand frozen over the screen of her tablet. She stared at the wreckage, thunderstruck, hair being tossed about in the wind blowing in around the body of the car from the autumnal London night outside.

"Are you *alright*?" she managed to breathe out as he straightened his blazer, standing erect like the picture of nobility.

"I'm *alive*!" Maxwell enthused. He glanced at her device, continuing, "And you're on a government-protected network! I beg you to send *one* message on your tablet!"

Maxwell withdrew his own device and stepped toward her to show her a system address.

"The message is simply: 'Ask Haden to fully merge'!"

The woman stared for a second into his wide, earnest, boyish eyes.

"Yeah, okay," she murmured as a whimsical, mesmerized smile played across her lips, her gaze finally dropping as she blushed, refocused, and began typing on her screen.

---

The two bullet-riddled edges of the window frame—and broken glass in their proximity—were evidence of the volume of fire Jayce and Gaines had been exchanging with their adversaries, though the duo had been badly outgunned.

"They're assessing our firepower and reducing our ammo!" Gaines hissed across to Jayce during this brief lull in combat.

Jayce had emptied the Sandbagger and was on his handgun's last clip, while Gaines had counted down to his final round. Suddenly, and with great precision, the first adversary the officer had spotted reappeared, joined by his partner as they stepped around the corner of the wall and let loose a hailstorm of automatic weapons fire toward the edge of the window by General Gaines' position—one always firing while the other was reloading. At the same instant, the two mercenaries at the right side of the clearing had stepped out from behind their cover and begun moving forward with the same approach, firing at the window frame next to Jayce.

All mercenaries advanced while the continuous gunfire kept Jayce and Gaines pinned down, the shooters holding their chins and elbows tucked, and the visor sections of their clear face shields lined up behind their raised firearms, this stance protecting the weakest points on their armor. The remnants of the window shattered inward, shards of glass flying everywhere. Lilian cried out and rolled behind one of the chairs as serrated slivers sprayed across her. Jayce grimaced, and Gaines looked heavenward, preparing to move out to engage the assailants through their incessant fire.

The adversaries were nearly at the house, and all hope seemed lost when a vehicle dropped out of the sky, slamming the mercenaries to the ground beneath it with the crunch of undercarriage striking armor.

Jayce and Lilian recognized it as their own AV, with both of the vehicle's doors nearest to the house sliding open.

"Need...lift?" FAILSAFE's voice broke through on their strips and the sedan's screens simultaneously.

Breathing out a heavy sigh of relief and enthusing, "Man, you are quite the guardian angel!" Jayce stepped through the empty window frame and then held out his hand for Lilian to join him.

Hearing continuous weapons fire from in front of the house, she willed herself to her feet and ran to the car through the cool night air that was now flooding through the improvised exit. Lilian slid onto the rear passenger bench and Gaines swiftly followed, pausing to withdraw the fob as he set one foot on the edge of the vehicle's entryway and pressed and held the device's single button.

The scene in front of the estate at that time was chaotic, with a half dozen of the mercenaries' bodies resting where they'd been thrown with great force up against the wall or across the courtyard. Three of the hired guns had taken up positions behind the ends of one of the vans, and gunmen were leaning out of the third van as it hovered at the roofline, allowing them to comb the area with the tactical lights mounted on their firearms. The Panther darted out from the tree line to the side of the unguarded van, where it obtained a small amount of cover as the airborne combatants once again rained down bullets all around it. Flattening itself and crawling beneath the vehicle with some difficulty, the dark machine then burst out from below the nose of the motionless AV and—touching down only twice—sailed through the front door of the house as projectiles spattered the side of the dwelling.

The trio by the rental car behind the mansion heard a galloping coming from the front of the domicile and then the low, dark shape of the Panther burst into the sitting room, broad shoulders barely fitting through the door as the cat sprang from the outer hearth of the fireplace across to elegantly land on the window ledge in front of General Gaines.

"Attaboy, Severance!" Gaines churred and waved the robot into the vehicle.

"Severance?" Jayce raised his brows in amusement while Lilian's eyes widened at the sight of the finely formed and yet bullet-scathed metallic cat, the young woman pressing herself against the far side of the AV to give the feline plenty of room.

The machine leaped onto the rear bench—smearing dirt and a bit of blood across the clean upholstery—and then perched itself heavily on the center console between the front seats. Its tail waved slightly next to Lilian's shoulder as the cat balanced and looked expectantly out the front windshield. Gaines chuckled and slid into the remaining space on the rear bench as Jayce climbed into the driver's seat, stashing the Sandbagger by his chair and politely trying not to run up against the robotic creature's shoulder with his own. Closing all doors and pulling the car away from the house, Jayce guided the crowded vehicle above the treetops to the rear of the estate.

Checking the mirrors, he growled, "They're coming up behind us!"

The van that had remained airborne had risen above the building's rooftop and was swinging its nose toward their fleeing vehicle as it accelerated, the second van rising into view behind it.

"Our best chance now is to make it to a news station!" General Gaines shouted. "They may halt pursuit once we're inside—*especially* if we can expose Jennings! At this point, it will only be our word against hers, but we have to try!"

Lilian lifted her head to call across the bulk of the Panther, "Not *just* our word against hers! I actually started recording on my strip when I realized communications were being blocked!"

"That's our Lilian!" Jayce acclaimed as Gaines curiously noted the woman's true name.

The Command Activated soldier then double-tapped his strip.

"FAILSAFE? You there?"

"...here...ifficult..." was all that came through their communications devices and the car's screens.

Jayce glanced in the rearview mirror, brow furrowing more deeply, and asked, "General can you get us to the nearest news station? You're familiar with this town, and I have something I need to *share* with our friends in the vans."

The general nodded, inserting his firearm back into its ankle holster. Jayce reclined the front passenger seat and asked Lilian to move forward, pulling his handgun from its holster and handing it to her after she'd secured herself.

"It's only got eleven rounds left, so use it sparingly," he advised.

Lilian gingerly took the weapon from Jayce. She was wishing now that she'd accepted Gunny's offer to equip her with a handgun as well so she could have contributed more to their present defenses, though even Jayce's basic lessons on the way to DC had not filled her with great confidence in her own abilities.

Still, the seasoned veteran had given her at least fundamental firearms training during their cross-country journey. Noticing Lilian's worried expression, Jayce soothingly reminded her, "Just like we went over on the trip from Colorado: lock your right thumb, cover that thumb with your left, cup left hand around right."

Lilian nodded, her expression already more resolute and focused.

Jayce nudged the Panther with his elbow, and as the large feline looked at him with head cocked, Jayce tossed his own head back diagonally.

"You gotta move over, big guy," he told it.

The machine obligingly scooted itself back into the right area of the rear bench, accompanied by the low whirring of its actuators as it tried to hunch over as tightly as possible in the confined space. Jayce double-checked that the accelerator was floored and set the autopilot before reclining his seat, then exchanged places with the general as quickly as possible.

As Gaines took the wheel and strapped himself in, returning the driver's seat to its upright position, Jayce pressed the button to lower the back of the rear seat, the Panther making a small sound of protestation as the seat levered the cat's rear end forward.

Jayce chuckled and said, "Sorry!" as the mechanical animal's nose was brought within centimeters of his due to the way it had to turn itself to avoid the lowering seat back—the feline's face bearing a distinctly distressed expression.

"These cars weren't designed to accommodate pets your size!" Jayce grinned and then ducked his torso into the trunk.

After a few seconds, he called out, "General, would you do me the favor of lifting our kilt?"

Gaines glanced in the mirror with a droll expression and thumbed the cargo access switch. As the hatch hissed open, Jayce raised himself on his elbows, catching sight of the lead van as it pulled up within just twenty meters of their AV sedan. The mercenary sitting in the front passenger seat was gesturing at Jayce as he turned to the other passengers.

Jayce grinned.

He was feeling oddly ebullient despite the danger, as though the action was therapeutic for the nagging, latent feelings of anger that had been steadily rising inside him again.

"No need to hold back my wrath here," he whispered, and then shouted, "Okay, boys. Let's *dance*!"

Hefting up the bulk of the belt-fed weapon he'd had stored in the trunk, Jayce adeptly released the bipod mounted below its barrel, flicked off the safety, activated its laser sight, and sent a barrage of bullets into the front of the nearest enemy transport—filling their own vehicle with the acrid smell of gun smoke. The pursuing driver had not had time to react before the stream of bullets had pounded across the vehicle's hood and begun mutilating the van's windshield.

As Jayce expected, the van was armored, and his weapon's standard rounds could not fully penetrate the protective glass, but the sheer volume of bullets he was pumping out was so scarring the other vehicle's windshield that it robbed the driver of the ability to see through it. The van started swerving and dipping wildly, turbines wailing as the driver fruitlessly attempted to both see and evade Jayce's relentless gunfire.

"Now *that's* what I'm talking about!" General Gaines crowed from the front of the car.

The officer was bringing the AV down to fly between the buildings now that they were entering downtown Washington, maintaining an elevation a few dozen meters above the street. The driver of the maimed van tried to follow but missed seeing a roof-mounted water tower until it was too late. The vehicle smashed into the reservoir with its front-right corner, sending the van spinning out of control until it painfully rebounded off a building on the opposite side of the street and tumbled to the empty pavement below.

"One down, one to go!" Jayce shouted as Lilian glanced back with her face beaming in elation and as Gaines exclaimed, "*Yes!*" through a broad grin.

The second van accelerated, starting to close the gap. To Jayce's dismay, it was joined by yet another black vehicle: this one a truck-style rig with an extended cab. The truck descended in a curving trajectory to swing into the position previously occupied by the first van.

"And now they've got reinforcements!" he growled as he swung his gun's barrel towards the truck and let loose more rounds, forcing the enemy vehicle to bob and weave.

# Chapter 16

*"Artificial intelligence is a powerful technology that can enhance the performance of all law enforcement operations—from its analytics to its weapons systems. AI can reduce human errors, biases, and casualties in police operations, with automated solutions being programmed to follow ethical and legal rules and to respect human rights and dignity. Additionally, AI will facilitate improved coordination and communication among law enforcement agents and agencies, improving the transparency and accountability of their actions."*

*- Law Enforcement General Training Handbook, District of Columbia, United States of America, Global Alliance*

"Heads up!" Gaines cried out, tilting his head forward as he spotted the undercarriage of another AV truck descending above them, catching sight of it just in time to see mercenaries lean out of the side doors and begin firing down on him.

His Panther lunged forward to place its front paws on the dash just as bullets traced across it, further aerating the windshield and pelting the robotic cat's head and shoulders. The black feline managed to take the worst of the incoming gunfire for Gaines, preventing a kill shot. Only two rounds had made it past the Panther's armored body, one ripping a wedge off the elevation control lever and the other profoundly burying itself in the general's thigh as he veered and rapidly decelerated, pulling the car up above the buildings that were flashing past on either side.

"You saved my neck, boy!" the general praised through a grimace of pain and gave the Panther a rub on its shoulder as it turned to look at him with apparent concern. Gaines sucked air in deeply as a sharper twinge of agony surged through him. "They managed to nail my leg, though!"

Lilian had been staring at the vehicle in front of them with dread, but at the general's words, she ducked her head down to look beneath the large metal animal, seeing blood pouring out of the officer's injury. Face grim, she stashed her weapon in the footwell and grabbed the cat's right shoulder, pulling hard.

The robot turned to look at her, and she shouted, "Back, please!"

Severance obligingly moved itself back with a sinuous motion, granting Lilian access to Gaines' wounded limb. Tearing the scarf off her neck and swiftly strapping it around the general's leg, Lilian tied the cloth into a tight band and stuffed the ends of the scarf into the inside edge of the binding material to add pressure to the wound, the officer hissing in pain as she did so.

The scarf was soon dyed a deep red.

Jayce had risen to his knees to maintain his view of the trailing AVs as their sedan had elevated, and he now continued his thunderous assault on the nearest vehicle's hood, windshield, and—provided a better angle—its turbines as well. The gunner's bullets sent sparks flying off of the front left propulsion unit and forced the driver to slue, decelerate, and increase elevation to avoid having flight capabilities disabled. Jayce's muscles were screaming from the exertion as he tried to hold the intensely shaking machine aloft and steady, his face rapidly flashing in the light of its spitfire.

"I'm going to try to give you an angle!" Gaines shouted to Lilian inside the AV as he nodded his head down toward the truck in front of them, the general forcing the words out between clenched teeth. "Aim just below the headrest!"

She scooped her weapon up out of the footwell and nodded, holding the firearm hesitantly in one hand and looking dolefully out at the adversary's vehicle as it was slowing down and elevating to come alongside them.

"Accelerating and descending...now!" the general shouted as Lilian lowered her window, filling the cabin with bracing cold and the deafening thunder of tortured air currents.

The mercenaries in the truck were aiming their firearms carefully back at Gaines and were thrown off by the sudden change in the car's speed and elevation, dropping their weapons' muzzles and trying to fire off a few rounds—the bullets embedding themselves in the front right side of the sedan. Lilian leaned out of the window, grasped the grip of the handgun firmly with both hands, and extended her arms as straight as she could as the vehicles came to level. She had to fight against the stinging wind as she directed the handgun's laser sight at the back of the enemy rig's driver seat.

Lilian hurriedly fired off round after round until the vehicle suddenly jerked, and the driver slumped forward. The truck careened off into a business building, crashing through the tinted glass of its fifth floor as a member of the cleaning crew inside threw himself out of the way. Glinting shards were pouring from the impact site like a waterfall of ice crystals glimmering in the lights of the night-bedecked city street.

"*Good!*" Gaines exulted through his gritted teeth as Lilian breathlessly withdrew her arms inside the vehicle, shooting the flag officer a look that was both relieved and troubled by what she'd done.

Unexpectedly, at that moment, the car's screens crackled, and then FAILSAFE's voice came through clearly, powerfully, and with a change in tone that Lilian could have sworn sounded triumphant.

"*Now powered by advanced subversion AI. HOUND held at bay.*"

Lilian gasped and shouted, "Is Max okay?!"

FAILSAFE responded, "*Max is safe. Get to reporters. Notified media outlet on corner of Connecticut and Ashmead. One kilometer ahead.*"

Eyes bulging in pain but having drunk in Lilian's exchange with this newly introduced entity, Gaines grunted out, "I'm guessing you're one of Max's AIs?"

The general glanced at Lilian, and she gave him a short nod of confirmation as FAILSAFE replied, "*Indeed, sir.*"

"Alright, I'm headed there now..." the general confirmed, and then, as he began descending onto the street below, he added, "...but you better tell them we're comin' in hot!"

Jayce had broken out in a sweat of exertion inside his layers of protective clothing, even with the icy night air battering his head and shoulders as it rushed around their speeding transport. He was sending out bursts of gunfire that were forcing the two remaining enemy AVs to keep their distance and decreasing the accuracy of the fire the vehicles' occupants were training on him.

The warrior took a quick glance inside his ammunition canister. The belt now filled only the last few centimeters of the container.

"Almost there!" the general shouted as his hand moved back to the lacerated elevation control lever on the AV's dashboard.

Lilian peered ahead at the next major intersection, trying to identify lights or a sign that indicated they were approaching a news broadcast building through the dim glow of city lights below. Unfortunately, the flashing lights that suddenly consumed nearly the entire road ahead—and the air above it—belonged instead to a tight formation of police AVs that were entirely barricading their path.

The Homeland analyst's heart practically stopped as she realized that the police units had raised the heavy machine gun turrets from the left- and right-front sections of their vehicles' frames, and these turrets were now focusing their laser sights on the trio's already bullet-riddled aerial machine. Dozens of red-tinted light emissions all brilliantly beamed into the nose of their car like a deadly modern art display.

Lilian, gripping the dash, cried out in desperation, "FAILSAFE! *Help!*"

---

After it had lost contact with Maxwell, FAILSAFE had taken the initiative and pursued a number of different approaches for breaking through HOUND's interference, using the techniques it had learned from interfacing with Haden's specialized infiltration model during the intrusion into the Command Activated network. FAILSAFE had managed to circumvent some of HOUND's devastating, focused denial-of-service attacks. It has also managed to overcome the way in which the enemy AI had commandeered security devices from key players providing the public network's backbone to intentionally filter FAILSAFE's communications.

Maxwell's creation had punched through these unbelievably sophisticated assaults just long enough to move its US-based allies' AV to the rear of the senator's house and onto the heads of their attackers. The determined artificial intelligence had caught a glimpse of the approaching vans before HOUND's interference had begun, and then made use of internally generated projections and the fragments of Jayce and Lilian's communications signals coming from the center rear of Senator Jennings' dwelling to define its targeting of the mercenaries and freeing of its allies from the enemies' grasp—at least so they could escape towards downtown DC.

Knowing it would have been Maxwell's desire, FAILSAFE had continued trying to reach the besieged associates as they fled their lethal foes while the AI was simultaneously dealing with the increasingly fierce attacks HOUND had been unleashing on every network route it could tie to FAILSAFE's activities. The corruption-combating AI had then estimated that within twenty minutes, HOUND would have sufficient data to identify FAILSAFE's source—the hosting facility in which its core logic centers existed—and then it would quickly be completely contained by the enemy AI. At that point in time, the likelihood of success given its available capabilities had been a dismal twenty-two percent.

Then a message had appeared on a particular command-and-control server: a system having a core purpose of extracting portions of incoming messages and combining them to reconstitute Maxwell's obfuscated instructions. If FAILSAFE had not developed sufficient approximation logic for problem-solving purposes, the intelligence might well have discarded the inbound message as incomprehensible; luckily, its human operator had equipped it to handle this type of contingency. According to the incoming order from the electronic entity's administrator, it had been time for FAILSAFE to rely on a different ally.

The advanced software construct had called Haden Juma's direct line, spoofing Maxwell's caller identification code.

"*Max?!*" the man had answered wearily. "We nearly in the clear?"

"This is FAILSAFE, Mr. Juma. Max is currently evading a group of lethal pursuers. He has asked me to request that you fully merge my model with the one you designed for offensive endeavors. Then, perhaps, by leveraging my recent expansion and adaptations, I can defeat the adversary that is attacking us both."

On the other end of the line, the security specialist had taken a moment to ponder the proposal, and then a sudden brightness and wicked grin had broken out across his previously fatigued face.

"Yeah, baby! Let's give it *hell!*"

---

Lilian knew that at any moment, the cruisers forming the police barricade were going to decimate their AV and everyone inside. Mind racing, she could think of no way to change what seemed like the inevitable outcome at this point. If they attempted to evade and tried to make it to another news outlet, the police would pursue and quickly disable their vehicle. Surrendering or seeking protection from another government entity would undoubtedly put them right into their enemies' lethal hands.

So, this is how it ends? Lilian thought as she closed her eyes.

After all we've overcome?

Amid the eerie glow of flashing lights, the law enforcement vehicles activated their heavy weapons, and bursts of flame accompanied the large-caliber projectiles escaping the armaments' barrels. The bullets flew through the air and horrifically mutilated the forward section of the trio's conveyance with a deafening thunder that resounded inside the vessel...but that was where it all stopped.

FAILSAFE punched through the adversaries' network defenses.

As the sedan's engine failed and the aerial vehicle began its inevitable return to Earth, the barricade ceased fire—lights frozen in state—and the cruisers dropped out of the air. The trio's AV sailed safely over the topmost craft in the barricade as they fell, Gaines unable to prevent the now-disabled car from careening down and striking the ground hard, gravity pulling the lower front and lower rear of the car down to ricochet off the ground several times with ever-increasing frequency. The mangled vehicle skidded and drifted down Connecticut Avenue until it finally ground to a screeching, tortured halt.

"*Police network infiltrated,*" FAILSAFE's synthesized voice resonated powerfully through the screens in the sudden, dim stillness. "*I believe that is called the 'nick of time.'*"

Gaines, Lilian, Jayce, and the Panther slowly raised their heads, their bodies having been forced down by the car's repeated impacts with the road and the two seated passengers' landing only having been partially softened by the deployment of the vehicle's airbags. Jayce had managed to brace himself against the interior walls of the trunk, allowing him to come away with only a healthy-sized gash across his forehead where the trunk hatch had made contact with it during their rough touchdown.

He pulled himself out of the trunk, looking back at the mess of law enforcement assets behind them, and then searched the dark sky for their pursuers. He saw that the mercenaries had risen to a higher elevation to avoid being in the kill zone for the police barricade's weapons fire. The hunters had shot past high overhead, but they were now circling and descending toward the disabled AV—the throbbing of their vehicles' turbines growing louder by the second.

"We gotta move!" he shouted as he saw his companions cautiously raising their heads in the main cabin area, the muscular man insistently banging on the car's composite frame as he hoisted his weapon out of the cargo hold.

The rear-right door of the sedan exploded off the vehicle, whirling across the street to impact a parked car near the western curb and then rocking and spinning slowly on the ground, crunching away on the debris till it finally lay still. Having thus kicked open an exit, the Panther turned itself around and clambered out of the car, crouching and drearily looking up at the mercenaries' approaching transports.

Lilian and Gaines unbuckled their harnesses and pulled the emergency release levers for the decrepit rental's exits, allowing them to manually slide open their doors and climb out of the vehicle. The general, looking up and seeing the mercenary rigs humming in only a city block away, started grunting and struggling quickly around the front of the vehicle as Lilian ran around to support him.

Jayce slammed the cargo hatch and threw the machine gun forward so its bipod rested on the curved surface of the hold, firing off a few bursts of bullets at the approaching enemies—sending glowing streaks up into the night sky like streaming fireworks and forcing the incoming opponents to veer off to seek landing sites nearby. Gaines and Lilian had almost made it to the front of the corner building that housed the DC office of the desired national news outlet, and from that building, a staff member was now running out the entrance to assist them. The woman became momentarily distracted, first by the sight of the large robotic beast keeping pace with General Gaines and then again by the sight of police cruisers scattered about in disarray down the road, officers starting to climb from the tangle of vehicles and a few taking some shaky steps in the evaders' direction.

Jayce hefted his weapon—now down to its final rounds—and jogged after his friends through the cool and humid night, catching up and overtaking them in time to stand in the motion-detection area of the slick glass doors of the entryway so the barriers slid open as the others moved through. They were quite the motley crew at this point, covered in cuts and contusions, disheveled, and smelling of combat.

The voluminous veteran hastily scanned the gray marble lobby and noted that it met up with a hallway leading toward the rear of the building, splitting where it reached a communal lounge at the center of the structure. Elevators were situated in protrusions encroaching on either side of the welcome area, with an electronically secured door to a stairwell situated on a wall nearer the central hall. The group made their way across the lobby as Jayce glanced back and noted that the access panel for the main doors now indicated that the ingress was in a locked state.

"Does that lead to a rear entrance?" he asked the staff member as he pointed at the proximate hallway. The woman nodded as she pushed a button on the wall by the elevators, causing the doors to one of the lifts to slide open.

Jayce continued pointing at the hall, now asking, "Another set of stairs back there?"

The woman anxiously nodded again as she urgently ushered the general and Lilian into the lift, but then stood in its doorway and added, "It's locked after hours, though."

Jayce nodded.

"That will at least slow them down."

Turning to Lilian, he soberly asked, "You and the general can handle everything upstairs?"

Lilian's brow furrowed, and she gave a short nod, worry lines radiating out in the skin around her eyes. Gaines, now gasping, perspiring despite the cold, and obviously wearied from loss of blood, said, "Take care of yourself, brother."

Jayce indicated his willingness to comply with that order and, looking down at Severance's raised face, asked, "It alright if I borrow your pet?"

"You'd *better!*" the general insisted with a weak smile. The media company employee stepped inside the elevator, and the door closed on the three passengers' anxious faces.

Jayce called out, "FAILSAFE, you there?"

The AI's newly intensified voice rang out from the speakers embedded in the lobby's ceiling.

"*Yes. I am here, Jayce.*"

The warrior tossed his head toward the central hallway.

"Let's you, me, and this crazy machine set up a li'l ambush," he said with a wide grin.

# Chapter 17

*"Why do I do what I do? The role of the media is crucial in a democratic society. When other institutions, including government agencies, lawmakers, or the criminal justice system as a whole fail to serve the public interest, the media can expose their wrongdoing and hold them accountable. We are the last resort when the system fails."*

*- From the notes of William Fuentes*

The most able officers from the police vehicles had made their way along the avenue and taken up positions along the outer wall of the office building adjoining the media company's office. The column of law enforcement personnel had been nearly ready to breach the building's entrance when a squad of mercenaries had come jogging around the corner from the adjoining street—armor clattering as the hired guns had moved in professional unison. The lead man in the newly arrived crew had held up a flat-palmed hand toward the officers as he'd glanced at the glass doors to his left, noting that the barrier had been locked after his prey's entry into the building.

Seeing no threats in the brightly lit lobby, the mercenary raised his massive shotgun to his shoulder and fired off a half dozen slugs into one of the doors. The hardened composite glass only cracked in fractal patterns under the force of the first few rounds, but the powerful weapon soon pounded through it with the cumulative force of a cannon.

As the glass shattered inward with a loud crash, pieces spinning out across the polished gray floor, the squad of hired guns quickly moved into the building with boots crunching across the debris. Splitting into two fire teams, each team skirted the walls and came up to a tactical halt where the walls extended out into the lobby to encompass the elevator shafts and stairwells.

The squad leader posted himself at the corner of the enclosure surrounding the southern elevators. Peering around the cover—his fire team lined up behind him along the wall—the man observed the well-lit central hallway, the locked stairwell entryway, and the elevator doors. Looking across at the opposite fire team lead, the squad leader drew three sides of a rectangle in the air, pointed at the door to the stairs on the other man's side of the building, and then ended by pointing a finger at the other lead.

The second lead nodded, waved his arm forward, and his column swept around the corner toward the stairs.

At the same instant, Jayce swung around the edge of the split hallway into the center of the building, stepping out from the right side of the division while squatting low and holding the machine gun at his hip. He adeptly aimed his heavy firearm's laser sight at the moving adversaries, letting loose a volley of shots that struck across the chest of the column's leader. As Jayce spun around into the protection of the left side of the split, dodging a slug fired by the squad leader from the southern side of the lobby, Jayce's target stumbled back and slammed into the man behind him.

Only the mercenary's thick armor prevented him from becoming a fatality. The somewhat shaken fire team leader quickly regained his footing and stepped to the side, allowing the second in the column to take his place at the lead so that the man's unscathed armor protected all behind him. As the damaged mercenary hastily stepped into the second position, the column advanced again, this time matched in their advance by the other fire team swiftly moving along the opposite wall.

They did not get far before Jayce leaned out from a standing stance. Having switched his weapon to grasp the grip with his left hand, almost none of his body was exposed as he fired off his last few rounds. Bullets embedded themselves in the shoulder armor of the new frontman for the second fire team, but the sound of Jayce's gun clicking on an empty chamber calamitously echoed through the lobby.

This sound was soon followed by the percussive racket created by a second squad of mercenaries as they bombarded the solid steel door at the rear of the building, the noise somewhat dampened by the distance it traveled through the hallways around the central lounge. Still, the sound seemed to represent the final nail in Jayce's coffin.

Now having reached the walls by the central hallway's entrance, a wicked smile cracked the face of the grizzled squad leader as he caught the eye of the fire team chief on the opposite side. The burly lead held up a hand and counted down from three to one before waving toward the hall. As the mercenary officer's hand deftly returned to his firearm's grip, he led his own fire team forward, and both columns streamed into the corridor.

Then FAILSAFE disabled the lights.

The mercenaries' visors were suddenly reduced to reliance upon only the weak light making its way in from the street and the dull glow coming through the glass of the lounge at the building's core. The optics built into the enemies' face shields quickly switched over to night vision mode, but not before Severance had leaped around the corner at full speed, ducking its head and levering upwards just below the squad leader's knees.

The big cat's upward motion sent the mercenary careening into the men behind him as he first ricocheted off the ceiling and then dropped down on top of his team members' heads, emitting a heavy grunt as the air was knocked out of his lungs with each blow. The fire team on the opposite side squeezed their triggers as they swung their weapons towards the robot in a panic, their gunfire flagging across the opposite team. Several of the gunmen on the other side of the narrow hallway cried out, having been wounded as bullets impacted more exposed portions of their bodies on the backs of their legs and in gaps at joints.

The Panther had pressed its right shoulder into the wall to quickly halt its forward movement and now ignored the projectiles rebounding off its reinforced shoulders and back, the cat kicking rearwards and to its left. Severance's hind paws caught the man at the front of the northern column at the hips and sent him flying like a ragdoll along the wall toward the lounge. The hired gun's flailing body careened across the split hall and made brutal contact with the heavy glass that surrounded the refreshment area beyond, the now-comatose man's form collapsing into a pile on the floor.

Partially illuminated by the residual light emanating from the salon behind him, Jayce swiftly stepped across the latest casualty's body and picked up the man's assault rifle from where it had landed. He swung the advanced weapon deftly up as he stepped to the right corner of the split hallway again, unleashing a dozen rounds into his previous victim's chest. That mercenary had caught sight of Jayce and had been bringing his own breaching shotgun around to face his human opponent, managing to get off one slug that cracked the glass of the tastefully decorated rejuvenation room behind the Command Activated warrior.

Despite this attempt, the mercenary's weakened armor rapidly broke down under Jayce's assault. He cried out and was thrown backward into his two remaining fire team members as a dying groan escaped his throat.

Severance had followed his rearward kick with a pounce on top of the column of mercenaries directly before him to further impede the men who were struggling to rise from the ground, wounds inflicted by friendly fire hindering their efforts. The squad leader's head was slammed down into the marble floor with such force that his brain ceased functioning, and the other team members were heavily shaken by the big cat's blow. The last two members of the still-upright fire team had stopped firing at the cat and had been preparing to step across to shoot upward into the robot's weaker points at close range when their team lead's body—having been riddled with Jayce's bullets—had been thrown into them, forcing them to twist and step back to regain their balance.

Having seen Jayce's gunfire, they tried to return fire at him, but he now emptied the current clip in the assault rifle into the next man in the column, taking that enemy down quickly and forcing the last man to retreat around the corner into the lobby.

The second mercenary in the squad leader's column was unable to move his arms under the brutal weight of the robotic feline and the unit officer's still form. However, only the legs and left shoulder of the man behind him were currently compressed. Though this third mercenary in the column had lost his assault rifle as he'd been thrown to the floor, he managed to unholster a heavy combat pistol from his leg, and he brought it up to fire off several rounds into Severance's neck, breaking away the composite armor material and tearing through some of the cat's exposed muscle fibers beneath.

The robotic beast yowled in distress and scrambled backward.

Jayce rapidly rotated his weapon's magazine to click its secondary clip into the rifle and brought his gun to bear on the shooter's arm, blowing the limb back and sending the pistol flying. The veteran's next rounds powerfully drilled through the man's chest armor until he lay still, and then Jayce adjusted his fire to sweep across the torso of the second mercenary in the team as the foe managed to free his assault rifle and strove to raise it to shoot toward the defending fighter.

As his second target expired with a loud cry, the ex-Marine moved his aim from there to fire into the submachine gun that the last member of that column was bringing to bear on Severance, the mercenary having just extracted himself from the tangle of his team members' bodies and taken up a quick crouching position. Jayce's bullets pounded the man's weapon downwards, and then the Command Activated soldier quickly shifted his aim to the right to strike the weaker armor at the seam between the man's chest and waist. That mercenary gave a bellowing cry, and he fell to the floor, clutching his hip in utter agony.

The lobby flooded with light again.

Severance kept its gaze on the last mercenary as the man glanced around the corner, spotted the cat looking straight at him, and hastily stepped back. Jayce took the opportunity to dash forward, snatching up the shotgun from the second column leader's lifeless hands, grasping its grip with his right hand as he rushed the corner and shoved the final enemy's weapon aside with his left.

Jayce brought the barrel of the shotgun up to the man's waistline, and the mercenary froze. Pulling the enemy's weapon from his unresisting hands, Jayce tossed it aside and grabbed the man's left wrist from its outer edge with his left hand, twisting the mercenary's arm around behind him and shifting the shotgun barrel to press up against the man's lower back. Jayce faced his hostage toward the hallway just as the leads of the two mercenary fire teams moving up from the rear of the building reached the corners where the hallway split.

"He doesn't have to *die* today!" Jayce shouted with a ferocity that rang out through the suddenly still space.

Severance, favoring its left shoulder and the neck area where it had been wounded, quietly padded forward into the lobby and then off to the other side of the hallway entrance, where the cat crouched and waited by the corner of the wall. The Panther intently eyed the members of the police force who had now started stepping carefully into the lobby from the street, weapons' laser sights trained on Jayce.

Before the second squad of hired guns could move forward, FAILSAFE's voice boomed through the building's sound system.

*"This man has been falsely accused. His friends are here to expose crimes committed by the very people who ordered their elimination. These friends are broadcasting the evidence now."*

The police officers behind Jayce paused in confusion as the two advancing mercenary fire team leads stalled and raised their eyes briefly to the ceiling. Realizing their time was running out, these two leads quickly recovered and began carefully stepping past their comrades' bodies into the hallway, weapons trained intently and meaningfully on the chest of Jayce's terrified hostage.

Then, the lobby was filled with the sound of the news broadcast that was taking place upstairs.

"...so, you have actual forensically sound evidence of Senator Jennings' crimes?" a woman's voice asked.

"Yes," General Gaines grunted out.

"And you want to play that for us now?" the woman questioned.

"Yes, I do!" Lilian said firmly. "This is playing from my strip."

After a moment, Senator Jennings' voice came through the speakers.

"...I've partnered with the owner of a rather large private security company, and he has added to the forces at my disposal in exchange for a major government contract..."

The mercenaries halted their approach as they listened.

---

Senator Jennings was standing by the desk in her safe room, having just finished applying a bandage to Shaeger's wound after extracting Gaines' bullet—the senator's guard now rolling his shoulder carefully and scowling.

The woman had gone still as a statue.

On the screen on her stately desk, an interface relaying combat communications from the mercenaries in the background was displayed.

In the foreground, a frame contained the video feed of General Gaines and Lilian being interviewed by a reporter, with Gaines' leg wound visibly bleeding onto his chair through its bandage.

The senator's own voice was very clear as it issued from the screen.

"Gaines, *you* at least should appreciate that I will transform the lives of these so-called *special needs* burdens on society into not only an asset to our country, but a *great* advantage! To maintain our nation's superiority, well...I will allow *no one* to stand in my way!"

Jennings' eyes widened in terror as her pupils dilated, staring off into some unseen hell.

"Shaeger, book me a flight to Cuba," she murmured.

---

In the lobby of the media building, the reporter's voice continued, "...and is it true that at this moment armed assailants are storming this building, sent by Jennings' accomplices to assassinate you?"

"That is, most assuredly, correct," Lilian confirmed, her voice straining with tension. "Our friend is downstairs, bravely facing them and the misinformed police officers supporting them, all to keep them from *murdering* us where we sit."

The lead police officer in the group that had warily been entering the lobby slowly adjusted the direction of her shotgun's laser sight to aim at the mercenaries, also leveling an almost lethally savage glare at them. The other law enforcement personnel adjusted their aim as well.

All members of the police force in the lobby had now created an array of a dozen firearms targeting the mercenary squad's leaders. Jayce, seeing the redirection of the police officers' focus, allowed a slight smile to twist the corners of his mouth as he slowly moved himself and his hostage off to his right—getting himself clear of the law enforcement agents' lines of sight toward the enemies in a situation of turnabout being fair play.

An officer at the back of the pack glanced up the street and called out, "SWAT just arrived! They're headed 'round back!"

The mercenaries' squad leader stood unmoving for a moment and then slowly straightened, lowering his weapon. Eyes glancing up and to the right attentively, he quietly said, "Yes, sir. Understood."

The leader turned to the rest of his team.

"We've been ordered to stand down," he barked, and the other mercenaries eagerly lowered their weapons. The man Jayce had been using as a shield also visibly sagged in relief, and his loud exhalation could be heard echoing throughout the expansive space.

The officers cautiously shuffled forward with weapons still raised, the lead woman calling out for the members of the armored group to toss their firearms aside. As the clatter of armaments hitting the marble floor resounded in the lobby, Jayce dropped the barrel of his shotgun to his side and pushed his hostage into the waiting hands of the police.

"If you don't mind, could you please disarm as well?" one nearby officer requested.

Jayce considered this, shrugged, and proceeded to drop the shotgun in a manner very reminiscent of someone dropping a microphone. The officer looked anxiously at the crouching figure of the Panther, the robotic beast's optics keenly appraising the law enforcement personnel.

"Is that thing safe?" the young officer queried, eyes betraying his significant disquietude.

Jayce chuckled.

"Aw, this big softie? He wouldn't hurt a *fly*!"

# Chapter 18

*"Restoring integrity and morality to a tainted organization—or our personal lives—is one of the most challenging tasks in human existence, but it also brings immense satisfaction and fulfillment. The process requires courage, honesty, and accountability as we confront wrongdoings or harmful attributes and rectify them, demanding a renewed commitment to ethical values and principles that guide our actions and decisions. When we succeed in purifying an organization—or our lives—from corruption, we better the world not only for ourselves but for the entirety of our society as well."*

*- Dr. Teresa Silva, 'The Principle of Restoration'*

It was early the next day, and General Rossi had just convened his first meeting of the morning. He sat at the head of the long, black glass table in his conference room like a king presiding over a court. The large man's hands rested comfortably at the corners of the table, an oily grin on his face as he regaled his minions with his sexual exploits—his descriptions avoiding explicit statements but the meaning of his words being apparent to all. The flag officer's eyes were jovial, yet they intently scanned across the faces of his subordinates to ensure that all of them were showing him deference and at least forced appreciation for his "incredible" power over women.

Rossi continued, "...and that's when I told her, 'Baby, I may be an *officer*, but let me get you home, and you'll see I *sure* ain't no *gentleman*!"

The general broke out into self-satisfied laughter, his cohorts dutifully laughing along with him.

Out in the general's reception area, his executive assistant was furiously typing away and trying her best not to listen to yet another of her boss' sickening tales when she noticed the approaching military police officers. Her hands stalled in the air as the glass doors of the reception area slid open, and the MPs stepped into the office from the long hallway beyond.

The two muscular men briskly approached her desk and then abruptly stopped, standing stiffly before her.

"We have a warrant for the arrest of General Honorius Rossi," the lead man announced.

The young woman slowly raised a finger to point back toward the conference room as she kept her face blank, and the MPs marched their way in to interrupt the general's meeting—over which a stillness had fallen at the sound of the man's name reverberating in from the lobby. The assistant was sincerely wishing she could have been in the room to witness the general's face when he'd seen the men enter. That would have been a memory to cherish for a *lifetime!*

They approached the senior officer, and the ranking MP began informing Rossi of his rights while the junior pulled out a pair of handcuffs and stepped forward to place a meaty palm meaningfully around the general's upper arm, firmly encouraging the older man to raise himself from his chair.

"I've *never* liked that man!" the assistant said with an infinitely poignant passion as she removed her tablet from its stand, collapsed its screen, and spun around to slip it into the pocket of her military dress coat.

The young enlisted service woman pulled her coat off the nearby rack and donned it swiftly. She was buttoning it up as the two MPs came back into view with the handcuffed Rossi scowling between them—the foul odor of his nauseating cologne permeating everything in the room as he passed. His bewildered gaze swung to his assistant and a hint of additional discomfiture crept into his expression as she happily smiled away, drinking in his exodus from the office like a heady elixir.

"*I'm finally free!*" she called out at his back as he was escorted down the hall past the concourse of shocked and, often, mirthful onlookers occupying the glass-fronted offices on either side of the corridor.

---

Senator Jennings was walking briskly through the terminal, dressed in an exquisitely crafted, silky blouse and tasteful slacks. She allowed her grand coat to flare out behind her as she strode purposefully down the passageway, utterly unimpugnable designer heels clicking like clockwork on the gleaming floor.

Her lustrous hair was done up in a tight bun beneath the wide-brimmed hat that shielded the upper half of her face from prying eyes, and she wore a fierce frown that dared any other travelers to speak to her. An expensive leather purse was draped over her left elbow, and she clutched a Cuban passport in the associated hand like a drowning swimmer clutches a lifeline.

Her departure gate was just ahead now, and with her first-class seat, she should be boarding in less than ten minutes. After that, she would start a new life abroad, someplace where people would give her the authority—and the deference—that a person in her class of cultivation, intelligence, and outstanding *patriotism* deserved!

Jennings' mind was yanked from this reverie by the sight of two dark-suited individuals walking down the wide hall toward her, spaced roughly equidistantly from the sides of the terminal and double that distance from each other. The two were each attempting to hold small devices out in a casual manner as they ambulated toward her.

*Nares!*

The senator stopped in her tracks, quickly scanning right and left for a possible detour or enclosure, but this stretch of hallway was void of gates, restaurants, or other facilities into which she could duck. She stepped back and began to turn in an attempt to abscond in the opposite direction, but she froze in her tracks mid-turn.

Flanked by two more such somberly-clad individuals, an agent stood a few meters away with his left hand tucked casually into his coat pocket. His right hand held a Nares out on display at his waist, the small device's red directional indicator arrow flashing brightly and pointing straight at Jennings.

The man looked extremely self-satisfied, as one would who had finally caught an evader after having previously experienced great public embarrassment due to a malfunctioning cleaning bot.

The senator's legs remained frozen where she stood. Her eyes had glazed over once again, only this time her jaw was moving—yet she was unable to make any sound. Her entire being had been overcome by incomprehensible terror at the realization that she had no possible means of escape.

The formerly unethically tasked law enforcement lead lingeringly extracted magnetic cuffs from his pocket as he jubilantly ambled toward her.

"Agnes Jennings, you are under arrest for kidnapping, unlawful restraint, coercion, misappropriation of government funds, conspiracy to commit fraud..."

---

Maxwell Clarke stood listening cheerfully in both a turtleneck and a smart blazer, hands clasped behind him, as the members of the oversight committee finished expressing their repulsion at the thought that those responsible for the shadow unit had been operating the clandestine program right under their noses, figuratively and, in some cases, literally speaking. One of the senior legislators was calling for onsite audits of all facilities on a regular basis going forward, while the previous speaker had sworn that she would see to it that every Command Activated troop's identity would be reviewed by the oversight body prior to each deployment.

Maxwell had already expressed his belief that the operations command staff—at least the core members—were not involved in the illicit scheme. He had also affirmed that he still had faith in the ability of the CA program as a whole to continue standing bravely for freedom and the protection of the innocent. He now waited for the right opening in the blustering antics of the bureaucrats into which he could insert a segue to take the meeting in a more meaningful direction.

"...I will not *rest* until I'm *certain* that the well-being of *all* our service members is protected!" exclaimed a senior medical adviser.

Hearing this, Maxwell raised a finger.

"Yes, about that..."

He kept his finger aloft until the clamor had died down, and he was certain he had their full attention.

"Over the past year, I have become well acquainted with one of the world's foremost experts on neurosurgical interventions for the remediation of mental health issues, particularly those associated with brain injuries."

Maxwell waited for the participants to process the implications of what he'd just shared, then pulled his tablet from his blazer pocket, expanded its screen, and continued, "I'm sending you all a copy of the results..." he paused as he swiped his finger up his screen toward the room's main display and, seeing the meeting participants starting to examine the file they'd received on their tablets, continued, "...from his latest testing on live subjects, as well as the simulation and extrapolation reports generated via sophisticated models."

He waited patiently once again as the oversight committee and senior program leadership scanned over the summaries of results.

The senior medical advisor was first to respond, commenting, "*Very* interesting. The testing methodology is solid, and the results are...well, they are effective to a greater extent than anything *I've* seen to date."

The Chief of Staff of the Army grunted.

"If I understand this correctly, the idea is that members of the program who have experienced brain trauma now have hope for being cured. Is that accurate?"

Maxwell nodded, tilting his head to the side and rejoining respectfully and with sympathy.

"Yes, sir. The issues that have plagued them—and so many others throughout the world—may now be resolvable. We can free humanity of a tremendous amount of psychological pain, and I'd like to start with the service members inside the CA program."

The Chief of Staff looked discomfited and tapped his thumb on the edge of his silvery tablet as his broad shoulders heaved, sending ripples through the stiff fabric of his dress green uniform—his numerous pins and medals shimmering.

"This is one *hell* of a time for miraculous healings," he muttered despondently.

Maxwell had anticipated the general's concern, and his voice was filled with understanding and yet also with heartfelt enthusiasm as he consoled the man.

"I realize that we are facing incredible, unprecedented stakes at the present juncture, for which we need the Command Activated more than ever. That being said, I believe that the overwhelming majority of our troops will voluntarily remain in the program after being treated, at least until we can find replacements for them.

"I firmly believe that we will not only find replacement soldiers but additional personnel when the current threats to democracy become apparent to our citizens and military service members. We just need to expand the scope of our recruiting to include those who desire to serve at a higher level of performance than they can at present—regardless of the absence of brain trauma.

"I believe that the impact of the CA program goes beyond that of any single project in the history of this world, with every aspect of human civilization now being tied directly to this one effort. We are now citizens of a world whose fate both depends on the Command Activated and for which the Command Activated will be a remedy for a wealth of ills. A Pangaea panacea, if you will."

He could see several people nodding their heads thoughtfully.

"We do owe it to our troops to offer them the opportunity to be healed, wouldn't you agree?" he asked, hands reaching out in an invitation for the listeners to join him in an inestimably worthy endeavor.

The senior-most Army officer sighed heavily, his weathered, older face and bulky frame visibly sagging in resignation.

"It's absolutely true," he breathed, "and I hope to God you're right about recruitment, because we may have just started a world war!"

---

The leadership meeting had finally ended, and Maxwell was very glad he'd had the foresight to turn down the temperature in the conference room before the session, as otherwise, he would have been sweating bullets by its conclusion. Though he was in such a fine mood that he doubted anything could bring him down, that had been a *highly* stressful meeting. Not only had he felt called upon to help guide the program to a more ethical future, but his poignantly deep investment in the eudaemonia of the service members for whose lives his AI—and he himself by extension—was continually responsible made every associated action feel absolutely critical.

Flapping the lapels of his blazer, he stepped through the conference room door as it hissed open, blinking as he exited the dim space into a brilliantly white and empty hallway in this military medical building, large windows at the far end allowing light to stream radiantly through. Voices and laughter could be heard pouring out of the open door of one of the recovery rooms situated a short way up the corridor. Maxwell smiled delightedly at the sound, striding to the open accessway.

As he approached the room, he could see that Ked was sitting on a sofa, an enormous grin decorating his face as he laughed again and again. The young man was positioned far forward on the Davenport with his elbows resting on his knees, his left hand dangling between his legs as he adjusted the angle at which the stump of his right forearm was extended a bit each time Jayce called attention to it.

The cap with which the medical team had covered Ked's wrist during its healing process shone white and plasticky. The cover bore the marks of many scuffs already, from times when Ked had forgotten his appendage was missing and had tried to use his right hand, painfully banging the cap into objects in each instance. According to the phalanx of assigned doctors, the young man's radiation exposure therapy was also going well, and no genetic damage had been detected.

Lilian sat close by Ked on the couch, her hand on his back and her chin resting warmly and protectively on his shoulder. Jayce was leaning easily against the sill of the room's picture window, hands playfully tapping its ceramic ledge as he continued his teasing of the younger man.

Jayce jovially jested, "...seriously, my brother! Once they attach that robotic hand, all the techie girls are going to be going *gaga* over you!"

Ked and Lilian burst into laughter again, faces beaming and worry-free. That was as beautiful a sight as Maxwell had ever seen.

The trio turned their faces and smiles to Maxwell as he entered, Lilian's eyes shining with a particular warmth and her nose crinkling in what he thought to be an absolutely adorable way as the corners of her mouth pulled up toward her now all-natural cheekbones.

He blushed a bit and made a show of straightening the collar of his turtleneck and brushing the front of his blazer flat, saying, "Well, we should have *more* than enough new regulatory measures to ensure the program gives birth to no additional shadowy children!"

Jayce and Lilian laughed heartily.

The burly Command Activated soldier then raised his eyebrows, gave a meaningfully angled nod, and said, "That's somethin' that I'm sure gonna appreciate as the program expands!"

He and Maxwell had talked about the fact that recent Command Activated operations had done more than just stirred the hornets' nest with the CEN. The lives of CA troops were about to become *very* busy—even if they were not fully conscious for the majority of the experience.

Maxwell smiled and then placed the knuckles of his hands against his hips, fingers splaying out behind.

"Jayce..." he opened, trying to contain the grin that threatened to overtake his face, "...one of the items discussed in that meeting had to do with a doctor friend of mine. An eminent neurosurgeon who I've recently helped to develop a cutting-edge new approach to the rectification of severe brain trauma."

Jayce's expression had gradually shifted from mirthful to astonished as Maxwell had spoken.

Maxwell beamed.

"He'd very much like to meet you!"

Several weeks had passed since Jayce had said his goodbyes to Maxwell and Lilian, their parting truly bittersweet despite their promises to stay in touch with each other.

His legs seemed to be moving without his conscious involvement as he slowly made his way up the sidewalk past the houses of old neighbors, his mind picking out subtle changes in their landscaping and signs of wear on the residences—differences that had appeared since he last saw them. To Jayce, it seemed his subconscious was taking over. That was not far from the truth, as his brain struggled to cope with the fears that roared through his mental landscape like ocean waves in a bitter storm as they crashed against cold and rocky cliffs.

Would his youngest boy even remember him? It was so hard to know whether kids as young as he had been when Jayce left would hold onto enough to help them recognize faces later.

Would they even *want* to remember him after what he'd done?

Would Alecia let him see them? He'd repeatedly mulled over the idea of calling her first, and there were definitely no small risks either way. In their final conversation before he had disappeared into the program, she *had* told him that she'd understood his decision, that she would always care about him, that he held a special place in her heart...

Whether that meant he still held a place in her *home* was a very important and separate question, and one on which he truly did not dare dwell. She could have remarried by now. He hadn't received any divorce papers, but there were likely exceptions that could be granted if one spouse was unreachable or in psychiatric care—if that's what you wanted to call his time in the Command Activated.

As he rounded the corner, the aroma of the pine tree that stood resolutely guarding the entrance to his old street released a flood of memories. Memories of walking and talking hand-in-hand with Alecia so many evenings as they'd circled this block. Memories of pushing his toddling Jaiden and brand-new Bronson in the double stroller as Jaiden had sung and laughed happily and Bronson had cooed. Memories of walking the street alone at night—and night after night—as he'd fought against the demons that had threatened not only his sanity but the lives of his beloved family members.

His feet slowed, then stopped. It wasn't too late to turn back. He could just return to the program and let the fantasies of some happy reunion in the future keep his hopes alive.

Maxwell's kind and sympathetic eyes and Lilian's thoughtful words returned to the center of his mental theater.

"You are one of the best people I have *ever* met," Lilian had whispered as she'd leaned in and embraced him tightly. "Whatever happens, whatever the situation with your family, they will still know that you have a good heart!"

And now he had a fully stable mind as well, thanks to Max.

Jayce willed his feet to move forward again, and as he moved, he started to hear the sounds of children's laughter up ahead. He passed the Nysons and saw that their yard was empty, and their kids were probably too old to sound like that anyway. He said a silent prayer that he would know how to handle whatever came next.

As he stepped past the hedge at the edge of the Nysons' property, his eyes were drawn to the figures of two little boys giggling and pelting each other with the pinecones that had blown over into their yard from the house beyond. Jayce's pace slowed until he reached the front gate of the waist-high picket fence, which was where he stopped, not daring to open it. His hand rested on the crest of the gate as he gazed at his boys, and he could not help smiling at their antics.

Bronson caught sight of Jayce first, as he was mid-throw, and he lost his grip on the large pinecone he had been swinging forward. He let it drop, forgotten, before his feet as his face lost its boyish grin and transitioned to wide-eyed curiosity. Jaiden realized his brother had gained a new focus. The boy wound down his chuckling as he turned and then he, too, began staring at Jayce. The child's expression showed some consternation, a bit of wonder, and a healthy dose of curiosity as well.

Jayce could hear footsteps faintly beating a rhythm toward the front entrance from inside the house. As the door swung open, Alecia laughingly announced, "When you boys go quiet, I *know* I'm in trouble!"

As she took in Jayce standing at the front gate, expression somber and unendingly apologetic as his suit, tie, and trench all seemed to try—unsuccessfully—to disguise the size of his muscles, the woman took a false step. She had been passing through the doorway and she now froze after catching hold of the door frame for support. Posture rigid, her eyes locked onto Jayce's for what seemed like an eternity. His brow furrowed, and his eyes full of questions, Jayce swallowed hard.

Alecia's body suddenly softened, in unison with the easing of her shocked and worried expression. The boys—who had turned to their mother as she had opened the door—were looking at her for guidance regarding what was allowed. Eyes turning to meet her children's, and with just a half nod at them, she lifted what felt like a tombstone off Jayce's heart.

The boys turned their faces back toward their father with their expressions of curiosity now tinged with a hint of nervousness. Jayce carefully unlatched the gate and stepped into the yard with what he hoped was a pacific bearing. Turning, he crouched until one knee braced him against the ground, trying not to let his frame shake with the tension.

"Hey, champs. I know it's been a while..." he began, but was cut off by Jaiden running to him and throwing his arms around his neck, Bronson soon barreling in behind.

"*Daddy!*"

END

**BENJAMIN GORDON CARD** is a former military intelligence special agent and Department of Defense consultant. He is a combat veteran and currently serves as a Chief Information Security Officer, penetration tester (aka, "gray hat hacker"), and—most importantly—husband, father, son, brother, nephew, cousin, friend, and member of the Church of Jesus Christ of Latter-Day Saints. His uncle, Orson Scott Card, set an example of how tragedy can be turned into inspiration. Benjamin Gordon Card's life experiences have allowed him to witness the heights and depths of human emotion and potential, and his objective is to let that joy and pain bleed through on every page of his works.

www.ingramcontent.com/pod-product-compliance
Lightning Source LLC
Chambersburg PA
CBHW020610310726
48979CB00008B/1415/J

* 9 7 9 8 9 9 0 9 5 8 9 9 9 *